DEATH IS A LONELY BUSINESS

DEATH IS A LONELY BUSINESS

RAY BRADBURY

BANTAM BOOKS
NEW YORK • TORONTO • LONDON • SYDNEY • AUCKLAND

*This edition contains the complete text
of the original hardcover edition.*
NOT ONE WORD HAS BEEN OMITTED.

DEATH IS A LONELY BUSINESS

*A Bantam Book / published by arrangement with
Alfred A. Knopf, Inc.*

PRINTING HISTORY
Knopf edition published October 1985
Bantam edition / January 1992

Library of Congress Cataloging-in-Publication Data

Bradbury, Ray, 1920–
    Death is a lonely business / Ray Bradbury.
        p.   cm.
    Originally published: New York : Knopf, 1985.
    ISBN 0-553-35462-0
    PS3503.R167D3   1992
    813'.54—dc20   91-16641
                                                CIP

Published simultaneously in the United States and Canada

*Bantam Books are published by Bantam Books, a division of Bantam
Doubleday Dell Publishing Group, Inc. Its trademark, consisting of the
words "Bantam Books" and the portrayal of a rooster, is Registered
in U.S. Patent and Trademark Office and in other countries. Marca
Registrada. Bantam Books, 666 Fifth Avenue, New York, New York 10103.*

PRINTED IN THE UNITED STATES OF AMERICA

FFG   0 9 8 7 6 5 4 3 2 1

With love
to
Don Congdon,
who caused it to happen.

And to the memory
of Raymond Chandler, Dashiell Hammett,
James M. Cain, and Ross Macdonald.

And to my friends and teachers
Leigh Brackett and Edmond Hamilton,
sorely missed.

DEATH IS A LONELY BUSINESS

Venice, California, in the old days had much to recommend it to people who liked to be sad. It had fog almost every night and along the shore the moaning of the oil well machinery and the slap of dark water in the canals and the hiss of sand against the windows of your house when the wind came up and sang among the open places and along the empty walks.

Those were the days when the Venice pier was falling apart and dying in the sea and you could find there the bones of a vast dinosaur, the rollercoaster, being covered by the shifting tides.

At the end of one long canal you could find old circus wagons that had been rolled and dumped, and in the cages, at midnight, if you looked, things lived—fish and crayfish moving with the tide; and it was all the circuses of time somehow gone to doom and rusting away.

And there was a loud avalanche of big red trolley car that rushed toward the sea every half-hour and at midnight skirled the curve and threw sparks on the high wires and rolled away with a moan which was like the dead turning in their sleep, as if the trolleys and the lonely men who swayed steering them knew that in another year they would be gone, the tracks covered with concrete and tar and the high spider-wire collected on rolls and spirited away.

And it was in that time, in one of those lonely years when the fogs never ended and the winds never stopped their laments, that riding the old red trolley, the high-bucketing thunder, one night I met up with Death's friend and didn't know it.

It was a raining night, with me reading a book in the back of the old, whining, roaring railcar on its way from one empty confetti-tossed transfer station to the next. Just me and the big, aching wooden car and the conductor up front slamming the brass controls and easing the brakes and letting out the hell-steam when needed.

And the man down the aisle who somehow had got there without my noticing.

I became aware of him finally because of him swaying, swaying, standing there behind me for a long time, as if unde-cided because there were forty empty seats and late at night it is hard with so much emptiness to decide which one to take. But finally I heard him sit and I knew he was there because I could smell him like the tidelands coming in across the fields. On top of the smell of his clothes, there was the odor of too much drink taken in too little time.

I did not look back at him. I learned long ago, looking only encourages.

I shut my eyes and kept my head firmly turned away. It didn't work.

"Oh," the man moaned.

I could feel him strain forward in his seat. I felt his hot breath on my neck. I held on to my knees and sank away.

"Oh," he moaned, even louder. It was like someone falling off a cliff, asking to be saved, or someone swimming far out in the storm, wanting to be seen.

"Ah!"

It was raining hard now as the big red trolley bucketed across a midnight stretch of meadow-grass and the rain banged the windows, drenching away the sight of open fields. We sailed through Culver City without seeing the film studio and ran on, the great car heaving, the floorboard whining under-foot, the empty seats creaking, the train whistle screaming.

And a blast of terrible air from behind me as the unseen man cried, "Death!"

The train whistle cut across his voice so he had to start over.

"Death—"

Another whistle.

"Death," said the voice behind me, "is a lonely business."

I thought he might weep. I stared ahead at the flashing rain that rushed to meet us. The train slowed. The man rose up in a fury of demand, as if he might beat at me if I didn't listen and at last turn. He wanted to be seen. He wished to drown me in his need. I felt his hand stretch out, and whether as fists or claws, to rake or beat me, I could not guess. I clutched the seat in front of me. His voice exploded.

"Oh, death!"

The train braked to a halt.

Go on, I thought, *finish* it!

"Is a lonely business!" he said, in a dreadful whisper, and moved away.

I heard the back door open. At last I turned.

The car was empty. The man had gone, taking his funeral with him. I heard gravel crunching on the path outside the train.

The unseen man was muttering out there to himself as the doors banged shut. I could still hear him through the window. Something about the grave. Something about the grave. Something about the lonely.

The train jerked and roared away through the long grass and the storm.

I threw the window up to lean out and stare back into wet darkness.

If there was a city back there, and people, or one man and his terrible sadness, I could not see, nor hear.

The train was headed for the ocean.

I had this awful feeling it would plunge in.

I slammed the window down and sat, shivering.

I had to remind myself all the rest of the way, you're only twenty-seven. You don't drink. But . . .

had a drink, anyway.

Here at this far lost end of the continent, where the trail wagons had stopped and the people with them, I found a last-stand saloon, empty save for a bartender in love with Hopalong Cassidy on late night TV.

"One double vodka, please."

I was astounded at my voice. Why was I drinking? For courage to call my girlfriend, Peg, two thousand miles away in Mexico City? To tell her that I was all right? But nothing had happened to me, had it?

Nothing but a train ride and cold rain and a dreadful voice behind me, exhaling vapors of fear. But I dreaded going back to my apartment bed, which was as empty as an icebox abandoned by the Okies on the way west.

The only thing emptier was my Great American Novelist's bank account in an old Roman temple bank building on the edge of the sea, about to be washed away in the next recession. The tellers waited in rowboats every morning, while the manager drowned himself in the nearest bar. I rarely saw any of them. With only an occasional sale to a pulp detective magazine, there was no cash to deposit. So . . .

I drank my vodka. I winced.

"Jesus," said the bartender, "you look like you never had booze before!"

"I never did."

"You look horrible."

"I *feel* horrible. You ever think something awful is going to happen, but you don't know what?"

"It's called the heebie-jeebies."

I swallowed more vodka and shivered.

"No, no. Something *really* terrible, closing in on you, is what I mean."

The bartender looked over my shoulder as if he saw the ghost of the man on the train there.

"Did you bring it in with you?"

"No."

"Then it's not here."

"But," I said, "he *spoke* to me—one of the Furies."

"*Furies?*"

"I didn't see his face. God, I feel worse now. Good night."

"Lay off the booze!"

But I was out the door and peering in all directions to catch the thing that was waiting for me. Which way home, so as not to meet up with darkness? I chose.

And knowing it was the wrong choice, I hurried along the dark rim of the old canal toward the drowned circus wagons.

How the lion cages got in the canal no one knew. For that matter, no one seemed to remember how the canals had gotten there in the middle of an old town somehow fallen to seed, the seeds rustling against the doors every night along with the sand and bits of seaweed and unravelings of tobacco from cigarettes tossed along the strand-shore as far back as 1910.

But there they were, the canals and, at the end of one, a dark green and oil scummed waterway, the ancient circus wagons and cages, flaking their white enamel and gold paint and rusting their thick bars.

A long time before, in the early Twenties, these cages had probably rolled by like bright summer storms with animals prowling them, lions opening their mouths to exhale hot meat breaths. Teams of white horses had dragged their pomp through Venice and across the fields long before MGM put up its false fronts and made a new kind of circus that would live forever on bits of film.

Now all that remained of the old parade had ended here. Some of the cage wagons stood upright in the deep waters of the canal, others were tilted flat over on their sides and buried in the tides that revealed them some dawns or covered them some midnights. Fish swarmed in and out of the bars. By day small boys came and danced about on the huge lost islands of steel and wood and sometimes popped inside and shook the bars and roared.

But now, long after midnight with the last trolley gone to destinations north along the empty sands, the canals lapped their black waters and sucked at the cages like old women sucking their empty gums.

I came running, head down against the rain which suddenly cleared and stopped. The moon broke through a rift of darkness like a great eye watching me. I walked on mirrors which showed me the same moon and clouds. I walked on the sky beneath, and—something happened. . . .

From somewhere a block or so away, a tidal surge of salt water came rolling black and smooth between the canal banks. Somewhere a sandbar had broken and let the sea in. And here the dark waters came. The tide reached a small overpass bridge at the same moment I reached the center.

The water hissed about the old lion cages.

I quickened. I seized the rail of the bridge.

For in one cage, directly below me, a dim phosphorescence bumped the inside of the bars.

A hand gestured from within the cage.

Some old lion-tamer, gone to sleep, had just wakened to find himself in a strange place.

An arm outstretched within the cage, behind the bars, languidly. The lion-tamer was coming full awake.

The water fell and rose again.

And a ghost pressed to the bars.

Bent over the rail, I could not believe.

But now the spirit-light took shape. Not only a hand, an arm, but an entire body sagged and loosely gesticulated, like an immense marionette, trapped in iron.

A pale face, with empty eyes which took light from the moon, and showed nothing else, was there like a silver mask.

Then the tide shrugged and sank. The body vanished.

Somewhere inside my head, the vast trolley rounded a curve of rusted track, chocked brakes, threw sparks, screamed to a halt as somewhere an unseen man jolted out those words with every run, jump, rush.

"Death—is a lonely—business."

No.

The tide rose again in a gesture like a seance remembered from some other night.

And the ghost shape rose again within the cage.

It was a dead man wanting out.

Somebody gave a terrible yell.

I knew it was me, when a dozen lights flashed on in the little houses along the rim of the dark canal.

"All right, stand back, stand back!"

More cars were arriving, more police, more lights going on, more people wandering out in their bathrobes, stunned with sleep, to stand with me, stunned with more than sleep. We looked like a mob of miserable clowns abandoned on the bridge, looking down at our drowned circus.

I stood shivering, staring at the cage, thinking, why didn't I look back? Why didn't I see that man who knew all about the man down there in the circus wagon?

My God, I thought, what if the man on the train had actually shoved this dead man *into* the cage?

Proof? None. All I had was five words repeated on a night train an hour after midnight. All I had was rain dripping on the high wire repeating those words. All I had was the way the cold water came like death along the canal to wash the cages and go back out colder than when it had arrived.

More strange clowns came out of the old bungalows.

"All right, folks, it's three in the morning. Clear away!"

It had begun to rain again, and the police when they had arrived had looked at me as if to say, why didn't you mind your own business? or wait until morning and phone it in, anonymous?

One of the policemen stood on the edge of the canal in a pair of black swim trunks, looking at the water with distaste. His body was white from not having been in the sun for a long while. He stood watching the tide move into the cage and lift the sleeper there, beckoning. A face showed behind the bars. The face was so gone-far-off-away it was sad. There was a terrible wrenching in my chest. I had to back off, because I heard the first trembling cough of grief start up in my throat.

And then the white flesh of the policeman cut the water. He sank.

I thought he had drowned, too. The rain fell on the oily surface of the canal.

And then the officer appeared, inside the cage, his face to the bars, gagging.

It shocked me, for I thought it was the dead man come there for a last in-sucked gasp of life.

A moment later, I saw the swimmer thrashing out of the far side of the cage, pulling a long ghost shape like a funeral streamer of pale seaweed.

Someone was mourning. Dear Jesus, it can't be me!

They had the body out on the canal bank now, and the swimmer was toweling himself. The lights were blinking off in the patrol cars. Three policemen bent over the body with flashlights, talking in low voices.

"—I'd say about twenty-four hours."

"—Where's the coroner?"

"—Phone's off the hook. Tom went to get him."

"Any wallet—I.D.?"

"He's clean. Probably a transient."

They started turning the pockets inside out.

"No, not a transient," I said, and stopped.

One of the policemen had turned to flash his light in my face. With great curiosity he examined my eyes, and heard the sounds buried in my throat.

"You know him?"

"No."

"Then why—?"

"Why am I feeling lousy? Because. He's dead, forever. Christ. And *I* found him."

My mind jumped.

On a brighter summer day years back I had rounded a corner to find a man sprawled under a braked car. The driver was leaping from the car to stand over the body. I stepped forward, then stopped.

Something pink lay on the sidewalk near my shoe.

I remembered it from some high school laboratory vat. A lonely bit of brain tissue.

A woman, passing, a stranger, stood for a long time staring at the body under the car. Then she did an impulsive thing she could not have anticipated. She bent slowly to kneel by the body. She patted his shoulder, touched him gently as if to say, oh there, there, there, oh, oh—there.

"Was he—killed?" I heard myself say.

The policeman turned. "What made you say that?"

"How would, I mean, how would he get in that cage—underwater—if someone didn't—*stuff* him there?"

The flashlight switched on again and touched over my face like a doctor's hand, probing for symptoms.

"You the one who phoned the call in?"

"No." I shivered. "I'm the one who yelled and made all the lights come on."

"Hey," someone whispered.

A plainclothes detective, short, balding, kneeled by the body and turned out the coat pockets. From them tumbled wads and clots of what looked like wet snowflakes, papier-mâché.

"What in hell's that?" someone said.

I know, I thought, but didn't say.

My hand trembling, I bent near the detective to pick up some of the wet paper mash. He was busy emptying the other pockets of more of the junk. I kept some of it in my palm and, as I rose, shoved it in my pocket, as the detective glanced up.

"You're soaked," he said. "Give your name and address to that officer over there and get home. Dry off."

It was beginning to rain again and I was shivering. I turned, gave the officer my name and address, and hurried away toward my apartment.

I had jogged along for about a block when a car pulled up and the door swung open. The short detective with the balding head blinked out at me.

"Christ, you look awful," he said.

"Someone else said that to me, just an hour ago."

"Get in."

"I only live another block—"

"Get *in!*"

I climbed in, shuddering, and he drove me the last two

blocks to my thirty-dollar-a-month, stale, crackerbox flat. I almost fell, getting out, I was so weak with trembling.

"Crumley," said the detective. "Elmo Crumley. Call me when you figure out what that paper junk is you stuck in your pocket."

I started guiltily. My hand went to that pocket. I nodded. "Sure."

"And stop worrying and looking sick," said Crumley. "He wasn't anybody—." He stopped, ashamed of what he had said, and ducked his head to start over.

"Why do I think he was *somebody?*" I said. "When I remember who, I'll call."

I stood frozen. I was afraid more terrible things were waiting just behind me. When I opened my apartment door, would black canal waters flood out?

"Jump!" and Elmo Crumley slammed his door.

His car was just two dots of red light going away in a fresh downpour that beat my eyelids shut.

I glanced across the street at the gas station phone booth which I used as my office to call editors who never phoned back. I rummaged my pockets for change, thinking, I'll call Mexico City, wake Peg, reverse the charges, tell her about the cage, the man, and—Christ—scare her to death!

Listen to the detective, I thought.

Jump.

I was shaking so violently now that I couldn't get the damn key in the lock.

Rain followed me inside.

Inside, waiting for me was . . .

An empty twenty-by-twenty studio apartment with a body-damaged sofa, a bookcase with fourteen books in it and lots of waiting space, an easy chair bought on the cheap from Goodwill Industries, a Sears, Roebuck unpainted pinewood desk with an unoiled 1934 Underwood Standard typewriter on it, as big as a player piano and as loud as wooden clogs on a carpetless floor.

In the typewriter was an anticipatory sheet of paper. In a wood box on one side was my collected literary output, all in one stack. There were copies of *Dime Detective, Detective Tales,* and *Black Mask,* each of which had paid me thirty or forty dollars per story. On the other side was another wooden box, waiting to be filled with manuscript. In it was a single page of a book that refused to begin.

UNTITLED NOVEL.

With my name under that. And the date, July 1, 1949.

Which was three months ago.

I shivered, stripped down, toweled myself off, got into a bathrobe, and came back to stand staring at my desk.

I touched the typewriter, wondering if it was a lost friend or a man or a mean mistress.

Somewhere back a few weeks it had made noises vaguely resembling the Muse. Now, more often than not, I sat at the damned machine as if someone had cut my hands off at the wrists. Three or four times a day I sat here and was victimized by literary heaves. Nothing came. Or if it did, it wound up on the floor in hairballs I swept up every night. I was going through that long desert known as Dry Spell, Arizona.

It had a lot to do with Peg so far away among all those catacomb mummies in Mexico, and my being lonely, and no sun in Venice for the three months, only mist and then fog and then rain and then fog and mist again. I wound myself up in cold cotton batting each midnight, and rolled out all fungus at dawn. My pillow was moist every morning, but I didn't know what I had dreamed to salt it that way.

I looked out the window at that telephone, which I listened

for all day every day, which never rang offering to bank my splendid novel if I could finish it last year.

I saw my fingers moving on the typewriter keys, fumbling. I thought they looked like the hands of the dead stranger in the cage, dangled out in the water moving like sea anemones, or like the hands, unseen, of the man behind me tonight on the train.

Both men gestured.

Slowly, slowly, I sat down.

Something thumped within my chest like someone bumping into the bars of an abandoned cage.

Someone breathed on my neck. . . .

I had to make both of them go away. I had to do something to quiet them so I could sleep.

A sound came out of my throat as if I were about to be sick. But I didn't throw up.

Instead, my fingers began to type, x-ing out the UNTITLED NOVEL until it was gone.

Then I went down a space and saw these words begin to jolt out on the paper:

DEATH and then IS A and then LONELY and then, at last, BUSINESS.

I grimaced wildly at the title, gasped, and didn't stop typing for an hour, until I got the storm-lightning train rolled away in the rain and let the lion cage fill with black sea water which poured forth and set the dead man free. . . .

Down and through my arms, along my hands, and out my cold fingertips onto the page.

In a flood, the darkness came.

I laughed, glad for its arrival.

And fell into bed.

As I tried to sleep, I began sneezing and sneezing and lay miserably using up a box of Kleenex, feeling the cold would never end.

During the night the fog thickened, and way out in the bay somewhere sunk and lost, a foghorn blew and blew again. It sounded like a great sea beast long dead and heading for its own grave away from shore, mourning along the way, with no one to care or follow.

During the night a wind moved in my apartment window and stirred the typed pages of my novel on the desk. I heard the paper whisper like the waters in the canal, like the breath on my neck, and at last I slept.

I awoke late to a blaze of sun. I sneezed my way to the door and flung it wide to step out into a blow of daylight so fierce it made me want to live forever, and so ashamed of the thought I wanted, like Ahab, to strike the sun. Instead I dressed quickly. My clothes from last night were still damp. I put on tennis shorts and a jacket, then turned the pockets of my damp coat out to find the clot of papier-mâché that had fallen from the dead man's suit only a few hours ago.

I touched the pieces with my fingernail, exhaling. I knew what they were. But I wasn't ready to face up to it yet.

I am not a runner. But I ran . . .

Away from the canal, the cage, the voice talking darkness on the train, away from my room and the fresh pages waiting to be read which had started to say it all, but I did not want to read them yet. I just ran blindly south on the beach.

Into Lost World country.

I slowed at last to stare at the forenoon feedings of strange mechanical beasts.

Oil wells. Oil pumps.

These great pterodactyls, I said to friends, had arrived by air, early in the century, gliding in late nights to build their nests. Startled, the shore people woke to hear the pumping sounds of vast hungers. People sat up in bed wakened by the creak, rustle, stir of skeletal shapes, the heave of earthbound, featherless wings rising, falling like primeval breaths at three a.m. Their smell, like time, blew along the shore, from an age before caves or the men who hid in caves, the smell of jungles falling to be buried in earth and ripening to oil.

I ran through this forest of brontosauri, imagining triceratops, and the picket-fence stegosaurus, treading black syrups, sinking in tar. Their laments echoed from the shore, where the surf tossed back their ancient thunders.

I ran past the little white cottages that came later to nest among the monsters, and the canals that had been dug and filled to mirror the bright skies of 1910 when the white gondolas sailed on clean tides and bridges strung with firefly lightbulbs promised future promenades that arrived like overnight ballet troupes and ran away never to return after the war. And the dark beasts just went on sucking the sand while the gondolas sank, taking the last of some party's laughter with them.

Some people stayed on, of course, hidden in shacks or locked in some few Mediterranean villas thrown in for architectural irony.

Running, I came to a full halt. I would have to turn back in a moment and go find that papier-mâché mulch and then go seek the name of its lost and dead owner.

But for now, one of the Mediterranean palaces, as blazing white as a full moon come to stay upon the sands, stood before me.

"Constance Rattigan," I whispered. "Can you come out and play?"

. . .

It was, in fact, a fiery white Arabian Moorish fortress facing the sea and daring the tides to come in and pull it down. It had minarets and turrets and blue and white tiles tilted precariously on the sand-shelves no more than one hundred feet from where the curious waves bowed to do obeisance, where the gulls circled down for a chance look, and where I stood now taking root.

"Constance Rattigan."

But no one came out.

Alone and special in this thunder-lizard territory, this palace guarded that special cinema queen.

A light burned in one tower window all night and all day. I had never seen it not on. Was she there now?

Yes!

For the quickest shadow had crossed the window, as if someone had come to stare down at me and gone away, like a moth.

I stood remembering.

Hers had been a swift year in the Twenties, with a quick drop down the mine shaft into the film vaults. Her director, old newsprint said, had found her in bed with the studio hairdresser, and cut Constance Rattigan's leg muscles with a knife so she would no longer be able to walk the way he loved. Then he had fled to swim straight west toward China. Constance Rattigan was never seen again. If she could walk no one knew.

God, I heard myself whisper.

I sensed that she had ventured forth in my world late nights and knew people I knew. There were breaths of near meetings between us.

Go, I thought, bang the brass lion knocker on her shorefront door.

No. I shook my head. I was afraid that only a black-and-white film ectoplasm might answer.

You do not really want to meet your special love, you only

want to dream that some night she'll step out and walk, with her footprints vanishing on the sand as the wind follows, to your apartment where she'll tap on your window and enter to unspool her spirit-light in long creeks of film on your ceiling.

Constance, dear Rattigan, I thought, run out! Jump in that big white Duesenberg parked bright and fiery in the sand, rev the motor, wave, and motor me away south to Coronado, down the sunlit coast!

No one revved a motor, no one waved, no one took me south to sun, away from that foghorn that buried itself at sea.

So I backed off, surprised to find salt water up over my tennis shoes, turned to walk back toward cold rain in cages, the greatest writer in the world, but no one knew, just me.

I had the moist confetti, the papier-mâché mulch, in my jacket pocket, when I stepped into the one place where I knew that I had to go.

It was where the old men gathered.

It was a small, dim shop facing the railway tracks where candy, cigarettes, and magazines were sold and tickets for the big red trolley cars that rushed from L.A. to the sea.

The tobacco-shed-smelling place was run by two nicotine-stained brothers who were always sniveling and bickering at each other like old maids. On a bench to one side, ignoring the arguments like crowds at a boring tennis match, a nest of old men stayed by the hour and the day, lying upward about their ages. One said he was eighty-two. Another bragged that he was ninety. A third said ninety-four. It changed from week to week, as each misremembered last month's lie.

And if you listened, as the big iron trains rolled by, you could hear the rust flake off the old men's bones and snow through their bloodstreams to shimmer for a moment in their dying gaze as they settled for long hours between sentences and tried to recall the subject they had started on at noon and might finish off at midnight, when the two brothers, bickering, shut up shop and went away sniveling to their bachelor beds.

Where the old men lived, nobody knew. Every night, after the brothers grouched off into the dark, the old men dispersed like tumbleweeds, blown every which way in the salt wind.

I stepped into the eternal dusk of the place and stood staring at the bench where the old men had sat since the beginning of time.

There was an empty place between the old men. Where there had always been four, now there were only three, and I could tell from their faces that something was wrong.

I looked at their feet, which were surrounded by not only scatterings of cigar ash, but a gentle snowfall of strange little paper-punchouts, the confetti from hundreds of trolley line tickets in various L and X and M shapes.

I took my hand out of my pocket and compared the now almost dried soggy mess with the snow on the floor. I bent and picked some of it up and let it sift from my fingers, an alphabet down the air.

I looked at the empty place on the bench.

"Where's that old gent—?" I stopped.

For the old men were staring at me as if I had fired a gun at their silence. Besides, their look said, I wasn't dressed right for a funeral.

One of the oldest lit his pipe and at last, puffing it, muttered, "He'll be along. Always *does*."

But the other two stirred uncomfortably, their faces shadowed.

"Where," I dared to say, "does he live?"

The old man stopped puffing. "Who wants to know?"

"Me," I said. "You know me. I've come in here for years."

The old men glanced at each other, nervously.

"It's urgent," I said.

The old man stirred a final time.

"Canaries," murmured the oldest man.

"What?"

"Canary lady." His pipe had gone out. He lit it again, his eyes troubled. "But don't bother him. He's all right. He's *not* sick. He'll be along."

He was protesting too much, which made the other old men writhe slowly, secretly, on the bench.

"His name—?" I asked.

That was a mistake. Not to know his name! My God, *everyone* knew that! The old men glared at me.

I flushed and backed off.

"Canary lady," I said, and ran out the door to be almost killed by an arriving Venice Short Line train thirty feet from the shop door.

"Jackass!" cried the motorman, leaning out and waving his fist.

"Canary lady!" I yelled, stupidly, shaking *my* fist to show I was alive.

And stumbled off to find her.

I knew her address from the sign in her window.

canaries for sale.

Venice was and is full of lost places where people put up for sale the last worn bits of their souls, hoping no one will buy.

There is hardly an old house with unwashed curtains which does not sport a sign in the window.

1927 NASH. REASONABLE. REAR.

Or

BRASS BED. HARDLY USED. CHEAP. UPSTAIRS.

Walking, one thinks, which side of the bed was used, and

how long on both sides, and how long never again, twenty, thirty years ago?

Or VIOLINS, GUITARS, MANDOLINS.

And in the window ancient instruments strung not with wire or cat-gut but spiderwebs, and inside an old man crouched over a workbench shaping wood, his head always turned away from the light, his hands moving; someone left over from the year when the gondolas were stranded in back-yards to become flower planters.

How long since he had sold a violin or guitar?

Knock at the door, the window. The old man goes on cutting and sandpapering, his face, his shoulders shaking. Is he laughing because you tap and he pretends not to hear?

You pass a window with a final sign.

ROOM WITH A VIEW.

The room looks over the sea. But for ten years no one has ever been up there. The sea might as well not exist.

I turned a final corner and what I was searching for was there.

It hung in the sunbrowned window, its fragile letters drawn in weathered lead pencil, as faint as lemon juice that had burned itself out, self-erased, oh God, some fifty years ago!

canaries for sale.

Yes, someone half a century ago had licked a pencil tip, lettered the cardboard and hung it to age, fixed with flypaper adhesive tape, and gone upstairs to tea in rooms where dust lacquered the banister in gums, choked the lightbulbs so they burned with an Oriental light; where pillows were balls of lint and shadows hung in closets from empty racks.

canaries for sale.

I did not knock. Years before, out of mindless curiosity, I had tried, and, feeling foolish, gone away.

I turned the ancient doorknob. The door glided in. The downstairs was empty. There was no furniture in any of the rooms. I called up through the dusty sunlight.

"Anyone home?"

I thought I heard an attic-whisper:

" . . . no one."

Flies lay dead in the windows. A few moths that had died the summer of 1929 dusted their wings on the front screens.

Somewhere far above, where ancient Rapunzel-without-hair was lost in her tower, a single feather fell and touched the air:

" . . . yes?"

A mouse sighed in the dark rafters:

" . . . come in."

I pushed the inner door wider. It gave with a great, grinding shriek. I had a feeling that it had been left unoiled so that anyone entering unannounced would be given away by rusty hinges.

A moth tapped at a dead lightbulb in the upper hall.

" . . . up here. . . ."

I stepped up toward twilight at noon, past mirrors that were turned to the wall. No glass could see me coming. No glass would see me go. . . .

" . . . *yes?*" A whisper.

I hesitated by the door at the top of the stairs. Perhaps I expected to look in and find a giant canary, stretched out on a carpet of dust, songless, capable only of heart murmurs for talk.

I stepped in.

I heard a gasp.

In the middle of an empty room stood a bed on which, eyes shut, mouth faintly breathing, lay an old woman.

Archaeopteryx, I thought.

I did. I really did.

I had seen such bones in a museum, the fragile reptilian wings of that lost and extinct bird, the shape of it touched on sandstone in etchings that might have been made by some Egyptian priest.

This bed, and its contents, was like the silt of a river that runs shallow. Traced now in its quiet flow was a jackstraw litter of chaff and thin skeleton.

She lay flat and strewn out so delicately I could not believe it was a living creature, but only a fossil undisturbed by eternity's tread.

"Yes?" The tiny yellowed head just above the coverlet opened its eyes. Tiny shards of light blinked at me.

"Canaries?" I heard myself say. "The sign in your window? The birds?"

"Oh," the old woman sighed. " . . . Dear."

She had forgotten. Perhaps she hadn't been downstairs in years. And I was the first, perhaps, to come upstairs in a thousand days.

"Oh," she whispered, "that was long ago. Canaries. Yes. I had some lovely ones."

"1920," again in the whisper. "1930—1931—." Her voice faded. The years stopped there.

Just the other morn. Just the other noon.

"They used to sing, my lands, how they sang. But no one ever came to buy. Why? I never sold *one*."

I glanced around. There was a birdcage in the far north corner of the room, and two more half-hidden in a closet.

"Sorry," she murmured. "I must have forgotten to take that sign out of my window. . . ."

I moved toward the cages. My hunch was right.

At the bottom of the first cage I saw papyrus from the *Los Angeles Times*, December 25, 1926.

HIROHITO ASCENDS THRONE
The young monarch, twenty-seven,
this afternoon . . .

I moved to the next cage and blinked. Memories of high school days flooded me with their fears.

ADDIS ABABA BOMBED
Mussolini claims triumph.
Haile Selassie protests. . . .

I shut my eyes and turned from that lost year. That long ago the feathers had stopped rustling and the warblers had ceased. I stood by the bed and the withered discard there. I heard myself say:

"You ever listen Sunday mornings to the 'Rocky Mountain Canary-Seed Hour'—?"

"With an organist that played and a studioful of canaries that sang *along!*" the old woman cried with a delight that rejuvenated her flesh and reared her head. Her eyes flickered like broken glass. " 'When It's Springtime in the Rockies'!"

" 'Sweet Sue.' 'My Blue Heaven,' " I said.

"Oh, weren't the birds *fine*!?"

"Fine." I had been nine then and tried to figure how in hell the birds could follow the music so well. "I once told my mom the birdcages must have been lined with dime-store song-sheets."

"You sound like a sensitive child." The old woman's head sank, exhausted, and she shut her eyes. "They don't make them that way any more."

They never did, I thought.

"But," she whispered, "you didn't *really* come see me about the canaries—?"

"No," I admitted. "It's about that old man who rents from you—"

"He's *dead.*"

Before I could speak, she went on, calmly, "I haven't heard him in the downstairs kitchen since early yesterday. Last night, the silence told me. When you opened the door down there just now, I knew it was someone come to tell me all that's bad."

"I'm sorry."

"Don't be. I never saw him save at Christmas. The lady next door takes care of me, comes and rearranges me twice a day, and puts out the food. So he's gone, is he? Did you know him well? Will there be a funeral? There's fifty cents there on the bureau. Buy him a little bouquet."

There was no money on the bureau. There was no bureau. I pretended that there was and pocketed some nonexistent money.

"You just come back in six months," she whispered. "I'll be well again. And the canaries will be on sale, and . . . you keep looking at the *door!* Must you go?"

"Yes'm," I said, guiltily. "May I suggest—your front door's unlocked."

"Why, what in the world would anyone want with an old thing like me?" She lifted her head a final time.

Her eyes flashed. Her face ached with something beating behind the flesh to pull free.

"No one'll ever come into this house, up those stairs," she cried.

Her voice faded like a radio station beyond the hills. She was slowly tuning herself out as her eyelids lowered.

My God, I thought, she *wants* someone to come up and do her a dreadful favor!

Not me! I thought.

Her eyes sprang wide. Had I said it aloud?

"No," she said, looking deep into my face. "You're not him."

"Who?"

"The one who stands outside my door. Every night." She sighed. "But he never comes in. Why doesn't he?"

She stopped like a clock. She still breathed, but she was waiting for me to go away.

I glanced over my shoulder.

The wind moved dust in the doorway like a mist, like someone waiting. The thing, the man, whatever, who came every night and stood in the hall.

I was in the way.

"Goodbye," I said.

Silence.

I should have stayed, had tea, dinner, breakfast with her. But you can't protect all of the people in all of the places all of the time, can you?

I waited at the door.

Goodbye.

Did she moan this in her old sleep? I only knew that her breath pushed me away.

Going downstairs I realized I still didn't know the name of the old man who had drowned in a lion cage with a handful of train ticket confetti uncelebrated in each pocket.

I found his room. But that didn't help.

His name wouldn't be there, any more than he was.

Things are good at their beginnings. But how rarely in the history of men and small towns or big cities is the ending good.

Then, things fall apart. Things turn to fat. Things sprawl. The time gets out of joint. The milk sours. By night the wires on the high poles tell evil tales in the dripping mist. The water in the canals goes blind with scum. Flint, struck, gives no spark. Women, touched, give no warmth.

Summer is suddenly over.

Winter snows in your hidden bones.

Then it is time for the wall.

The wall of a little room, that is, where the shudders of the big red trains go by like nightmares turning you on your cold steel bed in the trembled basement of the Not So Royal Lost Canary Apartments, where the numbers have fallen off the front portico, and the street sign at the corner has been twisted north to east so that people, if they ever came to find you, would turn away forever on the wrong boulevard.

But meanwhile there's that wall near your bed to be read with your watered eyes or reached out to and never touched, it is too far away and too deep and too empty.

I knew that once I found the old man's room, I would find that wall.

And I did.

The door, like all the doors in the house, was unlocked, waiting for wind or fog or some pale stranger to step in.

I stepped. I hesitated. Maybe I expected to find the old man's X-ray imprint spread out there on his empty cot. His place, like the canary lady's upstairs, looked like late in the day of a garage sale—for a nickel or a dime, everything had been stolen away.

There wasn't even a toothbrush on the floor, or soap, or a washrag. The old man must have bathed in the sea once a day, brushed his teeth with seaweed each noon, washed his only shirt in the salt tide and lain beside it on the dunes while it dried, if and when the sun came out.

I moved forward like a deep sea diver. When you know someone is dead, his abandoned air holds back every motion you make, even your breathing.

I gasped.

I had guessed wrong.

For there his name was, on the wall. I almost fell, leaning down to squint.

Over and over, his name was repeated, scrabbled on the plaster on the far side of his cot. Over and over, as if fearful of senility or oblivion, terrified at waking some dawn to find himself nameless, over and over he had scratched with a nicotine-stained fingernail.

William. And then *Willie.* And then *Will.* And beneath the three, *Bill.*

And then, again, again, again.

Smith. Smith. Smith. Smith.

And under that, *William Smith.*

And, *Smith, W.*

His multiplication table swam in and out of focus as I stared, for it was all the nights I ever dreaded to see somewhere up ahead in the dark ages of *my* future. Me, in 1999, alone, and my fingernail making mice-sound graffiti on plaster. . . .

"My God," I whispered. "Wait!"

The cot squealed like a cat touched in its sleep. I put my full weight down and probed with my fingerprints over the plaster. There were more words there. A message, a hint, a clue?

I remembered some boyhood magic where you had pals write quotes on pads and then tear off the quotes. But you took the pads out of the room and rubbed a soft pencil across the hidden indentations left on the blank pages and brought forth the words.

Now, I did just that. I found and rubbed the flat lead of my pencil gently across the wall surface. The nail scratches illusioned themselves forth, here a mouth, there an eye; shapes, forms, bits of an old man's half-dreams:

Four a.m. and no sleep.

And below that, a ghostly plea:

Please, God—sleep!

And a dawn despair:

Christ.

But then, at last, something that snapped my knees as I crouched lower. For here were these words:

He's standing in the hall again.

But that was me, I thought, outside the old woman's room five minutes ago, upstairs. That was me, outside this empty room, a moment ago. And . . .

Last night. In the dark rain, on the train. And the great railcar bucking the curves and groaning its wooden slats and shivering its tarnished brass as someone unseen swayed in the aisle behind me and mourned the funeral train's passage.

He's standing in the hall again.

He stood in the aisle on the train.

No, no. Too much!

It was no crime, was it, to stand in a train aisle moaning, or stand here in the hall, simply looking at a door and letting an old man know of your being there just with your silence?

Yes, but what if one night whoever it was came *into* the room?

And brought his lonely business with him?

I looked at the graffiti, as faint and faded as the canaries-for-sale sign in the window outside. I backed off, pulling away from that terrible sentence of loneliness and despair.

Outside in the hall, I stood feeling the air, trying to guess if another man had stood here again and again in the last month, with the bones showing behind his face.

I wanted to whirl and shout upstairs to rattle the empty birdcages, "If that man comes back, sweet Jesus! *Call* me!"

How? I saw an empty telephone stand nearby and a stack of Yellow Pages from 1933 under it.

Yell from your window, then!

But who would hear the sound of her voice like an old key turned in a rusted lock?

I'll come and stand guard, I thought. Why?

Because the dead sea-bottom mummy, that old autumn woman lying in funeral bandages up there, was praying for a cold wind to drift up the stairs.

Lock all the doors! I thought.

But when I tried to shut the front door, it wouldn't close.

And I could hear the cold wind, still whispering in.

I ran a ways and then slowed down and stopped, heading toward the police station.

Because the dead canaries had begun to rustle their dry wings just behind my ears.

They wanted out. Only I could save them.

And because I sensed, around me, the quiet waters rising in the Nile silt which would flow to erase ancient Nikotris, the Pharaoh's two-thousand-year-old daughter.

Only I could stop the dark Nile from sanding her away downstream.

I ran to my Underwood Standard typewriter.

I typed and saved the birds, I typed and saved the old dry bones.

Feeling guilty but triumphant, triumphant but guilty, I rolled them out of the platen and laid them out flat in the bottom of my birdcage-sandstone river-bottom novel box where they sang only when you read the words and whispered only when you turned the page.

Then, bright with salvation, I went away.

I headed for the police station filled with grand fancies, wild ideas, incredible clues, possible puzzles, evident solutions.

Arriving, I felt I was the finest acrobat performing on the highest trapeze suspended from the greatest balloon.

Little did I realize that Detective Lieutenant Elmo Crumley was armed with long needles and an air rifle.

He was coming out the front door of the station as I arrived. Something about my face must have warned him I was about to explode my notions, fancies, concepts, and clues all over him. He made a premature gesture of wiping his face, almost ducked back inside, and came warily down the walk as if approaching a landmine.

"What are *you* doing here?"

"Aren't citizens supposed to show up if they can solve a murder?"

"Where do you see murders?" Crumley eyed the landscape, and sure enough there were none. "Next subject?"

"You don't want to hear what I have to say?"

"I've heard it all before." Crumley brushed by me and headed for his car parked at the curb. "Every time anyone drops dead of a heart attack or trips over his shoelaces in Venice, there's someone there the next day to tell me, sixteen to the dozen, how to solve the stopped heart or retie the shoelaces. You've got the heart-attack shoelace look about you, and I didn't sleep last night."

He kept going and I ran after, for he was doing the Harry Truman 120-steps-to-the-minute march.

He heard me coming and called over his shoulder, "Tell you what, young Papa Hemingway—"

"You know what I *do* for a living?"

"Everyone in Venice knows. Every time you got a story in *Dime Detective* or *Flynn's Detective,* the whole town hears you yelling down at the liquor store newsrack, pointing at the magazines."

"Oh," I said, the last of the hot air going out of my balloon. Grounded, I stood across the car from Crumley, biting my lower lip.

Crumley saw this and got a look of paternal guilt.

"Jesus H. Christ," he sighed.

"What?"

"You know the one thing that gripes my gut about amateur detectives?" said Crumley.

"I'm not an amateur detective, I'm a professional writer with big antennae that work!"

"So you're a grasshopper who knows how to type," said Crumley, and waited for my wince to die. "But if you'd been around Venice and my office and the morgue as many years as I have, you'd know that every vagrant who wanders by or any drunk who stumbles in is full of theories, evidence, revelations enough to fill a Bible and sink a Baptist Sunday-outing picnic boat. If we listened to every maundering preacher who fell through the jail doors half the world would be under suspicion, one third under arrest, and the rest fried or hanged. That being so, why should I listen to some young scribe who hasn't even *begun* to make his name in literary history"—again my wince, again he waited—"who just because he finds a lion cage full of accidental drowning thinks he has stumbled on *Crime and Punishment* and feels like Raskolnikov's son. End of speech. Respond."

"You know *Raskolnikov?*" I said, in amaze.

"Almost before you were born. But that doesn't buy horseflakes. Plead your case."

"I'm a writer, I know more about feelings than you do."

"Balls. I'm a detective, I know more about facts than you do. You afraid a fact will confuse you?"

"I—"

"Tell me this, kiddo. Anything ever *happen* to you in your life?"

"Anything?"

"Yeah, I mean anything. Big, in between, small. Anything. Like sickness, rape, death, war, revolution, murder."

"My mother and father died—"

"Peacefully?"

"Yes. But I had an uncle shot in a holdup once—"

"You *see* him shot?"

"No, but—"

"Well, that don't count, unless you *see*. I mean, you ever find anything like men in lion cages ever before?"

"No," I said at last.

"Well, there you have it. You're still in shock. You don't know what life is. I was born and raised in the morgue. This is the first real touch of marble slab you ever had. So why don't you quiet down and go away."

He heard his own voice getting much too loud, shook his head, and said, "No, why don't *I* quiet down and go away."

Which he did. He opened the car door, jumped in, and before I could reinflate my balloon, was gone.

Cursing, I slammed into a telephone booth, dropped a dime in the slot, and called across five miles of Los Angeles. When someone picked up at the other end I heard a radio playing "La Raspa," a door slammed, a toilet flushed, but I could feel the sunlight that I needed, waiting there.

The lady, living in a tenement on the corner of Temple and Figueroa, nervous at the phone she held in her hand, at last cleared her throat and said:

"*Qué?*"

"Mrs. Gutierrez!" I shouted. I stopped, and started over. "Mrs. Gutierrez, this is the Crazy."

"Oh!" she gasped, and then laughed. "*Sí, sí!* You want to talk to Fannie?"

"No, no, just a few yells. Will you yell down, please, Mrs. Gutierrez?"

"I yell."

I heard her move. I heard the entire ramshackle, rickety tenement lean. Someday, a blackbird would land on the roof and the whole thing would go. I heard a small Chihuahua tap-dance on the linoleum after her, built like a bull bumblebee and barking.

I heard the tenement outer porch door open as Mrs. Gutierrez stepped out onto the third floor and leaned to call down through the sunshine at the second floor.

"*Aai*, Fannie! *Aai!* It's the Crazy."

I called into my end, "Tell her I *need* to come visit!"

Mrs. Gutierrez waited. I could hear the second-floor porch creak, as if a vast captain had rolled out onto its plankings to survey the world.

"*Aai*, Fannie, the Crazy needs to visit!"

A long silence. A voice sprang sweetly through the air above the tenement yard. I could not make out the words.

"Tell her I need *Tosca!*"

"*Tosca!*" Mrs. Gutierrez yelled down into the yard.

A long silence.

The whole tenement leaned again, the other way, like the earth turning in its noon slumbers.

The strains of the first act of *Tosca* moved up around Mrs. Gutierrez. She spoke.

"Fannie says—"

"I hear the music, Mrs. Gutierrez. That means 'Yes'!"

I hung up. At the same instant, a hundred thousand tons of salt water fell on the shore, a few yards away, with exquisite timing. I nodded at God's precision.

Making sure I had twenty cents in my pocket, I ran for the next train.

She was immense.

Her real name was Cora Smith, but she called herself Fannie Florianna, and no one ever called her otherwise. And I had known her, years ago, when I lived in the tenement, and stayed in touch with her after I moved out to the sea.

Fannie was so huge that she never slept lying down. Day and night she sat in a large-sized captain's chair fixed to the deck of her tenement apartment, with bruise marks and dents in the linoleum which her great weight had riveted there. She moved as little as possible, her breath churning in her lungs and throat as she sailed toward the door, and squeezed out to cross the hall to the narrow water-closet confines where she feared she might be ignominiously trapped one day. "My God," she often said, "wouldn't it be awful if we had to get the fire department to pry me out of there." And then back to her chair and her radio and her phonograph and, only a beckon away, a refrigerator filled with ice cream and butter and mayonnaise and all the wrong foods in the wrong amounts. She was always eating and always listening. Next to the refrigerator were bookshelves with no books, only thousands of recordings of Caruso and Galli-Curci and Swarthout and the rest. When the last songs were sung and the last record hissed to a stop at midnight, Fannie sank into herself, like an elephant shot with darkness. Her great bones settled in her vast flesh. Her round face was a moon watching over the vast territorial imperatives of her body. Propped up with pillows, her breath escaped and sucked back, escaped again, fearful of the avalanche that might happen if somehow she lay back too far, and her weight smothered her, her flesh engulfed and crushed her lungs, and put out her voice and light forever. She never spoke of it, but once when someone asked why there was no bed in her room, her eyes burned with a fearful light, and beds were never mentioned again. Fat, as Murderer, was always with her. She slept in her mountain, afraid, and woke in the morning glad for one more night gone, having made it through.

A piano box waited in the alley below the tenement.

"Mine," said Fannie. "The day I die, bring the piano box up, tuck me in, hoist me down. Mine. Oh, and while you're at it, there's a dear soul, hand me that mayonnaise jar and that *big* spoon."

I stood at the front door of the tenement, listening.

Her voice flowed down through the halls. It started out as pure as a stream of fresh mountain water and cascaded through the second to the first and then along the hall. I could almost drink her singing, it was that clear.

Fannie.

As I climbed up the first-floor steps she trilled a few lines from *La Traviata*. As I moved on the second flight, pausing, eyes shut, to listen, Madame Butterfly sang welcome to the bright ship in the harbor and the lieutenant in his whites.

It was the voice of a slender Japanese maiden on a hill on a spring afternoon. There was a picture of that maid, aged seventeen, on a table near the window leading out onto the second-floor tenement porch. The girl weighed 120 pounds at most, but that was a long time ago. It was her voice that pulled me up through the old stairwell—a promise of brightness to come.

I knew that when I got to the door, the singing would stop.

"Fannie," I'd say. "I heard someone singing up here just now."

"Did you?"

"Something from *Butterfly.*"

"How strange. I wonder who it could have been?"

We had played that game for years, talked music, discussed symphony/ballet/opera, listened to it on radios, played it on her old Edison crank-up phono, but never, never once in three thousand days, had Fannie ever sung when I was in the room with her.

But today was different.

As I reached the second floor her singing stopped. But she must have been thinking, planning. Maybe she had glanced out and seen the way I walked along the street. Maybe she read my skeleton through my flesh. Maybe my voice, calling far across town on the phone (impossible) had brought the sadness of the night and the rain with it. Anyway, a mighty intuition heaved itself aware in Fannie Florianna's summer bulk. She was ready with surprises.

I stood at her door, listening.

Creaks as of an immense ship blundering through tides. A great conscience stirred there.

A soft hissing: the phonograph!

I tapped on the door.

"Fannie," I called. "The Crazy is here."

"*Voilà!*"

She opened the door to a thunderclap of music. Great lady, she had put the shaved wooden needle on the hissing record, then surged to the door, held the knob, waiting. At the whisk of the baton *down*, she had flung the door *wide*. Puccini flooded out, gathered round, pulled me in. Fannie Florianna helped.

It was the first side of *Tosca*. Fannie planted me in a rickety chair, lifted my empty paw, put a glass of good wine in it. "I don't drink, Fannie."

"Nonsense. Look at your face. Drink!" She surged around like those wondrous hippos turned light as milkweed in *Fantasia*, and sank like a terribly strange bed upon her helpless chair.

By the end of the record I was crying.

"There, there," whispered Fannie, refilling my glass. "There, there."

"I always cry at Puccini, Fannie."

"Yes, dear man, but not so *hard.*"

"Not so hard, true." I drank half of the second glass. It was a 1938 St. Emilion from a good vineyard, brought and left by one of Fannie's rich friends who came clear across town for good talk, long laughs, better times for both, no matter whose income was higher. I had seen some of Toscanini's relatives going up the stairs one night, and waited. I had seen Lawrence Tibbett coming down, once, and we had nodded, passing. They always brought the best bottles with their talk, and they always left smiling. The center of the world can be anywhere. Here it was on the second floor of a tenement on the wrong side of L.A.

I wiped tears on my jacket cuff.

"Tell me," said the great fat lady.

"I found a dead man, Fannie. And no one will listen to me about it!"

"My God." Her round face got rounder as her mouth opened, her eyes went wide, then softened to commiseration. "Poor boy. Who?"

"It was one of those nice old men who sit in the ticket office

down at the Venice Short Line stop, been sitting there since
Billy Sunday thumped the Bible and William Jennings Bryan
made his Cross of Gold speech. I've seen them there since I was
a kid. Four old men. You felt they'd be there forever, glued to
the wooden benches. I don't think I ever saw one of them up
and around. They were there all day, all week, all year, smoking pipes or cigars, and talking politics thirteen to the dozen
and deciding what to do with the country. When I was fifteen
one of them looked at me and said, 'You going to grow up and
change the world only for the best, boy?' 'Yes, sir!' I said. 'I
think you'll do it,' he said. 'Won't he, gents?' 'Yes,' they all
said, and smiled at me. The old man who asked me that, he's
the one I found in the lion cage last night."

"In the *cage?*"

"Under water, in the canal."

"This calls for one more side of *Tosca.*"

Fannie was an avalanche getting up, a tide flowing to the
machine, a mighty force cranking the windup arm, and God's
whisper putting the needle down on a new surface.

As the music rose, she came back into her chair like a ghost
ship, regal and pale, quiet and concerned.

"I know one reason why you're taking this so hard," she
said. "Peg. She still in Mexico, studying?"

"Been gone three months. Might as well be three years,"
I said. "Christ, I'm lonely."

"And vulnerable," said Fannie. "Shouldn't you call her?"

"Christ, Fannie, I can't afford. And I don't want to reverse
the charges. I'll just have to hope she'll phone me in the next
day or so."

"Poor boy. Sick with love."

"Sick with death. The awful thing is, Fannie, I didn't even
know that old man's name! And isn't that a shame?"

The second side of *Tosca* really did it. I sat there, head

down, with the tears running off the tip of my nose into the wine.

"You've ruined your St. Emilion," said Fannie gently, when the record ended.

"Now I'm mad," I said.

"Why?" Fannie, standing, like a great pomegranate mother, by the phonograph, sharpened a new needle and found a happier record. "Why?"

"Someone *killed* him, Fannie. Someone stuffed him in that cage. There was no other way for him to have gotten in."

"Oh, dear," she murmured.

"When I was twelve, one of my uncles back east was shot in a holdup late at night, in his car. At his funeral, my brother and I vowed we'd find the murderer and do him in. But he's still in the world somewhere. And that was a long time back in another town. This time, it's here. Whoever drowned the old man lives within a few blocks of me in Venice. And when I find him—"

"You'll turn him over to the police." Fannie leaned forward in one massive but tender motion. "You'll feel better after a good sleep."

Then she read my face.

"No," she said at my funeral, "you won't feel better. Well, go on. Be the fool all men are. God, what lives we women lead, watching the fools kill each other and the killers kill the killers, and us over on the sidelines yelling stop and nobody listening. Can't *you* hear me, love?"

She put another record on and let the needle down like a loving kiss to the grooves, and came surging over to touch my cheek with her great pink chrysanthemum fingers.

"Oh, please, do be careful. I don't like Venice. Not enough streetlights. And those damned oil wells pumping all night long, no letup, with a case of the moans."

"Venice won't get me, Fannie, or whatever it is wandering around Venice."

Standing in halls, waiting, I thought, outside old men's and old women's doors.

Fannie became a giant glacier standing over me.

She must have seen my face again, where everything was given away, nothing hidden. Instinctively, she glanced at her own door, as if a shadow had passed outside. Her intuition stunned me.

"Whatever you do"—her voice was lost deep down in hundreds of pounds of suddenly haunted flesh—"don't bring it here."

"Death isn't a thing you can bring with you, Fannie."

"Oh, yes it is. Scrape your feet before coming in downstairs. Do you have money to get your suit dry-cleaned? I'll give you some. Shine your shoes. Brush your teeth. Don't ever look back. Eyes can kill. If you look at someone, and they see you want to be killed, they tag along. Come here, dear boy, but wash up first and look straight ahead."

"Horsefeathers, Fannie, and hogwash. That won't keep death away and you know it. Anyway, I wouldn't bring anything here to you but me; lots of years, Fannie, and love."

That melted the snow in the Himalayas.

She turned in a slow carousel motion. Suddenly we both heard the music that had long since started on the hissing record.

Carmen.

Fannie Florianna sank her fingers into her bosom and seized forth a black-lace fan, flitted it to full blossom, flirted it before her suddenly flamenco eyes, shut her lashes demurely, and let her lost voice spring forth reborn, fresh as cool mountain water, young as I had felt only last week.

She sang. And as she sang, she moved.

It was like watching the heavy curtain lift daintily high at the Metropolitan to be draped around the Rock of Gibraltar and whirled at the gesturings of a maniac conductor who knew how to electrify elephant ballets and call spirit-spout white whales from the deeps.

By the end of the first song, I was crying again.

This time, with laughter.

Only later did I think to myself, my God. For the first time. In her room. She sang.

For *me!*

Downstairs, it was afternoon.

I stood in the sunlit street, swaying, savoring the aftertaste of the wine, looking up at the second floor of the tenement.

The strains sounded of the song of farewell; the leave-taking of Butterfly by her young lieutenant, all in white, sailing away.

Fannie loomed on her porch, looking down at me, her little rosebud mouth smiling sadly, the young girl trapped in her round harvest-moon face, letting the music behind her speak our friendship and my leave-taking for now.

Seeing her there made me think of Constance Rattigan locked away in her Moorish fort by the sea. I wanted to call up and ask about the similarity.

But Fannie waved. I could only wave back.

I was ready for Venice in clear weather now.

Little balding man who doesn't look like a detective— Elmo Crumley, I thought, here I *come!*

But all I did was loiter in front of the Venice Police Station feeling like a gutless wonder.

I couldn't decide whether Crumley was Beauty or the Beast inside there.

Such indecision made me ache out on the sidewalk until

someone who looked like Crumley glanced out of an upstairs jail window.

I fled.

The thought of him opening his mouth like a blowtorch to scorch the peach fuzz off my cheeks made my heart fall over like a prune.

Christ, I thought, when will I face up to him at last to unload all the dark wonders that are collecting like tombstone dust in my manuscript box? When?

Soon.

During the night, it happened.

A small rainstorm arrived out front of my apartment about two in the morning.

Stupid! I thought, in bed, listening. A *small* rainstorm? How small? Three feet wide, six feet tall, all just in one spot? Rain drenching my doormat, falling nowhere else, and then, quickly, gone!

Hell!

I leaped to yank the door wide.

There wasn't a cloud in the sky. The stars were bright, with no mist, no fog. There was no way for rain to get there.

Yet there was a pool of water by my door.

And a set of footprints arriving, pointed toward me, and another set, barefoot, going away.

I must have stood there for a full ten seconds until I exploded. "Now, hold on!"

Someone had stood there, wet, for half a minute, almost ready to knock, wondering if I was awake, and then walked off to the sea.

No. I blinked. Not to the sea. The sea was on my right, to the west.

These naked footprints went to my left, east.

I followed them.

I ran as if I could catch up with the miniature storm.

Until I reached the canal.

Where the footprints stopped at the rim—

Jesus!

I stared down at the oily waters.

I could see where someone had climbed out and walked along the midnight street to my place, and then run back, the strides were bigger, to—

Dive in?

God, who would swim in those filthy waters?

Someone who didn't care, never worried about disease? Someone who loved night arrivals and dark departures for the hell, the fun, or the death of it?

I edged along the canal bank, adjusting my eyes, watchful to see if anything broke the black surface.

The tide went away and came back, surging through a lock that had rusted open. A herd of small seals drifted by, but it was only kelp going nowhere.

"You still *there?*" I whispered. "What did you come for? Why to my place?"

I sucked air and held it.

For in a hollowed-out concrete cache, under a small cement bunker, on the far side of a rickety bridge . . .

I thought I saw a greasy fringe of hair rise, and then an oiled brow. Eyes stared back at me. It could have been a sea-otter or a dog or a black porpoise somehow strayed and lost in the canal.

The head stayed for a long moment, half out of water.

And I remembered a thing I had read as a boy leafing African novels. About crocodiles that infested the subterranean caves under the rims of Congo riverbanks. The beasts sank down and never came up. Submerged, they slid to hide up inside the secret bank itself, waiting for someone foolish enough to swim by. Then the reptiles squirmed out of their underwater dens to feed.

Was I staring at a similar beast? Someone who loved night tides, who hid in caches under the banks to rise and step softly to leave rain where he walked?

I watched the dark head in the water. It watched me, with gleaming eyes.

No. That can't be a man!

I shivered. I jumped forward, as one jumps toward a horror to make it vanish, to scare spiders, rats, snakes away. Not bravery but fear made me stomp.

The dark head sank. The water rippled.

The head did not rise again.

Shuddering, I walked back along the trail of dark rain that had come to visit my doorstep.

The small pool of water was still there on my sill.

I bent and plucked up a small mound of seaweed from the middle of the pool.

Only then did I discover I had run to and from the canal dressed only in my jockey shorts.

I gasped, glanced swiftly around. The street was empty. I leaped in to slam the door.

Tomorrow, I thought, I'll go shake my fists at Elmo Crumley.

In my right fist, a handful of trolley ticket dust.

In my left, a clump of moist seaweed.

But not at the police station!

Jails, like hospitals, sank me to my knees in a faint.

Crumley's home was somewhere.

Shaking my fists. I'd find it.

For about 150 days a year in Venice, the sun doesn't show through the mist until noon.

For some sixty days a year the sun doesn't come out of the fog until it's ready to go down in the west, around four or five o'clock.

For some forty days it doesn't come out at all.

The rest of the time, if you're lucky, the sun rises, as it does for the rest of Los Angeles and California, at five-thirty or six in the morning and stays all day.

It's the forty- or sixty-day cycles that drip in the soul and make the riflemen clean their guns. Old ladies buy rat poison on the twelfth day of no sun. But on the thirteenth day, when they are about to arsenic their morning tea, the sun rises wondering what everyone is so upset about, and the old ladies feed the rats down by the canal, and lean back to their brandy.

During the forty-day cycles, the foghorn lost somewhere out in the bay sounds over and over again, and never stops, until you feel the people in the local graveyard beginning to stir. Or, late at night, when the foghorn gets going, some variety of amphibious beast rises in your id and swims toward land. It is swimming somewhere yearning, maybe only for sun. All the smart animals have gone south. You are left stranded on a cold dune with an empty typewriter, an abandoned bank account, and a half-warm bed. You expect the submersible beast to rise some night while you sleep. To get rid of him you get up at three a.m. and write a story about him, but don't send it out to any magazines for years because you are afraid. Not Death, but Rejection in Venice is what Thomas Mann should have written about.

All this being true, or imagined, the wise man lives as far

inland as possible. The Venice police jurisdiction ends as does the fog at about Lincoln Avenue.

There, at the very rim of official and bad weather territory, was a garden I had seen only once or twice.

If there was a house in the garden it was not visible. It was so surrounded by bushes, trees, tropical shrubs, palm fronds, bulrushes, and papyrus that you had to cut your way in with a reaper. There was no sidewalk, only a beaten path. A bungalow was in there, all right, sinking into a chin-high field of uncut grass, but so far away from the street it looked like an elephant foundering in a tar pit, soon to be gone forever. There was no mailbox out front. The mailman must have just tossed the mail in and beat it before something sprang out of the jungle to get him.

From this green place came the smell of oranges and apricots in season. And what wasn't orange or apricot was cactus or epiphyllum or night-blooming jasmine. No lawnmower ever sounded here. No scythe ever whispered. No fog ever came. On the boundary of Venice's damp eternal twilight, the bungalow survived amid lemons that glowed like Christmas tree lights all winter long.

And on occasion, walking by, you thought you heard okapi rushing and thumping a Serengeti Plain in there, or great sunset clouds of flamingos startled up and wheeling in pure fire.

And in that place, wise about the weather, and dedicated to the preservation of his eternally sunburned soul, lived a man some forty-four years old, with a balding head and a raspy voice, whose business, when he moved toward the sea and breathed the fog, was bruised customs, broken laws, and the occasional death that could be murder.

Elmo Crumley.

And I found him and his house because a series of people had listened to my queries, nodded, and pointed directions.

Everyone agreed that every late afternoon, the short detective ambled into that green jungle territory and disappeared amid the sounds of hippos rising and flamingos in descent.

What should I do? I thought. Stand on the edge of his wild country and shout his name?

But Crumley shouted first.

"Jesus Christ, is that *you?*"

He was coming out of his jungle compound and trekking along the weedpath, just as I arrived at his front gate.

"It's me."

As the detective trailblazed his own uncut path, I thought I heard the sounds I had always imagined as I passed: Thompson's gazelles on the leap, crossword-puzzle zebras panicked just beyond me, plus a smell of golden pee on the wind— lions.

"Seems to me," groused Crumley, "we played this scene yesterday. You come to apologize? You got stuff to say that's louder and funnier?"

"If you'd stop moving and listen," I said.

"Your voice carries, I'll say that. Lady I know, three blocks from where you found the body, said because of your yell that night, her cats still haven't come home. Okay, I'm *standing* here. And?"

With every one of his words, my fists had jammed deeper into my sports jacket pockets. Somehow, I couldn't pull them out. Head ducked, eyes averted, I tried to get my breath.

Crumley glanced at his wristwatch.

"There was a man behind me on the train that night," I cried, suddenly. "He was the one stuffed the old gentleman in the lion cage."

"Keep your voice down. How do you know?"

My fists worked in my pockets, squeezing. "I could feel his

hands stretched out behind me. I could feel his fingers working, pleading. He wanted me to turn and see him! Don't *all*
killers want to be found out?"

"That's what dime-store psychologists say. Why didn't
you look at him?"

"You don't make eye contact with drunks. They come sit
and breathe on you."

"Right." Crumley allowed himself a touch of curiosity. He
took out a tobacco pouch and paper and started rolling a cigarette, deliberately not looking at me. "And?"

"You should've heard his voice. You'd believe if you'd
heard. My God, it was like Hamlet's father's ghost, from the
bottom of the grave, crying out, remember me! But more than
that—*see* me, *know* me, *arrest* me!"

Crumley lit his cigarette and peered at me through the
smoke.

"His voice aged me ten years in a few seconds," I said. "I've
never been so sure of my *feelings* in my life!"

"Everybody in the world has feelings." Crumley examined
his cigarette as if he couldn't decide whether he liked it or not.
"Everyone's grandma writes Wheaties jingles and hums them
until you want to kick the barley-malt out of the old crone.
Songwriters, poets, amateur detectives, every damn fool thinks
he's all three. You know what you remind me of, son? That
mob of idiots that swarmed after Alexander Pope waving their
poems, novels, and essays, asking for advice, until Pope ran
mad and wrote his 'Essay on Criticism.' "

"You know Alexander *Pope?*"

Crumley gave an aggrieved sigh, tossed down his cigarette,
stepped on it.

"You think all detectives are gumshoes with glue between
their ears? Yeah, Pope, for Christ's sake. I read him under the
sheets late nights so my folks wouldn't think I was queer. Now,
get out of the way."

"You mean all this is for nothing," I cried. "You're not going to try to *save* the old man?"

I blushed, hearing what I had said.

"I meant—"

"I know what you meant," said Crumley, patiently.

He looked off along the street, as if he could see all the way to my apartment and the desk and the typewriter standing there.

"You've latched on to a good thing, or you think you have. So you run fevers. You want to get on that big red streetcar and ride back some night and catch that drunk and haul him in, but if you do, he won't be there, or if he is, not the same guy, or you won't know him. So right now, you've got bloody fingernails from beating your typewriter, and the stuff's coming good, as Hemingway says, and your intuition is growing long antennae that are ever so sensitive. That, and pigs' knuckles, buys me no sauerkraut!"

He started off around the front of his car in a replay of yesterday's disaster.

"Oh, no you don't!" I yelled. "Not again. You know what you are? Jealous!"

Crumley's head almost came off his shoulders. He whirled. "I'm what?"

I almost saw his fingers reach for a gun that wasn't there.

"And, and, and—" I floundered. "You—you're never going to *make* it!"

My insolence staggered him. His head swiveled to stare at me over the top of his car.

"Make *what?*" he said.

"Whatever it is you want to do, you—won't—do—it."

I jolted to a full stop, astounded. I couldn't remember ever having yelled like this at anyone. In school, I had been the prize custard. Every time some teacher slammed her jaws, my crust fell. But now—

"Unless you learn," I said, lamely, feeling my face fill up with hot color, "to—ah—listen to your stomach and not your head."

"Norman Rockwell's Philosophical Advice for Wayward Sleuths." Crumley leaned against his car as if it were the only thing in the world that held him up. A laugh burst from his mouth, which he capped with his palm, and he said, muffled, "Continue."

"You don't want to hear."

"Kid, I haven't had a laugh in days."

My mouth gummed itself shut. I closed my eyes.

"Go on," said Crumley, with a gentler tone.

"It's just," I said, slowly, "I learned years ago that the harder I thought, the worse my work got. Everyone thinks you have to go around thinking all the time. No, I go around feeling and put it down and feel again and write that down and, at the *end* of the day, *think* about it. Thinking comes later."

There was a curious light in Crumley's face. He tilted his head now this way to look at me, and then tilted it the other way, like a monkey in the zoo staring out through the bars and wondering what the hell that beast is there outside.

Then, without a word, or another laugh or smile, he simply slid into the front seat of his car, calmly turned on the ignition, softly pressed the gas, and slowly, slowly drove away.

About twenty yards down the line, he braked the car, thought for a moment, backed up, and leaned over to look at me and yelled:

"Jesus H. Christ! Proof! God damn it. Proof."

Which made me yank my right hand out of my jacket pocket so fast it almost tore the cloth.

I held my fist out at last and opened my trembling fingers.

"There!" I said. "You know what that is? No. Do *I* know

what it is? Yes. Do I know who the old man is? Yes. Do *you* know his name? No!"

Crumley put his head down on his crossed arms on the steering wheel. He sighed. "Okay, let's have it."

"These," I said, staring at the junk in my palm, "are little A's and small B's and tiny C's. Alphabets, letters, punched out of trolley paper transfers. Because you drive a car, you haven't seen any of this stuff for years. Because all *I* do, since I got off my rollerskates, is walk or take trains, I'm up to my armpits in these punchouts!"

Crumley lifted his head, slowly, not wanting to seem curious or eager.

I said, "This one old man, down at the trolley station, was always cramming his pockets with these. He'd throw this confetti on folks on New Year's Eve, or sometimes in July and yell Happy Fourth! When I saw you turn that poor old guy's pockets inside out I knew it had to be him. *Now* what do you say?"

There was a long silence.

"Shit." Crumley seemed to be praying to himself, his eyes shut, as mine had been only a minute ago. "God help me. Get in."

"What?"

"Get in, God damn it. You're going to prove what you just said. You think I'm an idiot?"

"Yes. I mean—no." I yanked the door open, struggling with my left fist in my left pocket. "I got this other stuff, seaweed, left by my door last night and—"

"Shut up and handle the map."

The car leaped forward.

I jumped in just in time to enjoy whiplash.

. . .

Elmo Crumley and I stepped into the tobacco smells of an eternally attic day.

Crumley stared at the empty space between the old men who leaned like dry wicker chairs against each other.

Crumley moved forward to hold out his hand and show them the dry-caked alphabet confetti.

The old men had had two days now to think about the empty seat between them.

"Son-of-a-bitch," one of them whispered.

"If a cop," murmured one of them, blinking at the mulch in his palm, "shows me something like that, it's gotta come from Willy's pockets. You want me to come identify him?"

The other two old men leaned away from this one who spoke, as if he had said something unclean.

Crumley nodded.

The old man shoved his cane under his trembling hands and hoisted himself up. Crumley tried to help, but the fiery look the old man shot him moved him away.

"Stand aside!"

The old man battered the hardwood floor with his cane, as if punishing it for the bad news, and was out the door.

We followed him out into that mist and fog and rain where God's light had just failed in Venice, southern California.

We walked into the morgue with a man eighty-two years old, but when we came out he was one hundred and ten, and could no longer use his cane. The fire was gone from his eyes, so he didn't even beat us off as we tried to help him out to the car and he was mourning over and over, "My God, who gave him that *awful* haircut? When did that happen?" He babbled because he needed to talk nonsense. "Did you do that to him?" he cried to no one. "Who did that? Who?"

I know, I thought, but didn't tell, as we got him out of the car and back to sit in his own place on that cold bench where the other old men waited, pretending not to notice our return, their eyes on the ceiling or the floor, waiting until we were gone so they could decide whether to stay away from the stranger their old friend had become or move closer to keep him warm.

Crumley and I were very quiet as we drove back to the as-good-as-empty canaries-for-sale house.

I stood outside the door while Crumley went in to look at the blank walls of the old man's room and look at the names, the names, the names, William, Willy, Will, Bill. Smith. Smith. Smith, fingernail-scratched there in the plaster, making himself immortal.

When he came out, Crumley stood blinking back into the terribly empty room.

"Christ," he murmured.

"Did you read the words on the wall?"

"All of them." Crumley looked around and was dismayed to find himself outside the door staring in. " 'He's standing in the hall.' Who stood here?" Crumley turned to measure me. "Was it you?"

"You know it wasn't," I said, edging back.

"I could arrest you for breaking and entering, I suppose."

"And you won't do that," I said, nervously. "The door, all the doors, have been open for years. Anyone could come in. Someone did."

Crumley glanced back into the silent room.

"How do I know you didn't scratch those words on that wall with your own damned fingernail, just to get my hair up and make me believe your cockamamie theory?"

"The writing on the wall is wobbly; an old man's scribble."

"You could have thought of that, and imitated an old man's scrawl."

"Could have done, but didn't do. My God, what do you need to convince you?"

"More than gooseflesh on my neck, I'll tell you that."

"Then," I said, my hands back in my pockets again, making fists, the seaweed still hidden but waiting, "the rest is upstairs. Go up. Look. Come down. Tell me what you see."

Crumley tilted his head to give me one of those monkey looks, then sighed and went up, like an old shoe salesman carrying an anvil in each hand.

At the top of the stairs he stood like Lord Carnarvon outside Tutankhamen's waiting tomb, for a long moment. Then he went in. I thought I heard the ghosts of old birds rustling and peering. I thought I heard a mummy whisper, rising from river dusts. But that was the old Muse in me, anxious for startlements.

What I heard was Crumley pacing the milkweed silt on the old woman's floor, which muffled his tread. A birdcage gave a metallic bell sound; he had touched it. Then what I heard was him bending over to lend an ear to a wind of time that moved from a dry and aching mouth.

And what I heard finally was the sound of the name on the wall whispered once, twice, three times, as if the old canary woman were reading the Egyptian hieroglyphs, symbol by symbol.

When Crumley came back down he was carrying the anvils in his stomach, and his face was tired.

"I'm getting out of this business," he said.

I waited.

"Hirohito ascends throne." He quoted the old newsprint he had just seen at the bottom of the cage.

"Addis Ababa?" I said.

"Was it really *that* long ago?"

"Now you've seen it all," I said. "What's your conclusion?"

"What conclusion should I have?"

"Didn't you read it in her face? Didn't you see?"

"What?"

"She's next."

"What?"

"It's all there, in her eyes. She knows about the man who stands in the hall. He's been up to her room, also, but hasn't gone in. She's simply waiting, and praying for him. I'm cold all over, and can't get warm."

"Just because you were right about the trolley ticket punchout junk, and found his place and I.D.'d the man, doesn't make you Tarot Card Champ of the Week. You're cold all over? *I'm* cold all over. Your hunch and my chill buys no dog food for a dead dog."

"If you don't post a guard here, she'll be dead in two days."

"If we posted guards over everybody who's going to be dead in two days, we'd have no more police. You want me to go tell the captain what to do with his men? He'd throw me downstairs and throw my badge after me. Look, she's nobody. I hate to say that. But that's the way the law runs. If she were somebody, maybe we'd post—"

"I'll do it myself, then."

"Think what you just said. You got to eat sometime, or sleep. You can't be here and you know it. The first time you run for a hotdog is when he, him, who, whomever, *if* he exists, will come in, make her sneeze, and she's gone. There was never any man here. It was only an old hairball blowing by in the night. The old guy heard it first. Mrs. Canary hears it now."

Crumley stared up the long, dark stairs toward the place of no birdsong, no springtime in the Rockies, no bad organist playing for his tiny yellow friends in some lost year.

"Give me time to think, kid," he said.

"And let you be an accessory to murder?"

"There you go again!" Crumley yanked the door so it

screamed on its hinges. "How come I spend half my time almost liking you and the rest being mad as hell?"

"Do I do that to you?" I said.

But he was gone.

Crumley did not call for twenty-four hours.

Grinding my teeth into a fine powder, I primed my Underwood and steamrollered Crumley into the platen.

"Speak!" I typed.

"How come," Crumley responded, typing from somewhere inside my amazing machine, "I spend half my time almost liking you and the rest being mad as hell?"

Then the machine typed, "I'll telephone you on the day the old canary lady dies."

It's obvious that years back I had pasted two gummed labels on my Underwood. One read: OFFICIAL OUIJA BOARD. The other, in large letters: DON'T *THINK*.

I didn't. I just let the old Ouija board bang and clatter.

"How soon do we work together on this problem?"

"You," responded Crumley in my fingertips, "are the problem!"

"Will you become a character in my novel?"

"I already am."

"Then help me."

"Fat chance."

"Damn!"

I tore the page out of the machine.

Just then, my private phone rang.

t seemed it took me ten miles of running to get there, thinking,

Peg!

All the women in my life have been librarians, teachers, writers, or booksellers. Peg was at least three of those, but she was far away now, and it terrified me.

She had been all summer in Mexico, finishing studies in Spanish literature, learning the language, traveling on trains with mean peons or busses with happy pigs, writing me love-scorched letters from Tamazunchale or bored ones from Acapulco where the sun was too bright and the gigolos not bright enough; not for her anyway, friend to Henry James and consultant to Voltaire and Benjamin Franklin. She carried a lunchbucket full of books everywhere. I often thought she ate the brothers Goncourt like high tea sandwiches in the late afternoons.

Peg.

Once a week she called from somewhere lost in the churchtowns or big cities, just come up out of the mummy catacombs at Guanajuato or gasping after a climb down Teotihuacán, and we listened to each other's heartbeats for three short minutes and said the same dumb things to each other over and over and over; the sort of litany that sounds fine no matter how long or often you say it.

Each week, when the call came, the sun blazed over the phone booth.

Each week, when the talk stopped, the sun died and the fog arose. I wanted to run pull the covers over my head. Instead, I punched my typewriter into bad poems, or wrote a tale about a Martian wife who, lovesick, dreams that an earthman drops from the sky to take her away, and gets shot for his trouble.

Peg.

Some weeks, as poor as I was, we pulled the old telephone tricks.

The operator, calling from Mexico City, would ask for me by name.

"Who?" I would say. "What was that again? Operator, speak up!"

I would hear Peg sigh, far away. The more I talked nonsense, the longer I was on the line.

"Just a moment, operator, let me get that again."

The operator repeated my name.

"Wait—let me see if he's here. Who's calling?"

And Peg's voice, swiftly, would respond from two thousand miles off. "Tell him it's Peg! Peg."

And I would pretend to go away and return.

"He's not here. Call back in an hour."

"An hour—" echoed Peg.

And click, buzz, hum, she was gone.

Peg.

I leaped into the booth and yanked the phone off the hook.

"Yes?" I yelled.

But it wasn't Peg.

Silence.

"Who is this?" I said.

Silence. But someone was there, not two thousand miles away, but very near. And the reception was so clear, I could hear the air move in the nostrils and mouth of the quiet one at the other end.

"Well?" I said.

Silence. And the sound that waiting makes on a telephone line. Whoever it was had his mouth open, close to the receiver. Whisper. Whisper.

Jesus God, I thought, this can't be a heavy-breather calling me in a phone booth. People don't call phone booths! No one knows this is my private office.

Silence. Breath. Silence. Breath.

I swear that cool air whispered from the receiver and froze my ear.

"No, thanks," I said.

And hung up.

I was halfway across the street, jogging with my eyes shut, when I heard the phone ring again.

I stood in the middle of the street, staring back at the phone, afraid to go touch it, afraid of the breathing.

But the longer I stood there in danger of being run down, the more the phone sounded like a funeral phone calling from a burial ground with bad telegram news. I had to go pick up the receiver.

"She's still alive," said a voice.

"Peg?" I yelled.

"Take it easy," said Elmo Crumley.

I fell against the side of the booth, fighting for breath, relieved but angry.

"Did you call a moment ago?" I gasped. "How'd you know this number?"

"Everyone in the whole goddamn town's heard that phone ring and seen you jumping for it."

"Who's alive?"

"The canary lady. Checked her late last night—"

"That was last night."

"That's not why I'm calling, damn it. Get over to my place late this afternoon. I might just rip your skin off."

"Why?"

"Three o'clock in the morning, what were you doing standing outside my house?"

"Me!"

"You better have a good alibi, by God. I don't like being spooked. I'll be home around five. If you talk fast you get maybe a beer. If you bat an eye, I kick ass."

"Crumley!" I yelled.

"*Be* there." And he hung up.

I walked slowly back toward my front door.

The phone rang again.

Peg!

Or the man with cold ice in his breath?

Or Crumley being mean?

I banged the door open, jumped in, slammed it, and then, with excruciating patience, rolled a fresh white sheet of Elmo Crumley into my Underwood and forced him to say only nice things to me.

Ten thousand tons of fog poured over Venice and touched at my windows and came in under the cracks in the door.

Every time it is a damp drear November in my soul I know it is high time to go from the sea again, and let someone cut my hair.

There is a thing in haircutting that assuages the blood and calms the heart and makes the nerves serene.

Beyond that, I heard the old man stumbling out of the morgue in the back of my mind, wailing, "My God, who gave him that *awful* haircut?"

Cal, of course, had done that awful job. So I had several reasons to go visit. Cal, the worst barber in Venice, maybe the world, but cheap, called across the tidal waves of fog, waiting with his dull scissors, brandishing his Bumblebee Electric clippers that shocked and stunned poor writers and innocent customers who wandered in.

Cal, I thought. Snip away the darkness.

Short in front. So I can see.

Short on the sides. So I can hear.

Short in back. So I can feel things creeping up on me.

Short!

But I didn't make it to Cal's, just then.

As I stepped out of my apartment into the fog, a parade of great dark elephants went by on Windward Avenue. Which is to say a pavane of black trucks with huge cranes and immense pile-pullers on the back. They were in full thunder, and heading for the pier to knock it down, or begin to knock it down. The rumors had been afloat for months. And now the day was here. Or tomorrow morning at the latest.

I had more of the day to wait to go see Crumley.

And Cal was not exactly the greatest lure in the world.

The elephants lumbered and groaned their machineries and shook the pavement, on their way to devour the fun house and the horses on the carousel.

Feeling like an old Russian writer, madly in love with killing winter and blizzards on the move, what could I do but follow?

By the time I got to the pier, half the trucks had lumbered down on the sand to move out toward the tides and catch the junk that would be tossed over the railings. The others had headed out toward China on the rotting planks, sawdusting the wooden mulch on the way.

I followed, sneezing and using Kleenex. I should be home lying with my cold, but the thought of going to bed with so many fog and mist and rain thoughts slogged me on.

I stood amazed at my own blindness, halfway down the

length of the pier, wondering at all the people here I had seen but never known. Half of the games were nailed shut with freshcut pine planks. A few stayed open, waiting for the bad weather to come in and toss hoops or knock milk bottles down. Outside half a dozen stalls, the young men who looked old or the old men who looked older stood watching those trucks growling out on the sea end of the pier, getting ready to tooth and nail sixty years of past time.

I looked around, realizing I had rarely seen behind the dropped flat doors or the rolled-down and battened canvasses.

I had the feeling again of being followed and spun about.

A big plume of fog came along the pier, ignored me, and passed on.

So much for premonition.

Here, halfway to the sea, there was a small dark shack that I had passed for at least ten years without seeing the window-shades up.

Today, for the first time, the shades were raised.

I looked in.

My God, I thought. There's a whole library there.

I walked swiftly over, wondering how many similar librar-ies were hidden away on the pier or lost in the old alleys of Venice.

I stood by the window, remembering nights when I had seen a light behind the shade and a shadow-hand turning pages in an invisible book, and heard a voice whispering the words, declaiming poetries, philosophizing on a dark universe. It had always sounded like a writer with second thoughts or an actor slipping downhill into a ghost repertory, Lear with two extra sets of mean daughters and only half the wits.

But now, at noon this day, the shades were up. Inside, a small light still burned in a room empty of occupants but filled with a desk, a chair, and an old-fashioned but huge leather couch. Around the couch, on all sides, towering to the ceiling, were cliffs and towers and parapets of books. There must have been a thousand of them, crammed and shoved up to the ceiling.

I stepped back and looked at the signs I had seen but not seen around and above the shack door.

TAROT CARDS. But the print was faded.

The next sign down read PALMISTRY.

The third one, in block letters, was PHRENOLOGY.

And beneath, HANDWRITING ANALYSIS.

And to one side, HYPNOTISM.

I sidled closer to the door, for there was a very small business card thumbtacked just above the doorknob.

I read the name of the shack's owner:

A. L. SHRANK.

And underneath the name, in pencil not quite so faint as *canaries for sale*, these words:

Practicing Psychologist.

A sextuple-threat man.

I put my ear to the door and listened.

In there, between precipice shelves of dusty books, did I hear Sigmund Freud whispering a penis is only a penis, but a good cigar is a smoke? Hamlet dying and taking everyone along? Virginia Woolf, like drowned Ophelia, stretched out to dry on that couch, telling her sad tale? Tarot cards being shuffled? Heads being felt like cantaloupes? Pens scratching?

"Let's peek," I said.

Again, I stared through the window, but all I saw was the empty couch with the outline of many bodies in its middle. It was the only bed. Nights, A. L. Shrank slept there. Days, did strangers lie there, holding on to their insides as if they were broken glass? I could not believe.

But the books were the things that fascinated me. They not only brimmed the shelves but filled the bathtub which I could glimpse through a half-open door to one side. There was no kitchen. If there had been, the icebox would have been filled, no doubt, with copies of *Peary at the North Pole* or *Byrd Alone in Antarctica*. A. L. Shrank, it was obvious, bathed in the sea, like many others here, and had his banquets at Herman's Hotdogs, down the way.

But it was not so much the presence of nine hundred or a thousand books, as it was their titles, their subjects, their incredible dark and doomed and awful names.

On the high, always midnight shelves stood Thomas Hardy in all his gloom next to *The Decline and Fall of the Roman Empire*, which leaned on dread Nietzsche and hopeless Schopenhauer cheek by jowl with *The Anatomy of Melancholy*, Edgar Allan Poe, Mary Shelley, Freud, the tragedies of Shakespeare (no comedies visible), the Marquis de Sade, Thomas De Quincey, Hitler's *Mein Kampf*, Spengler's *Decline of the West* . . . and on and on. . . .

Eugene O'Neill was there. Oscar Wilde, but only his sad prison essay, none of his lilac fluff or gentian laughs. Genghis Khan and Mussolini leaned on each other. Books with titles like *Suicide As an Answer* or *The Dark Night of Hamlet* or *Lemmings to the Sea* were on the high shelf in snows. On the floor lay *World War Two* and *Krakatoa, the Explosion Heard Round the World*, along with *India the Hungry* and *The Red Sun Rises*.

If you run your eye and mind along books like that, and run your stare along again, disbelieving, there is only one thing you can do. Like a bad film version of *Mourning Becomes Electra*, where one suicide follows another and murder tops murder, and incest incites incest, and blackmail supersedes poisoned apples and people fall down stairs or step on strychnine tacks, you finally snort, toss back your head, and . . .

Laugh!

"What's so funny?" said someone behind me.

I turned.

"I said, what's so *funny?*"

He stood with his thin pale face about six inches from the tip of my nose.

The man who slept on that analysis couch.

The man who owned all those end-of-the-world books.

A. L. SHRANK.

"Well?" he said.

" **Y**our library!" I stammered.

A. L. Shrank glared, waiting.

Luckily I sneezed, which erased my laugh and let me cover my confusion with a Kleenex.

"Forgive me, forgive," I said. "I own exactly fourteen books. It's not often you see the New York Public Library imported to Venice pier."

The flames went out in A. L. Shrank's tiny, bright-yellow fox eyes. His wire-thin shoulders sank. His tiny fists opened up. My praise caused him to glance through his own window like a stranger and gape.

"Why," he murmured, amazed, "yes, they're all mine."

I stood looking down at a man no taller than five-one or five-two, maybe less without his shoes. I had a terrible urge to check to see if he wore three-inch heels, but kept my eyes level with the top of his head. He was not even aware of my inspection, so proud was he of the proliferation of literary beasts that infested his dark shelves.

"I have five thousand nine hundred and ten books," he announced.

"You sure it's not five thousand nine hundred and *eleven?*"

He very carefully looked only in at his library and said, in a cold voice, "Why are you laughing?"

"The titles—"

"The titles?" He leaned closer to the window to search the shelves for some bright traitor among all those assassin books.

"Well," I said, lamely, "aren't there any summers, good weather, fair winds, in your library? Don't you own any glad books, happy finds like Leacock's *Sunshine Sketches of a Little Town? The Sun Is My Undoing? In the Good Old Summertime? June Laughter?*"

"No!" Shrank stood on tiptoe to say this, then caught himself and sank down. "No—"

"How about Peacock's *Headlong Hall,* or *Huck Finn, Three Men in a Boat, How Green Was My Father? Pickwick Papers?* Robert Benchley? James Thurber? S. J. Perelman—"

I machinegunned the titles. Shrank listened and almost cringed back at my recitation of joy. He let me run down.

"How about the *Savonarola Joke Book* or *The Funny Sayings of Jack the Ripper—.*" I stopped.

A. L. Shrank was all shadow and ice, turning away.

"Sorry," I said, and I was. "What I'd really like to do some day is come by to browse. That is, if you'll let me."

A. L. Shrank weighed this, decided I was repentant, and moved to touch his shop-front door. It whined softly open. He turned to examine me with his tiny, bright amber eyes, his thin fingers twitching at his sides.

"Why not now?" he said.

"I can't. Later, Mr.—"

"Shrank. A. L. Shrank. Consulting psychologist. No, not Shrink, as you might be thinking, as in psychiatrist. Just plain Shrank, meadow doctor to lost creatures."

He was imitating my banter. His thin smile was a weak-tea duplicate of my own. I felt it would vanish if I, in turn, shut my mouth. I glanced above him.

"How come you've left that old tarot card sign in place? And what about phrenology and hypnotism—"

"You forgot to mention my handwriting analysis sign. And the one mentioning numerology is just inside the door. Be my guest."

I moved, but stopped.

"Come along," said A. L. Shrank. "Come on," he said, really smiling now, the smile of a fish, however, not of a dog. "Step in."

At each gentle command, I inched forward, my eyes touching with all too obvious irony on the hypnotism sign above the tiny man's head. His eyes did not blink.

"Come," said A. L. Shrank, nodding at his library without looking at it.

I found the invitation irresistible, in spite of the car crashes, dirigible burnings, mine explosions, and mental delapidations I knew each book contained.

"Well," I said.

At which moment the entire pier shook. Far out at the end, in the fog, a great creature had struck the pier. It was like a whale brunting a ship, or the *Queen Mary* plowing into the ancient pilings. The big iron brutes out there, hidden, were beginning to tear the planks apart.

The vibrations knocked the planks and came up through my body and Shrank's body, with jolts of mortality and doom. Our bones shook in our blood. We both jerked our heads to try to stare through the fog at the devastation somewhere beyond. The mighty blows jarred me a modicum away from the door. The titanic buffeting trembled and shivered and inched A. L. Shrank on his sill like a lost toy. A paleness bloomed within the paleness of his face. He looked like a man panicked by an earthquake or a tidal wave rushing at the pier. Again and again the great machines hammered and pounded in the fog a hundred yards away, and invisible cracks seemed to appear in A. L. Shrank's milk-glass brow and cheeks. The war had begun! Soon the dark tanks would lumber along the pier, destroying as they came, a flood of carnival émigrés running before them toward land, A. L. Shrank soon to be among them as his house of dark tarot cards fell.

It was my chance to escape, but I failed.

Shrank's gaze had returned to me, as if I could save him from that invasion just beyond. In a moment he might seize my elbow for support.

The pier shook. I shut my eyes.

I thought I heard my secret office telephone ring. I almost cried out, my phone! it's for me!

But I was saved from that by a tide of men and women, and a few children, hurrying the other way, not toward land but rushing toward the sea end of the pier, a large man in a dark cloak and a floppy G. K. Chesterton hat leading the way.

"Last ride, last day, last time!" he yelled. "Last chance! Come *on!*"

"Shapeshade," whispered A. L. Shrank.

And that's who it was. Shapeshade, the sole owner and proprietor of the old Venice Cinema at the foot of the pier, which would be ground underfoot and turned to celluloid mulch within the week.

"*This* way!" called Shapeshade's voice from the mist.

I glanced at A. L. Shrank.

He shrugged and nodded, giving permission.

I ran off into the fog.

The long chattering clack and grind, the ascending slow clang, rattle, and roar, like some robot centipede of immense size scaling the side of a nightmare, pausing at the top for the merest breath, then cascading in a serpentine of squeal, rush, and thunderous roar, in scream, in human shriek down the abysmal span, there to attack, more swiftly this time, another hill, another ascending scale rising yet higher and higher to fall off into hysteria.

The rollercoaster.

I stood looking up at it through the mist.

In an hour, so they said, it would be dead.

It had been part of my life as long as I could remember. From here most nights you could hear people laughing and screaming as they soared up to the heights of so-called existence and plunged down toward an imaginary doom.

So this was to be a final ride late in the afternoon, just before the dynamite experts taped explosives to the dinosaur's legs and brought him to his knees.

"Jump in!" a boy yelled. "It's free!"

"Even free I never thought it was anything but torture," I said.

"Hey, look who's here in the front seat," someone called. "And behind!"

Mr. Shapeshade was there, cramming his vast black hat down over his ears, laughing. Back of him was Annie Oakley the rifle lady.

Back of her sat the man who had run the fun house; alongside him was the old lady who spun the pink cotton candy machine and sold illusion that melted in your mouth and left you hungry long before Chinese food.

Back of them were the Knock a Milk Bottle and the Toss a Hoop team, everyone looking like they were posing for a passport photo to eternity.

Only Mr. Shapeshade, as coxswain, was jubilant.

"As Captain Ahab said, don't be yellow!" he called.

That made me feel like a sheep.

I let the rollercoaster ticket-tearer help me into the coward's back row.

"This your first trip?" He laughed.

"And my last."

"Everyone set to scream?"

"Why not?" cried Shapeshade.

Let me out, I thought. We'll all die!

"Here goes," the ticketman yelled, "nothing!"

It was heaven going up and hell all the way down.

I had this terrible feeling they blew the legs out from under the rollercoaster as we descended.

When we hit bottom I glanced over. A. L. Shrank stood on the pier, staring up at us lunatics who had willingly boarded the *Titanic*. A. L. Shrank backed off in the fog.

But we were climbing again. Everyone screamed. *I* screamed. Christ, I thought, we sound as if we mean it!

When it was over, the celebrants wandered off in the fog, wiping their eyes, holding on to each other.

Mr. Shapeshade stood beside me as the dynamite men ran in to wrap their explosives around the girders and struts of the great ride.

"You going to stay and watch?" said Mr. Shapeshade, gently.

"I don't think I could stand it," I said. "I saw a film once where they shot an elephant right on screen. The way it fell down and over, collapsed, hurt me terribly. It was like watching someone bomb St. Peter's dome. I wanted to kill the hunters. No, thanks."

A flagman, anyway, was waving us off.

Shapeshade and I walked back through the fog. He took my elbow, like a good middle-European uncle advising his favorite nephew.

"Tonight. No explosions. No destructions. Only joy. Fun. Great old times. My theater. Maybe tonight is our last cinema night. Maybe tomorrow. Free. Gratis. Nice boy, *be* there."

He hugged me and plowed off through the fog like a great dark tugboat.

On my way past A. L. Shrank's I saw that his door was still wide open. But I didn't step in.

I wanted to run, call collect on my gas station telephone, but I feared that two thousand miles of silence would whisper back at me of deaths in sunlit streets, red meats hung in *carneceria* windows, and a loneliness so vast it was like an open wound.

My hair grayed. It grew an inch.

Cal! I thought. Dear, dreadful barber—here I come.

Cal's barber shop in Venice was situated right across the street from the city hall and next door to a bail bond shop where flies hung like dead trapeze artists from flypaper coils that had been left in the windows for ten years, and where men and women from the jail across the way went in like shadows and came out like uninhabited clothes. And next door to that was a little ma-and-pa grocery, but they were gone and their son sat on his pants in the window all day and sold maybe a can of soup and took horse-race telephone bets.

The barber shop, though it had a few flies in the window that had been dead no more than ten days, at least got a washdown once a month from Cal, who ran the place with well-oiled shears and unoiled elbows and spearmint gossip in his all-pink mouth. He acted like he was running a bee farm and afraid it would get out of hand as he wrestled the big, silver, bumbling insect around your ears until it suddenly froze, bit, and held on to your hair until Cal cursed and yanked back as if he were pulling teeth.

Which was why, along with economics, I had my hair cut only twice a year by Cal.

Twice yearly, also, because of all the barbers in the world, Cal talked, sprayed, gummed, cudgeled, advised, and droned more than most, which boggles the mind. Name a subject, he knew it all, top, side, and bottom, and in the middle of explaining dumb Einstein's theory would stop, shut one eye, cock his head, and ask the Great Question with No Safe Answer.

"Hey, did I ever tell you about me and old Scott Joplin? Why, old Scott and me, by God and by Jesus, listen. That day in 1915 when he taught me how to play the 'Maple Leaf Rag.' Let me tell you."

There was this picture of Scott Joplin on the wall, signed in ink a few centuries ago and fading like the canary lady's message. In that photo you could see a very young Cal, seated on a piano stool, and bent over him, Joplin, his big black hands covering those of the happy boy.

There was that joyous kid, forever on the wall, captured on film, hunched over to seize the piano keys, ready to leap on life, the world, the universe, eat it all. The look on that boy's face was such that it cracked my heart every time I saw it. So I didn't look at it often. It hurt enough to see Cal looking at it, gathering his spit to ask the age-old Great Question, and, with no begs or requests, dash for the piano to maple leaf that rag.

Cal.

Cal looked like a cowpuncher who now rode barber chairs. Think of Texas cowhands, lean, weatherbeaten, permanently dyed by sun, sleeping in their Stetsons, glued on for life, taking showers in the damn hats. That was Cal, circling the enemy, the customer, weapon in hand, eating the hair, chopping the sideburns, listening to the shears, admiring the Bumblebee

Electric's harmonics, talking, talking, as I imagined him cow-hand-naked dancing around my chair, Stetson jampack-nested above his ears, crave-itching to leap to that piano and rake its smile.

Sometimes I'd pretend I didn't see him throwing those mad stares, shuttling his love glances at the waiting black and white, white and black keys. But finally I'd heave a great masochistic sigh and cry, "Okay, Cal. Git."

Cal got.

Galvanized, he shot across the room, in a cowboy shamble, two of him, one in the mirror faster and brighter than the real one, yanking the piano lid up to show all that yellow dentistry just aching to have its music pulled.

"Listen to this, son. You ever hear anything, ever, ever in life, ever hear anything like—this?"

"No, Cal," I said, waiting in the chair with my head half-ruined. "No," I said, honestly, "I never did."

"My God," cried the old man coming out of the morgue a final time inside my head, "who gave him that *awful* haircut?"

I saw the guilty party standing in the window of his barber shop, gazing out at the fog, looking like one of those people in empty rooms or cafes or on street corners in paintings by Hopper.

Cal.

I had to force myself to pull open the front door and step in, gingerly, looking down.

There were curlicues of brown, black, and gray hair all over the place.

"Hey," I said, with false joviality. "Looks like you had a great day!"

"You know," said Cal, looking out the window, "that hair has been there five, six weeks. Ain't nobody in their right mind coming in that door save tramps, which isn't you, or fools, which isn't you, or bald men, which isn't you, asking directions to the madhouse, and poor people, which *is* you, so go sit down in the chair and prepare to be electrocuted, the electric clippers have been on the fritz for two months and I ain't had the cash to get the goddamn things fixed. Sit."

Obedient to my executioner, I bounded forward and sat and stared at the hair-strews on the floor, symbols of a silent past that must have meant something, but said nothing. Even looked at sidewise, I could figure no strange shapes or imminent forecasts.

At last Cal turned and waded across that forlorn porcelain and forelock sea to let his hands pick up, all by themselves, the comb and scissors. He hesitated behind me, like the axeman sad to have to chop some young king's head.

He asked how long I wanted it, or how ruined I wanted it, take your choice, but I was busy staring across the glaring white Arctic emptiness of the shop at—

Cal's piano.

For the first time in fifteen years it was covered. Its gray-yellow Oriental smile was invisible under a white mortuary bedsheet.

"Cal." My eyes were on the sheet. I had forgotten, for a moment, the old Venice ticket office man lying cold with a terrible haircut. "Cal," I said, "how come you're not maple leafing the old rag?"

Cal let his scissors snip-snip and then snip-snip around my neck.

"Cal?" I said.

"Something wrong?" I said.

"When does the dying stop?" said Cal, a long way off.

And now the bumblebee buzzed and stung my ears and

made the old chill ripple down my spine, and then Cal got busy hacking away with his dull scissors as if he were harvesting a wild wheat crop, cursing under his breath. I smelled a faint whiskey odor, but kept my eyes straight ahead.

"Cal?" I said.

"Shoot. No—shit is what I mean."

He threw the scissors, comb, and dead silver bumblebee on the shelf and shambled across the ocean of old hair to yank the sheet off the piano, which grinned like a big mindless shape as he sat down and laid his two hands like limp paintbrushes on the keys, ready to paint God knows what.

What came out was like broken teeth in a mashed jaw.

"Damn. Hell. Crud. I used to do it, used to play the living guts outa that thing Scott taught me, old Scott—Scott."

His voice died.

He had glanced up at the wall above the piano. He glanced away when he saw me looking, but it was too late.

For the first time in twenty years, that picture of Scott Joplin was gone.

I lurched forward in the chair, my mouth dropped wide.

At which time Cal forced himself to hurl the sheet back over the smile and return, a mourner at his own wake, to stand behind my chair and pick up the torture instruments again.

"Scott Joplin ninety-seven, Cal the barber zero," he said, describing a lost game.

He ran his trembling fingers over my head.

"Jesus, look what I done to you. My God, that's a lousy cut, and I'm not even halfway in. I ought to pay you for all the years you let me make you run around looking like an Airedale with mange. On top of which, let me tell you what I did to a customer three days ago. It's terrible. Maybe I made the poor son-of-a-bitch look so bad someone killed him to put him out of his misery!"

I lurched forward again, but Cal put me gently back.

"I should give Novocain, but I don't. About this old guy. Listen!"

"I'm listening, Cal," I said, for that was why I was here.

"Sat right where you are sitting now," said Cal. "Sat right there, just like you're sitting, looked in the mirror, and said, shoot the works. That's what he said. Cal, shoot the works. Biggest night of my life, he said. Myron's Ballroom, downtown L.A. Haven't been there in years. Called, said I'd won the grand prize, he said. For what? I said. Most important old resident of Venice, they said. Why's that a cause for celebration? Shut up and primp up, they said. So here I am, Cal. Short all around but don't billiard ball me. And some of that Tiger Tonic, shake it on me. I cut until hell wouldn't have it. Old man must've saved up two years of high, snow mountain hair. Drenched him with tonic until the fleas fled. Sent him out happy, leaving his last two bucks behind, I wouldn't wonder. Sitting right where you are.

"And now he's dead," Cal added.

"Dead!" I almost shouted.

"Somebody found him in a lion cage submerged under the canal waters. Dead."

"Somebody," I said. But didn't add, me!

"I figure the old man never had any champagne before or it was a long time back, got loaded, fell in. Cal, he said, the works. It just goes to show you, right? Could be me or you in that canal, just as likely, and now, hot damn and old breakfasts, he's alone forever. Don't it make you think? Hey, now, son. You don't look too well. I talk too much, right?"

"Did he say who was going to pick him up and how and when and why?" I said.

"Nothing fancy, far as I could tell. Someone coming on the big Venice Short Line train, pick him up, take him right down to Myron's Ballroom door. You ever get on the train Saturday nights around one? Old ladies and old gents piling out of Myron's in their mothball furs and green tuxedos, smelling of Ben Hur perfume and nickel panatelas, glad they didn't break a leg on the dance floor, bald heads sweating, mascara running, and the fox furs starting to spoil? I went once, and looked around and got out. I figured the streetcar might stop at Rose Lawn Cemetery, on the way to the sea, and half those folks get out. No, thanks. I talk too much, don't I? Just tell me if I do—

"Anyways," he went on at last, "he's dead and gone, and the awful thing is he'll be lying in the grave the next one thousand years remembering who in hell gave him his last awful haircut, and the answer is me.

"So it's been one of them weeks. People with bad haircuts disappear, wind up drowned, and at long last I know damn well my hands are no good for nothing, and—"

"You don't know who it was picked the old man up and took him to that dance?"

"Who knows? Who cares? Old man said whoever it was told him to meet him down front of the Venice Cinema at seven, see part of a show, have a dinner at Modesti's, the last cafe on the pier still open, boy howdy, and head downtown to the ballroom. For a fast waltz with a ninety-nine-year-old Rose Queen, what a night, hey? Then home to bed, forever! But why would you want to know all this, son? You—"

The telephone rang.

Cal looked at it, his face draining of color.

The telephone rang three times.

"Aren't you going to answer it, Cal?" I said.

Cal looked at it the same way I looked at my gas station office phone, and two thousand miles of silence and heavy breathing along the way. He shook his head.

"Why would I answer a phone when there's nothing but bad news on it?" he said.

"Some days, you feel that way," I said.

I pulled the apron from around my neck, slowly, and got up.

Automatically, Cal's hand went palm out for my cash. When he saw his hand there, he cursed and dropped his hand, turned and banged the cash register.

Up jumped NO SALE.

I looked at myself in the mirror and almost barked like a seal at what I saw.

"It's a great haircut, Cal," I said.

"Git outa here."

On the way out, I put my hand up to touch where the picture of Scott Joplin used to hang, playing great stuff with fingers like two bunches of big black bananas.

If Cal saw this, he didn't say.

I slipped on some old hair, going out.

I walked until I found sunshine and Crumley's buried-in-deep-grass bungalow.

I stood outside.

Crumley must have felt me there. He yanked the door open and said, "You doing *that* again?"

"I never did. I'm no good at being out scaring people at three o'clock in the morning," I said.

He looked down at his left hand and shoved it at me.

There was a small clot of oily green seaweed on his palm, his clench marks in it.

I held out my hand, like someone trumping an ace, and opened my fingers.

My identical clump of seaweed, drier, and brittle, lay in my palm.

Crumley's eyes moved from both our hands up to my eyes, my brow, my cheeks, my chin. He exhaled.

"Apricot pie, Halloween pumpkins, backyard tomatoes, late summer peaches, Santa Claus's California son, you look like all of them. With a face like that how can I yell guilty?"

He dropped his hands and stood aside.

"You do like beer, don't you?"

"Not much," I said.

"Would you rather I fix you a chocolate malt?"

"Could you?"

"No, goddamn it. You'll drink beer and like it. Get it in here." He wandered off, shaking his head, and I came in and shut the door, feeling like a high school student come back to visit his tenth-grade teacher.

Crumley was standing in his parlor window blinking out at the dry dirt path I had wandered up a moment ago.

"Three o'clock, by God," he muttered. "Three. Right out there. I heard someone weeping, how you figure that? Crying? Gave me the goosebumps. Sounded like a banshee woman. Hell. Let me look at your face again."

I showed him my face.

"Jesus," he said, "do you always blush that easily?"

"I can't help it."

"Christ, you could massacre half a Hindu village and still look like Peter Rabbit. What are you stuffed with?"

"Chocolate bars. And I keep six kinds of ice cream in my icebox, when I can afford it."

"I bet you buy it instead of bread."

I wanted to say no, but he would have caught the lie.

"Take a load off your feet and what kind of beer do you hate most? I got Budweiser which is awful, Budweiser which is dreadful, and Bud which is the worst. Take your pick. No, don't. Allow me." He ambled off to the kitchen and came back with two cans. "There's still a little sun. Let's get out of here."

He led the way into his backyard.

I couldn't believe Crumley's garden.

"Why not?" He steered me out the back door of his bungalow, into a green and luscious illumination of thousands of plants, ivies, papyrus, birds of paradise, succulents, cacti. Crumley beamed. "Got six dozen different species of epiphyllum over there, that's Iowa corn against the fence, that's a plum tree, that's apricot, that's orange. Want to know why?"

"Everyone in the world needs two, three jobs," I said, without hesitation. "One job isn't enough, just as one life isn't enough. I want to have a dozen of both."

"Bull's-eye. Doctors should dig ditches. Ditchdiggers ought to run kindergartens one day a week. Philosophers should wash dishes in a greasy spoon two nights out of ten. Mathematicians should blow whistles at high school gyms. Poets should drive trucks for a change of menu and police detectives—"

"Should own and operate the Garden of Eden," I said, quietly.

"Jesus." Crumley laughed and shook his head, and looked at the green seaweed he ground in his palm. "You're a pain-in-the-ass know-it-all. You think you got me figured? Surprise!" He bent and twisted a garden valve. "Hark, as they used to say. Hist!"

A soft rain sprang up in brilliant blooms that touched all around Eden with whispers that said, Soft. Quiet. Serenity. Stay. Live forever.

I felt all my bones diminish in my flesh. Something like a dark skin fell from my back.

Crumley tilted his head to one side to study my face. "Well?"

I shrugged. "You see so much rot every week, you need this."

"Trouble is, the guys over at the station won't try anything *like* this. Sad, huh? To just be a cop and nothing else, forever? Christ, I'd kill myself. You know what—I wish I could bring all the rot I see every week here and use it for fertilizer. Boy, what roses I'd grow!"

"Or Venus flytraps," I said.

He mused on that and nodded. "That earns you a beer."

He led the way into his kitchen and I stood looking out at the rainforest, taking deep breaths of the cool air, but not able to smell it because of my cold.

"I've passed your place for years," I said. "And wondered who could possibly live back in such a great homemade forest. Now that I've met you, I know it *had* to be you."

Crumley had to stop himself from falling on the floor and writhing with joy at the compliment. He controlled himself and opened two really terrible beers, one of which I managed to sip.

"Can't you make a better face than that?" he asked. "You *really* like malts better?"

"Yeah." I took a bigger sip and it gave me courage to ask, "One thing. What am I doing here? You asked me over because of that stuff you found out front of your house, that seaweed? Now here I am surveying your jungle and drinking your bad beer. No longer a suspect?"

"Oh, for Christ's sake." Crumley swigged his own drink, and blinked at me. "If I thought you were any kind of mad lion-tamer cage-filler-upper, you'd have been in the toilet two days ago. You think I don't know all about you?"

"There's not much to know," I said, sheepishly.

"Like hell there isn't. Listen." Crumley took another swig, shut his eyes, and read the details off the back of his eyelids.

"One block from your apartment's a liquor store, and an ice cream parlor, and next to that a Chinese grocery. They all think you're mad. The Nut, they call you. The Fool, on occasion. You talk loud and lots. They hear. Every time you sell a story to *Weird Tales* or *Astonishing Stories*, it's all over the pier because you open your window and yell. Christ. But the bottom line is, kid, they like you. You got no future, sure, they all agree, because who in hell is really going to go and land on the moon, when? Between now and the year 2000, will anyone give a damn about Mars? Only you, Flash Gordon. Only crazy nut you, Buck Rogers."

I was blushing furiously, head down, half-angry and somewhat embarrassed but somehow pleased at all this attention. I had been called Flash and Buck often, but somehow when Crumley did it, it went right by without wounding.

Crumley opened his eyes, saw my blush, and said, "Now, cut that *out*."

"Why would you have known all this about me, a long time before the old man was"—I stopped and changed it—"before he died?"

"I'm curious about everything."

"Most people aren't. I discovered that when I was fourteen. Everybody else gave up toys that year. I told my folks, no toys, no Christmas. So they kept on giving me toys every year. The other boys got shirts and ties. I took astronomy. Out of four thousand students in my high school there were only fifteen other boys and fourteen girls who looked at the sky with me. The rest were out running around the track and watching their feet. So, it follows that—"

I turned instinctively, for something had stirred in me. I found myself wandering across the kitchen.

"I got a hunch," I said. "Could I—?"

"What?" said Crumley.

"You got a workroom here?"

"Sure. Why?" Crumley frowned with faint alarm.

That only made me push a bit harder. "Mind if I see?"

"Well—"

I moved in the direction toward which Crumley's eyes had darted.

The room was right off the kitchen. It had once been a bedroom but now it was empty except for a desk, a chair, and a typewriter on the desk.

"I knew it," I said.

I went to stand behind the chair and look at the machine which was not an old beat-up Underwood Standard, but a fairly new Corona with a fresh ribbon in it, and a stack of yellow sheets waiting to one side.

"*That* explains why you look at me the way you do," I said. "Lord, yes, always tilting your head this way and that, scowling, narrowing your eyes!"

"Trying to X-ray that big head of yours, see if there's a brain in there, and how it does what it does," said Crumley, tilting his head now to the left, now to the right.

"Nobody knows how the brain works, not writers, no one. All I do is *throw* up every morning, *clean* up at noon."

"Bullshit," said Crumley, gently.

"Truth."

I looked at the desk, which had three drawers on either side of the cubby.

I put my hand out and down toward the bottom drawer on the left.

Crumley shook his head.

I shifted and reached over to touch the bottom drawer on the right.

Crumley nodded.

I pulled the drawer open, slowly.

Crumley exhaled.

There was a manuscript there in an open-top box. It looked

to be about 150 to 200 pages, beginning on page one, with no title page.

"How long's this been down here in the bottom drawer?" I asked. "Pardon."

"It's all right," said Crumley. "Five years."

"You're going to finish it now," I said.

"Like hell I am. Why?"

"Because I told you so. And I know."

"Shut the drawer," said Crumley.

"Not just yet." I pulled out the chair, sat, and rolled a sheet of yellow paper into the machine.

I typed five words on one line and then shifted down and wrote three more words.

Crumley squinted over my shoulder and read them aloud, quietly.

"Death Is a Lonely Business." He took a breath and finished it. "By Elmo Crumley." He had to repeat it. "By Elmo Crumley, by God."

"There." I placed my new title page down on top of his waiting manuscript and slid the drawer shut. "That's a gift. I'll find another title for my book. Now, you'll *have* to finish it."

I rolled another sheet of paper into the machine and asked, "What was the number of the last page on the bottom of your manuscript?"

"One hundred sixty-two," said Crumley.

I typed 163 and left the paper in the machine.

"There," I said. "It's waiting. Tomorrow morning you get out of bed, walk to the machine, no phone calls, no newspaper reading, don't even go to the bathroom, sit down, type, and Elmo Crumley is immortal."

"B.S.," said Crumley, but ever so quietly.

"God promises. But you got to work."

I got up and Crumley and I stood looking at his Corona as if it were the only child he would ever have.

"You giving me orders, kid?" said Crumley.

"No. Your brain is, if you'd just listen."

Crumley backed off, walked into the kitchen, got some more beer. I waited by his desk until I heard the back screen door bang.

I found Crumley in his garden letting the whirlaround water-tosser cover his face with cooling raindrops, for the day was warm now and the sun out full here on the rim of fog country.

"What is it," said Crumley, "forty stories you sold so far?"

"At thirty bucks apiece, yeah. The Rich Author."

"You *are* rich. I stood down at the magazine rack at Abe's Liquor yesterday and read that one you wrote about the man who finds he has a skeleton inside him and it scares hell out of him. Christ, it was a beaut. Where in hell do you get ideas like that?"

"I got a skeleton inside *me*," I said.

"Most people never notice." Crumley handed me a beer and watched me make yet another face. "The old man—"

"William Smith?"

"Yeah, William Smith, the autopsy report came in this morning. There was no water in his lungs."

"That means he didn't drown. That means he was killed up on the canal bank and shoved down into the cage after he was dead. That proves—"

"Don't jump ahead of the train, you'll get run down. And don't say I told you so, or I'll take that beer back."

I offered him the beer, gladly. He nudged my hand aside.

"What have you done about the haircut?" I said.

"What haircut?"

"Mr. Smith had a really lousy haircut the afternoon before he died. His friend moaned about it at the morgue, remember? I knew only one really lousy barber could have done it."

I told Crumley about Cal, the prizes promised William Smith, Myron's Ballroom, Modesti's, the big red train.

Crumley listened patiently, and said, "Flimsy."

"It's all we got," I said. "You want me to check the Venice Cinema to see if they saw him out front the night he disappeared?"

"No," said Crumley.

"You want me to check Modesti's, the train, Myron's Ballroom?"

"No," said Crumley.

"What do you want me to do, then?"

"Stay out of it."

"Why?"

"Because," said Crumley, and stopped. He glanced at the back door of his house. "Anything happens to you, my goddamn novel never gets finished. Somebody's got to read the damn thing, and I don't know anybody else."

"You forget," I said. "Whoever stood outside your house last night stands outside mine already. I can't let him do that, can I? I can't go on being spooked by that guy who gave me the title I just typed on your machine. Can I?"

Crumley looked at my face and I could see his thinking was, apricot pie, banana cake, and strawberry ice cream.

"Just be careful," he said, at last. "The old man may have slipped and knocked his head and was dead when he hit the water, which is why there was no water in his lungs."

"And then he swam over and put himself in the cage. Sure."

Crumley squinted at me, trying to guess my weight.

Silently, he went away into the jungle and was gone about a minute. I waited.

Then, far away, I heard an elephant trombone the wind. I turned slowly, into a drench of garden rain, listening. A lion, closer, opened his vast beehive valves and exhaled a killer swarm. A herd of antelopes and gazelles dusted by like a summer wind of sound, touching the dry earth, moving my heart to their run.

Crumley was suddenly on the path, smiling wildly, like a boy half-proud, half-ashamed of a madness unknown to all the world until now, this hour. He snorted and gestured two fresh beers up at six lilyhorn sound systems suspended like great dark flowers in the trees. From these, the antelopes, gazelles, and zebras circled our lives and protected us from the nameless beasts out beyond the bungalow fences. The elephant blew his nose once more and knocked my soul flat.

"African recordings," said Crumley, unnecessarily.

"Swell," I said. "Hey, what's that?"

Ten thousand African flamingos airlifted from a bright freshwater lagoon back five thousand days ago when I was a high school kid and Martin and Osa Johnson were flying in from the wildebeest African trails to walk among us plain folks in California and tell great tales.

And then I remembered.

The day I was supposed to run full speed to hear Martin Johnson speak, he had been killed in a plane crash just outside L.A.

But right now, in Elmo Crumley's jungle compound Eden retreat, there were Martin Johnson's birds.

My heart went with them.

I looked at the sky and said, "What are *you* going to do, Crumley?"

"Nothing," he said. "The old canary lady is going to live forever. You can bet on it."

"I'm broke," I said.

When the drowned people showed up later that day, it really spoiled the picnics all up and down the beach. People were indignant, packed their hampers, went home. Dogs that ran eagerly down to look at the strangers lying on the shore were called back by angry women or irritable men. Children were herded away and sent off with a reprimand, not to associate with such peculiar strangers ever again.

Drowning, after all, was a forbidden subject. Like sex, it was never discussed. It followed then that when a drowned person dared touch shore, he or she was persona non grata. Children might dash down to hold dark ceremonies in their minds, but the ladies who remained after the families had cringed off and gone away raised their parasols and turned their backs, as if someone with unruly breath had called from the surf. Nothing in Emily Post could help the situation. Very simply the lost surfers had come without invite, permission, or warning and like unwanted relatives had to be hustled off to mysterious ice-houses inland, at a double dogtrot.

But no sooner was one surf-stranger gone than you heard the sandpiping children's voices crying, "Look, Mommy, oh, look!"

"Git away! Get!"

And you heard the rush of feet running away from the still-warm landmines on the shore.

Walking back from Crumley's I heard about the unwelcome visitors, the drowned ones.

I had hated to leave the sun which seemed to shine forever in Crumley's orchard.

Reaching the sea was like touching another country. The fog came as if glad for all the bad shoreline news. The drownings had had nothing to do with police, night traumas, or dark surprises in canals that sucked their teeth all night. It was simply riptides.

The shore was empty now. But I had an even emptier feeling when I lifted my gaze to the old Venice pier.

"Bad rice!" I heard someone whisper. Me.

An old Chinese imprecation, shouted at the edges of crops to guarantee a good harvest against the devastation of the envious gods.

"Bad rice—"

For someone had at last stepped on the big snake.

Someone had stomped it down.

The rollercoaster was gone forever from the far end of the pier.

What was left of it now lay in the late day, like a great strewn jackstraws game. But only a big steamshovel was playing that game now, snorting, bending down to snap up the bones and find them good.

"When does the dying stop?" I had heard Cal say a few hours back.

With the empty pier-end ahead, its skeleton being flensed, and a tidal wave of fog storming toward shore, I felt a fusillade of cold darts in my back. I was being followed. I spun.

But it wasn't me being pursued by nothing.

Across the street, I saw A. L. Shrank. He ran along, hands deep in overcoat pockets, head sunk in his dark collar, glancing back, like a rat before hounds.

God, I thought, now I know who he reminds me of.

Poe!

The famous photographs, the somber portraits of Edgar Allan with his vast milk-glass lampglow brow and brooding night-fire eyes and the doomed and lost mouth buried under the dark moustache, his tie askew on his untidy collar, over his always convulsing and swallowing throat.

Edgar Allan Poe.

Poe ran. *Shrank* ran, glancing back at a swift fog with no shape.

Christ, I thought, it's after *all* of us.

By the time I reached the Venice Cinema, the fog, impatient, had already gone in.

M r. Shapeshade's old Venice Cinema was special because it was the last of a series of night riverboats, afloat on the edge of the tide, anywhere in the world.

The front part of the cinema was on the concrete walk that leads from Venice down toward Ocean Park and Santa Monica.

The back half of it stuck out on the pier so that its rear end was over the water.

I stood in front of the movie house at this late hour of the day, glanced up at the marquee, and gasped.

There were no films listed. Only one huge two-foot-high word.

GOODBYE.

It was like being stabbed in the stomach.

I stepped forward to the ticket booth.

Shapeshade was there smiling at me with manic good will as he waved.

"Goodbye?" I said, mournfully.

"Sure!" Shapeshade laughed. "Ta-ta, toodle-oo. Farewell. And it's free! Go in! Any friend of Douglas Fairbanks, Thomas Meighan, Milton Sills, and Charles Ray is a friend of mine."

I melted at the names from my childhood; people I had seen flickering on ancient screens when I was two, three, four on my mother's knee in a cool movie house in northern Illinois before the bad rice came and we steamed west in an old beat-up Kissel, ahead of the Okies, my dad looking for a twelve-buck-a-week job.

"I *can't* go in, Mr. Shapeshade."

"Look at the boy who won't!" Shapeshade threw his hands to the heavens and rolled his eyeballs like Stromboli, irritated by Pinocchio and itching to cut his strings. "Why not?"

"When I come out of movies in daylight, I get depressed. Nothing's right."

"So where's the sun?" cried Shapeshade. "By the time you exit, it's night!"

"Anyway, I wanted to ask you about three nights ago," I said. "Did you by any chance see that old ticket office man, Bill, Willy, William Smith, waiting out front here that night?"

"I yelled at him, yes. What happened to your head? I said. Did a grizzly bear claw your wig off? I said. His hair was a laugh riot. So who took a lawnmower to him? Demon Cal?"

"Yeah. Did you see someone meet William Smith and take him away?"

"I got busy. All of a sudden, six people came for tickets, six! When I looked around, Mr. Smith, Willie, was gone. Why?"

My shoulders sank. My frustration must have shown in my face. Shapeshade quickened with sympathy and enunciated his Sen-Sen breath through the ticket booth's glass speak-hole.

"Guess who's inside on the big 1922 moth-hole-sieved silver screen? Fairbanks! *The Black Pirate.* Gish! *Broken Blossoms.* Lon Chaney! *Phantom of the Opera.* Who was greater?"

"Lord, Mr. Shapeshade, those are all silent."

"So? Where were you in 1928 you didn't notice? The more talkie the less movie! *Statues*, they played. Mouths moved and your feet went to sleep. So, these last nights, silence, hmm?

Quiet, yes? Silence and gestures forty feet across and scowls and leers twenty feet high. Quiet phantoms. Mum's-the-word pirates. Gargoyles and hunchbacks who talked in winds and rains and let the organ speak for them, eh? Plenty of seats. Go."

He thumped his brass ticket key.

The machine stuck a nice fresh orange ticket out at me.

"Yes." I took the ticket and looked into the face of this old man who hadn't been out in sun for forty years, who loved films madly, and would rather read *Silver Screen* than the *Encyclopaedia Britannica*. His eyes were gently mad with his love of old faces on yesterday's posters.

"Is Shapeshade your real name?" I said, at last.

"It means a house like this where shades are shaped and all shapes are shadows. You got a better name?"

"No, sir, Mr. Shapeshade." And I hadn't.

"What—" I started to ask.

But Shapeshade guessed with relish. "What happens to *me* tomorrow when they knock my movie house down! Say, not to worry! I got protection! So have my films, all three hundred of them up in the booth now, but soon, down the beach one mile south, the basement there where I go run films and laugh."

"Constance Rattigan!" I cried. "I've often seen that funny light flickering in her basement window or up in her front parlor, late nights. Was that *you?*"

"Who else?" beamed Shapeshade. "For years now, when I finish here I just foxtrot along the shore with twenty pounds of film under each arm. Sleeps all day, Constance does, watches films and eats popcorn with me all night, that's Rattigan, and we sit and hold hands like two crazy kids, and rob the film vaults, and cry sometimes so much we can't see to rewind the spools."

I looked out at the beach beyond the cinema front and

could not help but see Mr. Shapeshade jogging the surf in the dark, toting popcorn and Mary Pickford, Holloway Suckers and Tom Mix, on his way to that ancient queen to be her subservient lover of multifold darks and lights that sprocketed the dream screen with just as many sunrises as sunsets.

And then Shapeshade watching just before dawn as Constance Rattigan, so the rumors said, ran naked to leap into the cold salt waves and rise with healthfood seaweeds in her straight white teeth and regally braiding her hair, while Shapeshade limped home in the rising sun, drunk on remembrance, mumming and humming the drones of the mighty Wurlitzer in his marrow, soul, heart, and happy mouth.

"Listen." He leaned forward like Ernest Thesiger in the dim halls of *The Old Dark House* or as Dr. Praetorius looming in *Bride of Frankenstein*. "Inside, go up behind the screen, have you ever? No. Climb up on stage in the night behind the screen. What an experience! Like being in Caligari's lopsided chambers. You'll thank me forever."

I shook his hand and stared.

"My gosh," I cried, "that hand of yours. Isn't that the paw that slid out of the dark behind the library bookshelves in *The Cat and the Canary* to grab and vanish the lawyer before he could read the will?"

Shapeshade stared down at his hand cradled in mine, and beamed.

"Aren't you a nice boy?" he said.

"I try, Mr. Shapeshade," I said. "I try."

Inside, I blundered down the aisle until I felt my way to the brass rail and half-flopped up the proscenium steps onto an always-midnight stage to duck behind the screen and look at the great ghosts.

And ghosts they were, the tall, pale, and black-eyed shadow phantoms of time, twisted like white taffy from the slanted angle at which I saw them, gesturing and mouthing in the silence, waiting for the organ music, which had not yet begun.

And there in swift clip after chop after clip was Fairbanks with an askew face and Gish wax-melting down the screen, and Fattie Arbuckle thinned from this sideview and knocking his starved head against the top of the frame and slithering off into the dark while I stood feeling the tide move under the floor, the pier, the theater which foundered in swarming waters, now tilting and creaking and shivering, with the smell of salt coming up through the boards and more pictures, white as cream, dark as ink, blinking across the screen as the theater lifted like a bellows and sank down exhaling like a bellows, and me sunk with it.

Just then, the organ exploded.

It was like that moment a few hours ago when the great unseen steamliner had plunged to strike the pier.

The theater careened, heaved up, and fell as if on a roller-coastal tide.

The organ shouted and brayed and ricocheted a Bach prelude so that dust flew off the ancient chandeliers, the curtains stirred restlessly like funeral gowns, and myself behind the screen reaching out to hold on to something but terrified that something might touch back.

Above me, the pale images ached and gibbered their mouths and the Phantom strode down the stairs at the Paris Opera in his white-skull mask and plumed hat, even as Shapeshade, a moment before, must have strode down the dark aisle to rattle and chime the brass rings holding the short curtain around the organ, and seat himself like Destiny and Doom to spider the keys and shut his eyes and gape his mouth to let Bach out.

Afraid to look behind, I stared out past the thirty-foot phantoms at an audience unseen, riveted in place, shuddering with music, drawn by terrible images, lifted and then jolted down by the night tide under the theater deck.

Among all those pale faces, fixing their eyes upon the flickering past, was he there? The mourner on the train, the pacer along the canal rim, the leaver of three-in-the-morning rains, was that his face over here, or that one over there? Colorless moons trembling in the dark, a cluster of souls in front, another back halfway, fifty, sixty people, dreadful suspects on yet another fog excursion rushing to collide with nightmare and sink with no sound, only the great suck of the sea going back for reinforcements.

Among all these night travelers, which was he, I wondered, and what could I shout to panic him up the aisles, with me in wild pursuit?

The giant skull smiled from the screen, the lovers fled to the Opera roof, the Phantom pursued to unfurl his cape and overhear their fearful love-talk and grin; the organ shrieked, the theater bucked and heaved with heavy waters celebrating sea burials should the planks gape and drop us down through.

My eyes raced from dimly upturned face to face, and up, up, to the little window of the projectionist's booth, where a section of brow and a maniac eye peered down at the delicious dooms painted on the screen in geysers of light and dark.

Poe's raven eye.

Or rather, Shrank!

Tarot card reader, psychologist, phrenologist, numerologist, and . . .

Film projectionist.

Someone had to run the film while Shapeshade clawed the organ in paroxysms of delight. Most nights, the old man ran from ticket booth to projection room to organ, bouncing off each like a manic boy disguised as rambling man.

But now—?

Who else for a late night menu of hunchbacks, striding

skeletons, and hairy paws snatching moon-pearls from a sleeping woman's neck?

Shrank.

The organ music peaked. The phantom vanished. A new clip, from *Jekyll and Hyde*, 1920, jittered across the screen.

I leaped down off the stage and ran up the aisle, among all the fiends and murderers.

The Poe eye in the projectionist's window was gone.

By the time I reached the projection booth, it was empty. The film unspooled itself in the firefly machine. Jekyll, on his way to becoming Hyde, slid down the lightbeams to strike a hairball on the screen.

The music stopped.

Downstairs, on the way out, I found an exhausted but happy Shapeshade back in the ticket booth, selling seats to the fog.

I thrust my hands in to grab his and squeeze.

"No bad rice for *you*, huh?"

"What!" cried Shapeshade, complimented but not knowing why.

"You'll live forever," I said.

"What do you know that God doesn't?" asked Shapeshade. "Come back later. One in the morning, Veidt in *Caligari*. Two, Chaney in *Laugh Clown Laugh*. Three, *The Gorilla*. Four, *The Bat*. Who could ask for more?"

"Not me, Mr. Shapeshade."

I moved off into the mist.

"You're not depressed?" he yelled after.

"I don't think so."

"If you got to think about it, you're not!"

Full night had arrived.

I saw that Modesti's Cafe had closed early, or forever, I didn't know which. I couldn't ask questions there about William Smith and celebratory haircuts and dinners.

The pier was dark. Only a single light shone in A. L. Shrank's tarot card shack window.

I blinked.

Scared, the damn light went out.

" **B** ad rice?" said Crumley, on the phone. But his voice was bright, hearing that it was me. "What kind of talk is that?"

"Crumley," I said, swallowing hard, "I got another name to add to our list."

"What list?"

"Along with the canary lady—"

"That's not our list, it's yours—"

"Shrank," I said.

"What!"

"A. L. Shrank, the Venice pier psychologist—"

"—Tarot card reader, weirdo librarian, amateur numerologist, Fifth Horseman of the Apocalypse?"

"You know him?"

"Kid, I know everyone up, down, above, in, and under the pier, every weight lifter kicking sand, every dead bum on the night beach resurrected by the smell of seventy-nine-cent muscatel comes the dawn. A. L. Shrank, that measly dwarf? No way."

"Don't hang up! I can see it in his face. He's asking for it. He's next. I wrote a story last year, in *Dime Detective,* about two trains in a station, going opposite ways, stopped at a siding for a minute. One man looks across at another man, they trade stares, and the one man realizes he should never have looked across, because the man on the other train is a murderer. The murderer looks back and smiles. That's all. Smiles. And my hero realizes that he himself is doomed. He looks away, trying to save himself. But the other man, the killer, keeps staring. And when my hero looks up again, the train window across the way is empty. He realizes that the killer has gone to get off the train. A minute later, the killer appears on my hero's train, in his car, walks down the aisle, and sits in a seat right behind my hero. Panic, huh? Panic."

"Great idea, but it don't happen that way," said Crumley.

"More often than you think. A friend of mine drove a Rolls-Royce across country last year. On the way, he was almost run off the road six times, through Oklahoma and Kansas and Missouri and Illinois, by men who resented that expensive car. If they had succeeded, it would have been murder and no one the wiser."

"That's different. An expensive car is an expensive car. They didn't care who was in it. Kill. But what you're saying is—"

"There are murderers and murderees in this world. The old man in the trolley waiting room was a murderee, so is the canary lady. It's in their eyes: take me, it said, favor me, spoil me away forever.

"Shrank," I finished. "I'd bet my life on it."

"Don't," said Crumley, suddenly quieter. "You're a good kid, but God you're wet behind the ears."

"Shrank," I said. "Now that the pier's collapsing, he's got to collapse, too. If someone doesn't kill him, he'll tie *Decline of the West* and *Anatomy of Melancholy* around his neck and jump off what's left of the far end of the pier. Shrank."

As if agreeing with me, a lion roared, hungry for blood, off in Crumley's African territory.

"Just when you and I were beginning to get along so well," said Crumley.

And hung up.

All over Venice, windowshades were going up for the first time in weeks, months, or years.

It was as if the ocean town were coming awake just before going to sleep forever.

A windowshade right across from my apartment, in a little white-flake-painted bungalow, had lifted during the day, and . . .

As I entered my apartment that night, I glanced over and was fascinated.

The eyes were staring at me.

Not just one pair, but a dozen, not a dozen but a hundred or more.

The eyes were glass and lay in shining paths or were displayed on small pedestals.

The eyes were blue and brown and green and hazel and yellow.

I walked across my narrow street and stood looking down and in at the fabulous aggie-marble display.

"What a game that would make in the schoolyard dirt," I said, just to me.

The eyes said nothing. They rested on their stands or strewn in little clusters on a white velvet cloth, fixing their gaze through and beyond me, at some cold future just over my shoulder and down my spine.

Who had made the glass eyes and who had put them in the window and who waited inside to sell them and pop them into people's sockets, I could not say.

Whoever it was was another of Venice's unseen manufacturers and salesmen. I had, on occasion, far back in the cavern reaches of this bungalow, seen a piercing blue-white flame and someone's hands working at teardrops of melting glass. But the old man (everyone is old in Venice, California) had his face hidden behind a thick metal-and-glass fire-torch mask. All you could see, far off, was a new stare coming to life, a blind eye being brought to focus in flame, to be laid out like a bright bonbon in the window next day.

Whether anyone ever came to buy this special jewelry, that also I did not know. I had never seen anyone blundering into the place or striding out with a fresher gaze. The windowshade had only been raised once or twice a month during the last year.

Looking down, I thought, strange eyes, do you see the lost canaries? and where did they go?

And added, watch my place, yes? During the night, stay alert. The weather may change. Rain may come. Shadows may touch my doorbell. Much note, please, and long remember.

The shiny agate-marble-mib long-years-ago schoolyard companions did not so much as blink.

At which point, a hand like a magician's slid from the shadows behind the display and pulled the lid down over the eyes.

It was as if the glass blower resented my staring at his stares.

Or perhaps he feared I might sneeze out one eye and come in for a refill.

A customer! That might spoil his perfect record. Ten years of blowing glass and not a single sale.

As a sideline, I wondered, does he sell bathing suits from 1910?

Back in my apartment, I glanced out.

The shade had gone back up again, now that I was not the Inquisition standing outside.

The eyes were bright and waiting.

What, I wondered, will they see tonight?

"With nothing trembles—"
    Instantly, I awoke.
"What," I said to the empty ceiling.
Had Lady Macbeth said that?
With nothing trembles.
To be afraid of nothing for no reason.
And having to live with that nothing until dawn.
I listened.
Was that the fog bruising my door? Was that the mist testing my keyhole? And was that the special miniature rainstorm prowling my doormat, leaving seaweed?
I was afraid to go look.
I opened my eyes. I looked at the hall which led to my two-by-four kitchen and my two-by-two Singer's Midgets bathroom.
I had hung an old torn white bathrobe there last night.
But now the robe wasn't a robe. With my glasses off and lying on the floor by my cot—my vision being what it was, almost legally blind—the robe had . . . changed.
It was the Beast.
When I was five years old, living east in Illinois, and had to go up some dark stairs in the middle of the night to go to the bathroom, the Beast was always at the top of the stairs, unless the small stairwell light was lit. Sometimes my mother would forget to turn it on. I would try terribly hard to make it to the top without looking up. But always I was afraid, and I had to look up. And the Beast was always there, with the sound of the dark locomotives rushing by far out in night country, funeral trains taking dear cousins or uncles away. And stood at the bottom of the stairs and . . .
    Screamed.

Now the Beast was hanging here on the edge of my door leading into darkness, the hall, the kitchen, the bathroom.

Beast, I thought, go away.

Beast, I said to the shape. I know you're not there. You're nothing. You're my old bathrobe.

The trouble was, I couldn't see it clearly.

If I could just reach my glasses, I thought, get them on, jump up.

Lying there, I was eight and then seven and then five and then four years old, getting smaller, smaller and smaller as the Beast on the door got bigger and darker and longer.

I was afraid to so much as blink. Afraid that that motion would make the Beast float softly down to . . .

"Ah!" someone yelled.

Because the phone, across the street, rang.

Shut up! I thought. You'll make the Beast move.

The phone rang. Four in the morning. Four! Christ. Who—?

Peg? Trapped in a Mexican catacomb? Lost?

The phone rang.

Crumley? With an autopsy report I would hate to hear?

The phone rang.

Or a voice of cold rain and running night and raw alcohol raving in the storm and mourning terrible events, as the great train shrieked on a curve?

The phone stopped.

With my eyes clenched, my teeth gritted, the covers over my head, turned away against the sweaty pillow. I thought I heard a drifting whisper. I froze.

I kept my breath, I stopped my heart.

For, just now, at that very instant . . .

Hadn't I felt something touch and—weigh itself . . .

On the end of my bed?

A. L. Shrank was not the next victim.
Nor did the canary lady suddenly fly around her room once and expire.

Someone else vanished.

And, not long after dawn, the bright glass eyes across the street from my tired apartment saw the arrival of the evidence.

A truck pulled up outside.

Sleepless and exhausted, I heard it, stirred.

Someone knocked on my coffin door.

I managed to levitate and balloon-drift over to crack the door and peer gum-eyed into the face of a great beefy ox. The face named me, I assented to the name, the ox told me to sign here, I signed something that looked like a D.O.A. slip and watched the delivery man hoof back to his half-truck and wrestle a familiar, bundled object off the back and wheel it along the walk.

"My God," I said. "What is it? Who—?"

But the big rolling bundle struck the doorjamb and gave off a musical chord. I slumped, knowing the answer.

"Where do you want it?" said the ox, glancing around Groucho Marx's overcrowded stateroom. "This as good as any?"

He heaved the wrapped object to one side against the wall, looked around with contempt at my Goodwill sofa, my rugless floor, and my typewriter, and cattle-trotted back out to his truck, leaving the door wide.

Over the way, I saw the ten dozen bright blue, brown, hazel glass eyes watching, even as I ripped away the covering to stare at . . .

The Smile.

"My God!" I cried. "That's the piano that I heard playing—"

The "Maple Leaf Rag."

Wham. The truck door slammed. The truck roared away.

I collapsed on my already collapsed sofa, totally disbelieving that big, vacant, ivory smile.

Crumley, I said in my mind. I felt the lousy haircut too high in back, too short on the sides. My fingers were numb.

Yeah, kid? said Crumley.

I changed my mind. I thought, Crumley, it's not going to be Shrank or the old bird lady who vanishes.

Gosh, said Crumley, who?

Cal, the barber.

Silence. A sigh. Then . . .

Click. Buzz.

Which is why, gazing at this relic from Scott Joplin years, I did not race forth to telephone my police detective friend.

All the glass eyes across the street examined my haircut and watched me shut my door.

God, I thought, I can't even play "Chopsticks."

The barber shop was open and empty. The ants, the bees, the termites, and the relatives had been there before noon.

I stood in the front door looking at the total evisceration. It was as if someone had shoved a gigantic vacuum cleaner through the front door and sucked everything out.

The piano, of course, had come to me. I wondered who had gotten, or would want, the barber chair, the liniments, the ointments, the lotions that used to color the mirrored wall with their tints and tinctures. I wondered who got all the hair.

There was a man in the middle of the barber shop, the landlord, I seemed to recall, a man in his fifties moving a pushbroom over no hair, just gliding over the empty tiles for no obvious reason. He looked up and saw me.

"Cal's gone," he said.

"So I see," I said.

"Bastard ran off owing me four months' rent."

"Business was that bad, was it?"

"It wasn't the business so much as the haircuts. Even for two bucks they were the lousiest, won awards, in the whole state."

I felt the top of my head and the nape of my neck and nodded.

"Bastard ran off owing me five months' rent. I heard from the groceryman next door Cal was here at seven this morning. Goodwill came at eight for the barber chair. Salvation Army got all the rest. Who knows who got the piano. I'd like to find and sell that, get some of my money." The landlord looked at me.

I said nothing. The piano was the piano. For whatever reasons, Cal had sent it to me.

"Where you think he's gone?" I said.

"Got relatives in Oklahoma, Kansas, Missouri, I hear. Someone was just in said he heard Cal say two days ago he was going to drive until the land gave out and then pitch right into the Atlantic."

"Cal wouldn't do that."

"No, he more likely will sink somewhere in the Cherokee Strip country and good riddance. Jesus, that was bad haircutting."

I wandered in over the clean white tiles through no-hair territory, not knowing what I was looking for.

"Who are you?" said the landlord, half-raising his broom into artillery position.

"The writer," I said. "You know me. The Crazy."

"Hell, I didn't recognize you. Did Cal do *that* to you?"

He stared at my hairline. I felt blood rush along my scalp. "Only yesterday," I said.

"He could be shot for that."

I wandered across and around behind a thin wooden partition that hid the backside of the barber shop, the trash barrels, and the restroom.

I stared down into the trash barrel and saw what I was looking for there.

The photograph of Cal and Scott Joplin, covered with a month's supply of hair, which was not much.

I reached down and picked up the photo.

In the next five or six seconds my whole body turned to ice.

Because Scott Joplin was gone.

Cal was still there, forever young, smiling, his thin fingers spidering the piano keys.

But the man who stood over him, grinning.

It wasn't Joplin.

It was another man, black, younger, more sinful looking.

I peered very close.

There were marks of old dry glue where Scott's head had once been.

Jesus God have mercy on Cal, I thought. None of us ever thought to look close. And, of course, the picture was always under glass and hung rather high on the wall, not easy to reach or take down.

Sometime, a long while ago, Cal had found a picture of Scott Joplin, razor cut around it, and pasted it over this other guy's face, head on head. He must have forged the signature as well. And all these years we had looked at it and sighed and clucked and said, "Hey, Cal, great! Aren't you special? Looky there!"

And all those years Cal had looked at it and known what a fraud it was and he was and cut hair so you looked as if you'd been blown dry by a Kansas twister and combed by a maniac wheat harvester run amok.

I turned the photograph over and reached down into the barrel, trying to find Scott Joplin's decapitated and missing part.

I knew I would not find it.

Someone had taken it.

And whoever had peeled it off the photo had telephoned and sent a message to Cal. You are known! You are naked! You are *revealed!* I remembered Cal's phone ringing. And Cal, afraid, refusing to answer.

And coming into his barber shop, what? Two days, three days ago, casually checking the photograph, Cal had been kicked in the gut. With Joplin's head gone, Cal was gone.

All he could do was Goodwill the barber chair, Salvation Army the tonics, piano me his piano.

I stopped searching. I folded the photograph of Cal without Joplin and went out to watch the landlord broom the hairless tiles.

"Cal," I said.

The landlord paused his broom.

"Cal didn't," I said. "I mean, Cal wouldn't, I mean, Cal's still alive?"

"Crud," said the landlord. "Alive about four hundred miles east of here by now, still owing seven months' rent."

Thank God, I thought. I won't have to tell Crumley about this one. Not now, anyway. Going away isn't murder, or being murdered.

No?

Going east? Isn't Cal a dead man, driving a car?

I went out the door.

"Boy," said the landlord. "You look bad coming and going."

Not as bad as some people, I thought.

Where do I go now? I wondered, now that the smile is there, filling up my bed-sitting-room and me only able to play an Underwood Standard?

The gas station telephone rang at two-thirty that afternoon. Exhausted by no sleep the night before, I had gone back to bed.

I lay listening.

The phone wouldn't stop.

It rang for two minutes and then three. The more it rang, the colder I got. By the time I lunged out of bed and floundered into my bathing trunks and trudged across the street, I was shuddering like someone in a snowstorm.

When I lifted the receiver, I could feel Crumley a long way off at the far end, and without his speaking I could guess his news.

"It's happened, hasn't it?" I said.

"How did you know?" Crumley sounded as if he had been up all night, too.

"What made you go by there?" I asked.

"While I was shaving an hour ago, I had a hunch, Jesus, like the ones you talk about. I'm still here, waiting for the coroner. You coming by to say I told you so?"

"No, but I'll be there."

I hung up.

Back in my apartment, Nothing still hung on the hall door leading to the bathroom. I yanked it off the door, hurled it to the floor, and stepped on it. It seemed only right, since it had gone off during the night to visit the canary lady and come back without telling me, just before dawn.

Christ, I thought, standing numbly on the bathrobe, all the cages are empty now!

rumley stood on one side of the Lower Nile, the dry riverbed. I stood on the other. One police car and the morgue van were waiting downstairs.

"You're not going to like this," said Crumley.

He paused, waiting for me to nod him to pull back the sheet. I said, "Did you call me in the middle of the night?"

Crumley shook his head.

"How long has she been dead?"

"We figure about eleven hours."

I ran my thoughts back. Four in the morning. When the phone had rung across the street in the night. When Nothing had called to tell me something. If I had run to answer, a cold wind would have blown out of the receiver to tell me—this.

I nodded. Crumley pulled back the sheet.

The canaries-for-sale lady was there and not there. Part of her had fled in the dark. What was left was terrible to see.

Her eyes were fixed on some dreadful Nothing, the thing on the top of my hall door, the invisible weight at the end of my bed. The mouth that had once whispered open, saying, come up, come in, welcome, was now gaped in shock, in protest. It wanted something to go away, get out, not stay!

Holding the sheet in his fingers, Crumley glanced at me.

"I guess I owe you an apology."

"For what?"

It was hard to talk, for she was staring up between us at some terror on the ceiling.

"For guessing right, that was you. For doubting, that was me."

"It wasn't hard to guess. That's my brother, dead. That's

my grandfather and my aunts dead. And my mother and father. All deaths are the same, aren't they?"

"Yeah." Crumley let the sheet drift down, a snowfall over the Nile Valley on an autumn day. "But this is just a simple death, kid. Not a murder. That look on her face you can find on all kinds of people when they feel their heart coming out of their chest with an attack."

I wanted to shout arguments. I bit my tongue. Something seen from the corner of my eye made me turn away and move over to the empty birdcages. It took a few moments for me to see what I was looking at:

"Jesus," I whispered. "Hirohito. Addis Ababa. They're gone."

I turned to stare at Crumley and point.

"Someone's taken the old newspaper headlines out of the cages. Whoever came up here not only scared her to death, but took the papers. My God, he's a souvenir collector. I bet he's got a pocketful of train ticket punchout confetti and Scott Joplin's peeled-off head, too."

"Scott Joplin's what?"

He didn't want to, but at last Crumley came to look at the bottoms of the cages.

"Find those newspapers and you'll find him," I said.

"Easy as pie." Crumley sighed.

He led me down past the turned-to-the-wall mirrors that had not seen anyone come up during the night and did not see him go. In the downstairs stairwell area was the dusty window with the sign in it. For no reason I could figure, I reached out and pulled the sign away from its flaking Scotch-taped frame. Crumley was watching me.

"Can I have this?" I asked.

"It'll hurt you, every time you look at it," said Crumley. "Oh, hell. Keep it."

I folded it and tucked it in my pocket.

Upstairs, the birdcages sang no songs.

The coroner stepped in, full of mid-afternoon beer and whistling.

J t had begun to rain. It rained all across Venice as Crumley's car drove us away from her house, away from my house, away from phones that rang at the wrong hours, away from the gray sea and the empty shore and the remembrance of drowned swimmers. The car windshield was like a great eye, weeping and drying itself, weeping again, as the wiper shuttled and stopped, shuttled and stopped and squeaked to shuttle again. I stared straight ahead.

Inside his jungle bungalow, Crumley looked in my face, guessed at a brandy instead of a beer, gave me that, and nodded at the telephone in his bedroom.

"You got any money to call Mexico City?"

I shook my head.

"Now you have," said Crumley. "Call. Talk to your girl. Shut the door and talk."

I grabbed his hand and almost broke every bone in it, gasping. Then I called Mexico.

"Peg!"

"Who is this?"

"It's me, me!"

"My God, you sound so strange, so far away."

"I am far away."

"You're alive, thank God."

"Sure."

"I had this terrible feeling last night. I couldn't sleep."

"What time, Peg, what time?"

"Four o'clock, why?"

"Jesus."

"Why?"

"Nothing. I couldn't sleep either. How's Mexico City?"

"Full of death."

"God, I thought it was all here."

"What?"

"Nothing. Lord, it's good to hear your voice."

"Say something."

I said something.

"Say it again!"

"Why are you shouting, Peg?"

"I don't know. Yes, I do. When are you going to ask me to marry you, damn it!"

"Peg," I said, in dismay.

"Well, when?"

"On thirty dollars a week, forty when I'm lucky, some weeks nothing, some months not a damn thing?"

"I'll take a vow of poverty."

"Sure."

"I will. I'll be home in ten days and take both vows."

"Ten days, ten years."

"Why do women always have to ask men for their hands?"

"Because we're cowards and more afraid than you."

"I'll protect you."

"Some conversation this." I thought of the door last night and the thing hanging on the door and the thing on the end of my bed. "You'd better hurry."

"Do you remember my face?" she said suddenly.

"What?"

"You do remember it, don't you, because, God, just an hour ago this terrible, horrible thing happened, I couldn't remember yours, or the color of your eyes, and I realized what a dumb fool I was not to bring your picture along, and it was all gone. That scares me, to think I could forget. You'll never forget me, will you?"

I didn't tell her I had forgotten the color of her eyes just the day before and how that had shaken me for an hour and that it was a kind of death but me not being able to figure who had died first, Peg or me.

"Does my voice help?"

"Yes."

"Am I there with you? Do you see my eyes?"

"Yes."

"For God's sake, first thing you do when you hang up, mail me a picture. I don't want to be afraid any more—"

"All I have is a lousy twenty-five-cent photo machine picture I—"

"Send it!"

"I should never have come down here and left you alone up there, unprotected."

"You make me sound like your kid."

"What else *are* you?"

"I don't know. Can love protect people, Peg?"

"It must. If it doesn't protect you, I'll never forgive God. Let's keep talking. As long as we talk, love's there and you're okay."

"I'm okay already. You've made me well. I was sick today, Peg. Nothing serious. Something I ate. But I'm right now."

"I'm moving in with you when I get home, no matter what you say. If we get married, fine. You'll just have to get used to my working while you finish the Great American Epic, and to hell with it, shut up. Someday, later on, you support me!"

"Are you ordering me around?"

"Sure, because I hate to hang up and I just want this to go on all day and I know it's costing you a mint. Say some more, the things I want to hear."

I said some more.

And she was gone, the telephone line humming and me left with a piece of wire cable two thousand miles long and a billion shadow whispers lingering there, heading toward me. I cut them off before they could reach my ear and slide inside my head.

I opened the door and stepped out to find Crumley waiting by the icebox, reaching in for sustenance.

"You look surprised?" He laughed. "Forget you were in my house, you were so busy yakking?"

"Forgot," I said.

And took anything he handed me, out of the fridge, my nose running, my cold making me miserable.

"Grab some Kleenex, kid," said Crumley. "Take the whole box."

"And while you're at it," he added, "give me the rest of your list."

"*Our* list," I said.

He narrowed his eyes, wiped his balding head with a nervous hand, and nodded.

"Those who will die next, in order of execution."

He shut his eyes, heavily burdened.

"Our list," he said.

I did not immediately tell him about Cal.

"**A**nd while you're at it"—Crumley sipped another beer—"write down the name of the murderer."

"It would have to be someone who knows everyone in Venice, California," I said.

"That could be me," said Crumley.

"Don't say that."

"Why?"

"Because," I said, "it scares me."

I made the list.

I made two lists.

And then suddenly discovered myself making three.

The first list was short and full of possible murderers, none of which I believed.

The second was Choose Your Victim, and went on at some length, on who would vanish in short order.

And in the middle of it I realized it had been some while since I trapped all the wandering people of Venice. So I did a page on Cal the barber before he fled out of my mind, and another on Shrank running down the street, and another on all those people on the rollercoaster with me plummeting into hell, and yet another on the big night steamboat theater crossing the Styx to ram the Isle of the Dead and (unthinkable!) sink Mr. Shapeshade!

I did a final sermon on Miss Birdsong, and a page about the glass eyes, and took all these pages and put them in my Talking Box. That was the box I kept by my typewriter where my ideas lay and spoke to me early mornings to tell me where they wanted to go and what they wanted to do. I lay half-asleep, listening, and then got up and went to help them, with my typewriter, to go where they most needed to go to do some special wild thing; so my stories got written. Sometimes it was a dog that needed to dig a graveyard. Sometimes it was a time machine that had to go backward. Sometimes it was a man with green wings who had to fly at night lest he be seen. Sometimes it was me, missing Peg in my tombstone bed.

I took one of the lists back to Crumley.

"How come you didn't use *my* typewriter?" said Crumley.

"Yours isn't used to me yet, and would only get in the way. Mine is way ahead of me, and I run to catch up. Read that."

Crumley read my list of possible victims.

"Christ," he murmured, "you got half the Venice Chamber of Commerce, the Lion's Club, the flea circus, and the Pier Carnival Owners of America on here."

He folded it and put it in his pocket.

"Why don't you throw in some friends from where you once lived in downtown L.A.?"

An ice-frog jumped in my chest.

I thought of the tenement and the dark halls and nice Mrs. Gutierrez and lovely Fannie.

The frog jumped again.

"Don't say that," I said.

"Where's the other list, of murderers? You got the Chamber of Commerce on that, too?"

I shook my head.

"Afraid to show it to me because I'm in the lineup with the rest of them?" asked Crumley.

I took that list out of my pocket, glanced at it, and tore it up.

"Where's your wastebasket?" I said.

Even as I had been talking, the fog had arrived across the street from Crumley's. It hesitated, as if searching for me, and then, to verify my paranoid suspicions, sneaked across and blanketed his garden, dousing the Christmas lights in his oranges and lemons and drowning the flowers so they shut their mouths.

"How dare it come here?" I said.

"Everything does," said Crumley.

"**Q**ué? Is this the Crazy?"

"*Sí*, Mrs. Gutierrez!"

"Do I call the office?"

"*Sí*, Mrs. Gutierrez."

"Fannie is calling outside on her porch!"

"I hear her, Mrs. Gutierrez—"

Far away in the sun inland where there was no fog or mist or rain, and no surf to bring strange visitors in, was the tenement, and Fannie's soprano calling like the Sirens.

"Tell him," I heard her sing, "I have a new recording of Mozart's *The Magic Flute*!"

"She says—"

"Her voice carries, Mrs. Gutierrez. Tell her, thank God, that's a happy one."

"She wants you to come see, she misses you and hopes you forgive her, she says."

For what? I tried to remember.

"She says—"

Fannie's voice floated on the warm clear air.

"Tell him to come but don't bring anyone with!"

That knocked the air out of me. The ghosts of old ice creams rose in my blood. When had I ever done that? I wondered. Who did she think I might bring along, uninvited?

And then I remembered.

The bathrobe hanging on the door late nights. Leave it there. Canaries for sale. Don't fetch the empty cages. The lion cage. Don't roll it through the streets. Lon Chaney. Don't peel him off the silver screen and hide him in your pocket. Don't.

My God, Fannie, I thought, is the fog rolling inland toward you? Will the mist reach your tenement? Will the rain touch on your door?

I shouted so loudly over the phone, Fannie could have heard it, downstairs.

"Tell her, Mrs. Gutierrez, I come alone. *Alone.* But tell her only maybe I come. I have no money, not even for train fare. Maybe I come tomorrow—"

"Fannie say, if you come, she give you money."

"Swell, but meantime, my pockets, empty."

Just then I saw the postman cross the street and stick an envelope in my mailbox.

"Hold on," I yelled, and ran.

The letter was from New York with a check for thirty dollars in it for a story I had just sold to *Bizarre Tales*, about a man who feared the wind that had followed him around the world from the Himalayas and now shook his house late at night, hungry for his soul.

I ran back to the telephone and shouted, "If I make it to the bank—tonight I will come!"

Fannie got the translation and sang three notes from the "Bell Song" from *Lakmé* before her translator hung up.

I ran for the bank.

Graveyard fog, I thought, don't get on the train ahead of me, headed for Fannie.

If the pier was a great *Titanic* on its way to meet an iceberg in the night, with people busy rearranging the deck chairs, and someone singing "Nearer My God to Thee" as he rammed the plunger on the TNT detonator . . .

Then the tenement at the corner of Temple and Figueroa was still afloat down the middle of the barrio, with curtains, people, and underwear hanging out of most windows, laundry being churned to death in back-porch machines, and the smell of tacos and delicatessen corned beef in the halls.

All to itself it was a small Ellis Island, adrift with people from some sixteen countries. On Saturday nights there were enchilada festivals on the top floor and conga lines dancing through the halls, but most of the week the doors were shut and people turned in early because they all worked, downtown in the dress lofts or the dime stores or in what was left of the defense industry in the valley or in Olvera Street selling junk jewelry.

Nobody was in charge of the tenement. The landlady, Mrs. O'Brien, came to visit as rarely as possible; fearful of purse snatchers, terrified for her seventy-two-year-old virtue. If anyone was in charge of the tenement it was Fannie Florianna, who from her second-floor opera balcony could singsong orders so sweetly that even the boys in the poolhall across the street stopped preening like pigeons and roosters and came, cues in hand, to wave up and cry *"Olé!"*

There were three Chinese on the first floor along with the usual Chicanos, and on the second floor one Japanese gentleman and six young men from Mexico City who owned one white ice cream suit—each got to wear it one night a week. There were also some Portuguese men, a night watchman from Haiti, two salesmen from the Philippines, and more Chicanos. Mrs. Gutierrez, with the only phone in the tenement, was there, yes, on the third floor.

The second was mostly Fannie and her 380 pounds, along with two old maid sisters from Spain, a jewelry salesman from Egypt, and two ladies from Monterey who, it was rumored, sold their favors at no great price, to any lost and lustful pool player who happened to stumble upstairs, uncaring, late Friday nights. Every rat to his warren, as Fannie said.

I was glad to stand outside the tenement at dusk, glad to hear all the live radios playing from all the windows, glad to smell all the cooking smells and hear the laughter.

Glad to go in and meet all the people.

Some people's lives can be summed so swiftly it's no more than a door slammed or someone coughing out on a dark street late at night.

You glance from the window; the street's empty. Whoever coughed is gone.

There are some people who live to be thirty-five or forty, but because no one ever notices, their lives are candle-brief, invisible-small.

In and around the tenement were various such invisible or half-visible people who lived but did not exactly live in the tenement.

There was Sam and there was Jimmy and there was Pietro Massinello and there was the very special blind man, Henry, as dark as the halls he wandered through with his Negro pride.

All or most of them would vanish in a few days, and each in a different way. Since their vanishing occurred with such regularity and variety, no one took notice. Even I almost missed the significance of their last farewells.

Sam.

Sam was a wetback wandered up from Mexico to wash dishes, beg quarters, buy cheap wine, and lie doggo for days, then up like the night-prowling dead to wash more dishes, cadge more quarters, and sink into vino, toted in a brown-bag valise. His Spanish was bad and his English worse because it was always filtered through muscatel. Nobody knew what he said, nobody cared. He slept in the basement, out of harm's way.

So much for Sam.

Jimmy you couldn't understand either, not as a result of wine but because someone had stolen his bite. His teeth, delivered gratis by the city's health department, had vanished one night when he was careless enough to dime himself into a Main Street flophouse. The teeth had been stolen from a water glass by his pillow. When he woke his great white grin was gone forever. Jimmy, gape-mouthed but convivial on gin, came back to the tenement, pointing at his pink gums and laughing. And what with the loss of his dentures and his immigrant Czech accent, he was, like Sam, unintelligible. He slept in empty tenement bathtubs at three in the morning, and did odd jobs around the place each day, laughing a lot at nothing in particular.

So much for Jimmy.

Pietro Massinello was a circus of one, allowed, like the others, to move his feast of dogs, cats, geese, and parakeets from the roof, where they lived in summer, to a basement lumber room in December, where they survived in a medley of barks, cackles, riots, and slumbers through the years. You could see him running along Los Angeles streets with his herd of adoring beasts in his wake, the dogs frisking, a bird on each shoulder, a duck pursuing, as he toted a portable windup phonograph which he set down at street corners to play *Tales from the Vienna Woods* and dance his dogs for whatever people threw him. He was a tiny man with bells on his hat, black mascara around his wide innocent mad eyes, and chimes sewn on his cuffs and lapels. He did not speak to people, he *sang*.

The sign outside his lean-to basement lumber room read MANGER, and love filled the place, the love of beautifully treated and petted and spoiled animals for their incredible master.

So much for Pietro Massinello.

Henry, the blind colored man, was even more special. Special because he not only spoke clean and clear, but walked without canes through our lives and survived when the others had gone, without trumpets, off in the night.

He was waiting for me when I came in the downstairs entrance to the tenement.

He was waiting for me in the dark, hid back against the wall, his face so black it was unseen.

It was his eyes, blind but white rimmed, which startled me.

I jumped and gasped.

"Henry. Is that you?"

"Scare you, did I?" Henry smiled, then remembered why he was there. "I been waiting on you," he said, lowering his voice, looking around as if he could actually see the shadows.

"Something wrong, Henry?"

"Yes. No. I don't know. Things is changing. The old place ain't the same. People is nervous. Even me."

I saw his right hand fumble down in the dark to touch and twitch a peppermint-striped cane. I had never seen him carry a cane before. My eye ran down to the tip, which was rounded with what looked to be a good weight of lead. It was not a blind man's guide. It was a weapon.

"Henry," I whispered.

And we stood for a moment while I looked him over and saw what had always been there.

Blind Henry.

He had everything memorized. In his pride he had counted and could recall every pace in this block and the next and the next, and how many steps across at this intersection or that. And he could name the streets he strode past, with sovereign certainty, by the butcher or shoeshine or drugstore or poolhall smokes and smells. And even when the shops were shut, he would "see" the kosher pickle scents or the boxed tobaccos, or the locked-away African ivory aromas of the billiard balls in their nests, or the aphrodisiac whiff from the gas station when some tank flooded, and Henry walking, staring straight ahead, no dark glasses, no cane, his mouth counting the beats, to turn in at Al's Beer and walk steadily and unswervingly through the crowded tables toward an empty piano stool, there to sit and reach up for the beer that was automatically popped in place by Al before his arrival, to play exactly three tunes—including the "Maple Leaf" sadly better than Cal the barber—drink the one beer, and stride out into a night he owned with his paces and counts, heading home, calling out to unseen voices, naming names, proud of his shuttered genius, only his nose steering the way and his legs firm and muscled from ten miles of strides per day.

If you tried to help him across the street, which I made the mistake of doing once, he yanked his elbow away and stared at you so angrily that your face burned.

"Don't touch," he whispered. "Don't confuse. You put me off now. Where was I?" He threw some abacus beads in his dark head. He counted cornrows on his skull. "Yeah. Now. Thirty-five across, thirty-seven over." And on he went alone, leaving you on the curb, his own parade, thirty-five steps across Temple this way, and thirty-seven the other, across Figueroa. An invisible cane tapped cadence for him. He marched, by God, he truly marched.

And it was Henry with No Last Name, Henry the Blind who heard the wind and knew the cracks in the sidewalk and snuffed the dust of the night tenement, who gave the first warnings of things waiting on the stairs or too much midnight leaning heavy on the roof, or a wrong perspiration in the halls.

And here he was now, flattened back against the cracked plaster of the tenement entryway, with full night outside and in the halls. His eyes wobbled and shut, his nostrils flared, he seemed to bend a bit at the knees as if someone had struck him on the head. His cane twitched in his dark fingers. He listened, listened so hard that I turned to stare down the long cavernous hall to the far end of the tenement where the back door stood wide and more night waited.

"What's wrong, Henry?" I said again.

"Promise you won't tell Florianna? Fannie takes on fits, you tell her too much wrong stuff. Promise?"

"I won't give her fits, Henry."

"Where you been last few days?"

"I had my own troubles, Henry, and I was broke. I could have hitchhiked in, but—well."

"Lots goes on in just forty-eight hours. Pietro, him and his dogs and birds and geese, you know his cats?"

"What about Pietro?"

"Someone turned him in, called the police. Nuisance, they said. Police come, take all his pets away, take him away. He was able to give some of them to folks. I got his cat up in my room. Mrs. Gutierrez got a new dog. When they led him out, Pietro, he was crying. I never heard a man cry so hard before. It was terrible."

"Who turned him in, Henry?" I was upset myself. I saw the dogs adoring Pietro, I saw the cats and the geese that lovingly followed and the canaries on his bell-chiming hat and him dancing on street corners through half of my life.

"Who turned him in?"

"Trouble is, no one knows. Cops just come and said, 'Here!' and all the pets gone forever and Pietro in jail, a nuisance, or maybe he kicked up a fuss out front there, hit somebody, striking a cop. Nobody knows. But somebody did. That ain't all—"

"What else?" I said, leaning against the wall.

"Sam."

"What about him?"

"He's in the hospital. Booze. Someone gave him two quarts of the hard stuff; damn fool drank it all. What they call it? Acute alcoholism? If he lives tomorrow, it's God's will. No one knows who gave him the booze. Then there's Jimmy, that's the worst!"

"God," I whispered. "Let me sit down." I sat on the edge of the steps leading up to the second floor. *"No News or What Killed the Dog."*

"Huh?"

"An old seventy-eight rpm record when I was a kid. "No News or What Killed the Dog." Dog ate burned horseflakes from the burned-down barn. How did the barn burn down? Sparks from the house blew over and burned down the barn. Sparks from the house? From inside the house, the candles around the coffin. Candles around the coffin? Someone's uncle died. On and on. It all ends with the dog in the barn eating the burned horseflakes and dying. Or, "No News or What Killed the Dog." Your stories are getting to me, Henry. Sorry."

"Sorry is right. Jimmy, now. You know how he sleeps from floor to floor nights, and once a week he just up and strips down and takes a bath in the third-floor tub? Or the first-floor washroom? Sure! Well last night he got in the full tub, drunk, turned over, and drowned."

"Drowned!"

"Drowned. Ain't that silly. Ain't that a terrible thing to put on your obit-tombstone, save he won't *have* a tombstone. Potter's field. Found in a bathtub of dirty water. Turned over, so drunk he slept himself into the grave. And him with new false teeth just this week. And the teeth gone, how you figure that, when they found him in the tub! Drowned."

"Oh my Christ," I said, stifling a laugh and a sob in one.

"Yes, *name* Christ, God help us all." Henry's voice trembled. "Now, you see what I don't want you to tell Fannie? We'll let her know, one at a time, spread it out over weeks. Pietro Massinello in jail, his dogs lost forever, his cats driven away, his geese cooked. Sam in the hospital. Jimmy drowned.

And *me?* Looky this handkerchief, all wet from my eyes, balled in my fist. I don't feel so good."

"Nobody's feeling very good, right now."

"Now." Henry put his hand out, unerringly toward my voice and took hold of my shoulder gently. "Go on up, and be cheerful. With Fannie."

I tapped on Fannie's door.

"Thank God," I heard her cry.

A steamboat came upriver, flung wide the door, and churned back downstream over the linoleum.

When Fannie had crashed into her chair she looked into my face and asked, "What's wrong?"

"Wrong? Oh." I turned to blink at the doorknob in my hand. "Do you leave your door unlocked all the time?"

"Why not? Who would want to come in and storm the Bastille?" But she did not laugh. She was watchful. Like Henry, she had a powerful nose. And I was perspiring.

I shut the door and sank into a chair.

"Who died?" said Fannie.

"What do you mean, who died?" I stammered.

"You look like you just came back from a Chinese funeral and were hungry all over again." She tried to smile and blinky-blink her eyes.

"Oh." I thought quickly. "Henry just scared me in the hall, is all. You know Henry. You come along a hall and can't see him for the night."

"You're a terrible liar," said Fannie. "Where have you been? I am exhausted, waiting for you to come visit. Are you ever tired, just worn out, with waiting? I've waited, dear young man, fearful for you. Have you been sad?"

"Very sad, Fannie."

"There. I knew it. It was that dreadful old man in the lion cage, wasn't it? How dare he make you sad?"

"He couldn't help it, Fannie." I sighed. "I imagine he would much rather have been down at the Pacific Electric ticket office counting the punch-confetti on his vest."

"Well, Fannie will cheer you up. Would you put the needle on the record there, my dear? Yes, that's it. Mozart to dance and sing to. We must invite Pietro Massinello up, mustn't we, some day soon. *The Magic Flute* is just his cup of tea, and let him bring his pets."

"Yes, Fannie," I said.

I put the needle on a record which hissed with promise.

"Poor boy," said Fannie. "You *do* look sad."

There was a faint scratching on the door.

"That's Henry," said Fannie. "He never knocks."

I went to the door but before I could open it, Henry's voice behind it said, "Only me."

I opened the door and Henry sniffed. "Spearmint gum. That's how I know you. You ever chew anything else?"

"Not even tobacco."

"Your cab's here," said Henry.

"My what?"

"Since when can you afford a taxi?" asked Fannie, her cheeks pink, her eyes bright. We had had a glorious two hours with Mozart and the very air was luminous around the big lady. "So?"

"Yeah, since when can I afford—" I said, but stopped, for Henry, outside the door, was shaking his head once: no. His finger went to his lips with caution.

"It's your friend," he said. "Taxi driver knows you, from Venice. Okay?"

"Okay," I said, frowning. "If you say so."

"Oh, and here. This is for Fannie. Pietro said give it over. He's so crammed full downstairs, no room for this."

He handed over a plump purring calico cat.

I took and carried the sweet burden back to Fannie, who began to purr herself when she held the beast.

"Oh, my dear!" she cried, happy with Mozart and calico. "What a dream cat, what a dream!"

Henry nodded to her, nodded to me, and went away down the hall.

I went to give Fannie a big hug.

"Listen, oh listen to his motor," she cried, holding the pillow cat up for a kiss.

"Lock your door, Fannie," I said.

"What?" she said. "What?"

Coming back downstairs, I found Henry still waiting in the dark, half-hidden against the wall.

"Henry, for God's sake, what're you doing?"

"Listening," he said.

"For what?"

"This house, this place. Shh. Careful. Now."

His cane came up and pointed like an antenna along the hall.

"There. You—hear?"

Far away a wind stirred. Far away a breeze wandered the dark. The beams settled. Someone breathed. A door creaked.

"I don't hear anything."

"That's 'cause you trying. Don't try. Just be. Just listen. Now."

I listened and my spine chilled.

"Someone in this house," whispered Henry. "Don't belong here. I got this sense. I'm no fool. Someone up there, wandering around, up to no good."

"Can't be, Henry."

"Is," he whispered. "A blind man tells you. Stranger underfoot. Henry has the word. You don't hear me, you fall downstairs or—"

Drown in a bathtub, I thought. But what I said was, "You going to stay here all night?"

"Someone's got to stand guard."

A blind man? I thought.

He read my mind. He nodded. "Old Henry, sure. Now run along. It's a big fancy-smelling Duesenberg out front. No taxi. I lied. Who would be picking you up this late, know anyone with a fancy car?"

"No one."

"Get on out. I'll mind Fannie for us. But who'll mind Jimmy now, not even Jim. Not even Sam—"

I started out from one night into another.

"Oh, one last thing."

I paused. Henry said:

"What was the bad news you brought tonight and didn't tell? Not to me. Not to Fannie."

I gasped.

"How did you know?"

I thought of the old woman sinking in the riverbed, silent, in her sheets, out of sight. I thought of Cal, the piano lid slammed on his maple leaf hands.

"Even though," explained Henry with good reason, "you chew spearmint gum, your breath was sour tonight, young sir. Which means you're not digesting your food proper. Which means a bad day for writers come inland with no roots."

"It was a bad day for everyone, Henry."

"I'm still huffing and puffing." Henry stood tall and shook

his cane at the darkening halls where the lightbulbs were burning out and the souls were guttering low. "Watchdog Henry. You, now—git!"

I went out the door toward something that not only smelled but looked like a 1928 Duesenberg.

It was Constance Rattigan's limousine.

It was as long and bright and beautiful as a Fifth Avenue shop window somehow arrived on the wrong side of L.A.

The back door of the limo was open. The chauffeur was in the front seat, hat crammed down over his eyes, staring straight ahead. He didn't look at me. I tried to get his attention, but the limousine was waiting, its motor humming, and I was wasting time.

I had never been in such a vehicle in my life.

It might be my one and only chance.

I leaped in.

No sooner had I hit the back seat than the limousine swerved in one boa-constrictor glide away from the curb. The back door slammed shut on me and we were up to sixty by the time we reached the end of the block. Tearing up Temple Hill we made something like seventy-five. We managed to make all of the green lights to Vermont where we wheeled over to Wilshire and took it out as far as Westwood for no special reason, maybe because it was scenic.

I sat in the back seat like Robert Armstrong on King Kong's lap, crowing and babbling to myself, knowing where I was going but wondering why I deserved all this.

Then I remembered the nights when I had come up to call on Fannie and met this very same smell of Chanel and leather and Paris nights in the air outside her door. Constance Rattigan had been there only a few minutes before. We had missed colliding by one or two hairs of mink and an exhalation of Grand Marnier.

As we prepared to turn at Westwood we passed a cemetery which was so placed that if you weren't careful, you drove into a parking lot. Or was it that some days, looking for a parking lot, you mistakenly motored between tombstones? A confusion.

Before I could give it great mind, the cemetery and the parking lot were left behind and we were halfway to the sea.

At Venice and Windward we wheeled south along the shore. We passed like a slight rainfall, that quiet and swift, not far from my small apartment. I saw my typewriter window lit with a faint light. I wonder if I am in there, dreaming this? I thought. And we left behind my deserted office telephone booth with Peg two thousand miles away at the end of the silent line. Peg, I thought, if you could see me now!

We swerved in behind the big, bone-white Moorish fort at exactly midnight and the limousine stopped as easily as a wave sinks in sand and the limo door banged and the chauffeur, still quiet after the long, silent glide, streaked into the backside of the fort and did not appear again.

I waited a full minute for something to happen. When it did not, I slid out of the back of the limousine, like a shoplifter, guilty for no reason and wondering whether to escape.

I saw a dark figure upstairs in the house. Lights went on as the chauffeur moved about the Moorish fort on the Venice sands.

I stayed quietly, anyway. I looked at my watch. As the minute hand counted off the last second of the last minute, the front portico lights went on.

I walked up to the open front door and stepped into an empty house. At a distance down a hall I saw a small figure darting about the kitchen making drinks. A small girl in a maid's outfit. She waved at me and ran.

I walked into a living room filled with a menagerie of pillows of every size from Pomeranian to Great Dane. I sat on the biggest one and sank down even as my soul kept sinking in me.

The maid ran in, put down two drinks on a tray, and ran out before I could see her (there was only candlelight in this room). Over her shoulder she threw away "Drink!" in what was or was not a French accent.

It was a cool white wine and a good one and I needed it. My cold was worse. I was sneezing and honking and sneezing all the time.

In the year 2078 they excavated an old tomb or what they thought to be a tomb on the shoreline of California where, it was rumored, queens and kings once ruled, then went away with the tides along the flats. Some were buried with their chariots, it was said. Some with relics of their arrogance and magnificence. Some left behind only images of themselves in strange canisters which, held to the light and spun on a shuttle, talked in tongues and tossed black-and-white shadow-shows on empty tapestry screens.

One of the tombs found and opened was the tomb of a queen and in that vault was not a speck of dust, nor furniture, just pillows in mid-floor and all around, row on row, rising to the ceiling, and stack on stack, reaching to touch that ceiling, canisters labeled with the lives that the queen had lived and none of these lives were true but they seemed true. They were tinned and prisoned dreams. They were containers from which djinns screamed forth or into which princesses fled to hide for eternity from the reality that killed.

And the address of the tomb was 27 Speedway, Ocean

Front, Venice, California, in a lost year under sand and water. And the name of the queen with her film in cans from floor to roof was Rattigan.

And I was there now, waiting and thinking:

I hope she's not like the canary lady. I hope she's not a mummy with dust in her eyes.

I stopped hoping.

The second Egyptian queen had arrived. And not with a grand entrance at all, and she wasn't wearing a silver lamé evening gown, or even a smart dress and scarf or tailored slacks.

I felt her in the door across the room before she spoke, and what was she? A woman about five feet tall, in a black bathing suit, incredibly suntanned all over her body, and with a face dark as nutmeg and cinnamon. Her hair was cropped and a kind of blonde gray brown and tousled as if, what the hell, she had given it a try with a comb and let it go. The body was neat and firm and quick, and the tendons of her legs had not been cut. She ran quickly, barefoot, across the floor and stood looking down at me with flashing eyes.

"You a good swimmer?"

"Not bad."

"How many laps of my pool could you do?" She nodded to the great emerald lake outside the French doors.

"Twenty."

"I can go forty-five. Any man I know has got to do forty, before he goes to bed with me."

"I just flunked the test," I said.

"Constance Rattigan." She grabbed my hand and pumped it.

"I know," I said.

She stood back and eyed me up and down.

"So you're the one who chews spearmint and likes *Tosca*," she said.

"You been talking to both Henry the blind man and Florianna?"

"Right! Wait here. If I don't have my night dip, I'll go to sleep on you."

Before I could speak, she plunged out the French doors, skirted the pool, and headed for the ocean. She vanished into the first wave and swam out of sight.

I had a feeling she wouldn't want wine when she came back. I wandered out to the kitchen, which was Dutch, cream white, sky blue, and found a percolator in full perk, and the smell of coffee brewing for the start of a new day. I checked my cheap watch: almost one in the morning. I poured coffee for two and took it out to wait for her on the veranda overlooking the incredibly greeny-blue swimming pool.

"Yes!" was her answer as she ran to shake herself like a dog on the tiles.

She grabbed the coffee and should have burned her mouth drinking it. Between gasps she said, "This *starts* my day."

"What time do you go to bed?"

"Sunrise, sometimes, like the vampires. Noon's not for me."

"How do you get such a tan?"

"Sunlamp in the basement. Why are you staring?"

"Because," I said. "You're so different from the way I thought you would be. I imagined someone like Norma Desmond in that movie that just came out. You see it?"

"Hell, I *lived* it. Half of the film's me, the rest bilge. That dimwit Norma wants a new career. All I want most days is to hole up and not come out. I've had it with his-hand-on-my-knee producers and mattress-spring directors, timid writers, and cowardly scripts. No offense. You a writer?"

"I damn well am."

"You got spunk, kid. Stay away from films. They'll screw

you. Where was I? Oh, yeah, I gave most of my fancy gowns to Hollywood Volunteer Sales years ago. I go to maybe one premiere a year, disguised as someone else. Once every eight weeks, if it's some old chum, I have lunch at Sardi's or the Derby, then hole in again. Fannie I see about once a month, usually around this time. She's a night-owl like yours truly."

She finished her coffee and toweled herself off with a huge soft yellow towel that went well with her dark tan. She draped it over her shoulders and gave me another stare. I had time to study this woman who was and wasn't Constance Rattigan, the great empress from my childhood. On screen, twenty feet of gliding, villainous, man-trapping woman, dark haired, ravishing in her slenderness. Here, a sunblasted desert mouse, quick, nimble, ageless, all cinnamon and nutmeg and honey as we stood in the night wind out in front of her mosque by her Mediterranean pool. I looked at that house and thought, no radios, no television, no newspapers. She was quick with her telepathy.

"Right! Only the projector and the films in the parlor. Time only works well in one direction. Back. I control the past. I'll be damned if I know what to do with the present, and to hell with the future. I'm not going to be there, don't want to go there, and would hate you if you made me. It's a perfect life."

I looked at all the lit windows of her house and all the rooms behind the windows and then over at the abandoned limousine to one side of the mosque.

This made her nervous enough that suddenly she was gone and came running back with the white wine. She poured it, and muttered, "What the hell. Drink this. I'll—"

Quite suddenly, as she handed me my glass of wine, I began to laugh. Laugh, hell, I exploded, I guffawed.

"What's the joke?" she asked, half-taking the wine back. "What's funny?"

"You," I roared, "and the chauffeur. *And* the maid. The maid, the chauffeur! And you!"

I pointed at the kitchen, out at the limousine, and back at her.

She knew she was trapped and joined my hilarity, throwing her head back and giving a delicious yell.

"Jesus Christ, kid, you caught on! But—I thought I was good."

"You are!" I cried. "You're terrific. But when you handed me my drink, there was something in your wrist motion. I saw the chauffeur's hands on the steering wheel. I saw the maid's fingers on the serving tray. Constance, I mean Miss Rattigan—"

"Constance."

"You could have carried the masquerade on for days," I said. "It was just the smallest thing about your hands and wrists."

She ran out of the room, scampered back, frisky as a lap dog, wearing the chauffeur's cap, took it off, put on the maid's, cheeks pink, eyes flashing.

"You want to pinch the chauffeur's bum? Or the maid's?"

"All three of you have terrific bums!"

She refilled my glass, tossed the two caps aside, and said, "It's the only fun I have. No jobs in years, so I make my own jobs. Drive around town nights, incognito. Shop evenings, as the maid, ditto. I also run the projection equipment here in the parlor, and wash the limo. I'm not a bad courtesan, either, if you like courtesans. I used to make fifty bucks a night, much moola, in 1923, when a buck was a buck and two bits bought dinner."

We stopped laughing as we went back inside and sank into the pillows.

"Why all the mystery, why those late nights?" I asked. "Do you ever go out by day?"

"Only to funerals. You see"—Constance sipped her coffee and lay back among the pillows, which resembled a kennel of dogs—"I don't much like people. I started turning cranky young. I guess I have too many producers' fingerprints on my skin. Anyway, it's not bad, playing house alone."

"What am I doing here?" I asked.

"You're Fannie's friend, one. And, two, you look like a good kid. Bright but brainless, I mean innocent. Those big blue eyes full of naivete. Life hasn't got to you yet? I hope it never does. You look safe to me, and rather nice, and fun. No phys. ed., though, as they say, no phys. ed. Which means I'm not going to tackle you into the bedroom, your virginity is safe."

"I'm no virgin."

"No, but you sure as hell look it."

I blushed furiously.

"You still haven't said. Why am I here?"

Constance Rattigan put her coffee cup down and leaned forward to stare straight into my face.

"Fannie," she said, "is frightened. Terrified. Spooked. Are you, I wonder, the one responsible?"

For a little while I had forgotten.

The drive to the beach had blown the darkness out of my head. Being in this house, standing by the pool, watching this woman dive in the sea and return, feeling the night wind on my face and the wine in my mouth had made the last forty-eight hours vanish.

I suddenly realized I hadn't laughed really hard in a good many weeks. This strange lady's laughter had aged me back to where I should have been: twenty-seven years old, not ninety the way I had felt getting up this morning.

"Are you the one responsible for scaring Fannie?" she repeated, and stopped.

"My God," said Constance Rattigan. "You look as if I had just run over your pet dog." She grabbed my hand and squeezed. "Did I just kick you in the kishkas?"

"Kish—?"

"Meatballs. Sorry."

She let go of me. I didn't fall off the cliff. So she said, "It's just, I'm protective as hell about Fannie. I don't think you know how often I've been down to that ratty tenement to visit."

"I never saw you there."

"Sure you did, but didn't know. One night a year ago, Cinco de Mayo, there was a mariachi Mexican Spanish Pachuco conga lineup through the halls and down through the tenement, gassed on wine and enchiladas. I headed the conga line dolled up as Rio Rita; nobody knew who I was, which is the only way to have a good time. You were at the far end of the line, out of step. We never met. After an hour I had a small chat with Fannie and vamoosed. Most of the time I arrive there at two in the morning because Fannie and I go back to Chicago Opera and Art Institute days, when I was painting and in the opera chorus free, and Fannie sang a few leads. We knew Caruso and were both skinny as rails, can you believe that? Fannie? Skinny! But what a voice! God, we were young. Well, you know the rest. I came a long way with mattress marks on my back. When the marks got too numerous, I retired to pump money here in my backyard."

She indicated at least four oil-rig machineries heaving and sighing out back of the kitchen, wonderful pets for a good life.

"Fannie? She had a lousy love affair which cracked her permanently in half and blew her up to the size you see now. No man, not me, not life, could coax her back to beauty. We all just gave up on that and stayed friends."

"A good friend from the sound of your voice."

"Well, it works both ways. She's a talented, dear, eccentric lost lady. I Chihuahua-caper to her mammoth gavotte. Lots of good honest laughs at the four-o'clock-in-the-morning world. We don't kid each other about the facts of life. We know we'll never come back out into it, she for her reasons, me for mine. She saw one man too close, I saw too many, quickly. Retirement takes many forms, as you can see by my disguises, as you can see by Fannie's Montgolfier balloon shape."

"The way you talk about men, I mean, you're talking to a real live one here, now," I said.

"You're not one of them, I can tell. You couldn't rape a chorus line, or use your agent's desk for a bed. You couldn't knock your grandma downstairs to cadge the insurance. Maybe you're a sap, I don't know, or a fool, but I've come to prefer saps and fools, guys who don't raise tarantulas or yank wings off hummingbirds. Silly writers who dream about going to Mars and never coming back to our stupid daytime world."

She stopped, hearing herself.

"Christ, I talk a lot. Let's get back to Fannie. She doesn't scare often, been living in that old firetrap for twenty years now, door open to one and all, and the mayonnaise jar in hand, but now something's wrong. She jumps when fleas sneeze. So—?"

"Last night all we did was play opera and try to joke. She didn't say."

"Maybe she didn't want to bother the Martian, that's one of the things she calls you, right? I know by the way her skin shakes. You know horses at all? Ever see the skin on a horse twitch and jerk when flies land on it? Invisible flies are landing on Fannie all the time now, and she just firms her mouth and shakes her flesh. Seems her astrology chart is out of whack. Her hourglass is malfunctioning, someone has put funeral-urn ashes in it instead of sand. There are odd whispers in her icebox door. The ice falls inside the fridge at midnight and sounds like the wrong kind of laughter. The toilet across the hall gargles all night. The termites under her chair are going to gnaw through and drop her to hell. The spiders in the wall are mending her shroud. How's that for a list? All intuition. No facts. Would get thrown out of court fast. You understand?"

With nothing trembles.

I thought that, but didn't say it. Instead I said, "You talked to Henry about this?"

"Henry thinks he's the world's greatest blind man. That don't catsup any beans for me. He hints. Something's up, but he won't say. Can you help? Then I can write Fannie or call her through the Gutierrez lady or drop by tomorrow night and tell her everything's Jake. Can do?"

"Can I have some more wine, please?"

She poured, never taking her eyes off me.

"Okay," she said, "start lying."

"Something *is* going on, but it's too early to tell."

"By the time you tell, it may be too late." Constance Rattigan jumped up and paced around the room, turning at last to rifle-shot me with a stare. "Why won't you talk when you know Fannie's scared gutless?"

"Because I'm tired of being afraid of every shadow, myself. Because I've been a coward all of my life and I'm sick of me. When I know more, I'll call you!"

"Jesus." Constance Rattigan snorted a laugh. "You got a loud voice. I'll move back and give you air. I know you love Fannie. You think she should come live with me here for a few days, a week, to protect her?"

I looked around at the grand pillows, the bright elephant herd of satin surfaces with goosedown stuffings, so much in shape and size like Florianna.

I shook my head. "That's her nest. I've tried to get her out to movies, to plays, even to operas. Forget it. She hasn't been out on the street in over ten years. To take her away from the tenement, her big elephant boneyard, well—"

Constance Rattigan sighed and refilled my glass.

"It wouldn't do any good anyway, would it?"

She was reading my profile. I was reading the dark surf out beyond the French windows where the tidal sands turned in their sleep, in their own good time.

"It's always too late, isn't it?" Constance Rattigan went on. "There's no way to protect Fannie or anyone, not if someone wants to hurt or kill you."

"Who said anything about killing?" I protested.

"You've got the kind of plain pink pumpkin face that shows everything. When I told fortunes it wasn't tea leaves, it was obvious eyes and vulnerable mouths. Fannie's spooked and that spooks me. For the first time in years, when I swim at night, I figure a big wave will take me so far out I'll never make it back. Christ, I hate to have my one really big enjoyment spoiled like this." Then she added, swiftly, "You wouldn't be the spoiler, would you?"

"What?"

Suddenly she sounded like Crumley, or Fannie telling me not to "bring anyone with."

I must have looked so startled that she barked a laugh.

"Hell, no. You're just one of those guys who kill people on paper so's not to kill for real. Sorry."

But I was on my feet now, bursting to say something, tell wild things, but I wasn't sure what.

"Look," I said. "It's been a crazy month. I'm beginning to notice things maybe I never noticed before. I never read the obituaries, ever. Now I do. You ever have weeks or months when too many friends go mad, or go away, or drop dead?"

"At sixty"—Constance Rattigan laughed ironically— "there are whole years like that. I'm afraid to go down any flight of stairs; friend broke his neck that way. Afraid of eating;

two friends choked. The ocean? Three friends drowned. Air-
planes? Six friends smashed. Cars, twenty. Sleeping? Hell, yes.
Ten friends died in their sleep, said what the hell and quit.
Drinking? Fourteen friends with cirrhosis. List me some lists.
It's only begun for you. I've got a phone book here, look."

She grabbed a small black book off the table near the door
and tossed it to me.

"Book of the dead."

"What?"

I turned the pages, saw the names. There were little red
crosses by fifty percent of the names on each page.

"That personal phone book is thirty-five years old. So half
the people in it have been gone quite a while, and I don't have
the guts to finally erase or yank out the names. It would be like
a final death. So I guess I'm the same sort of custard you are,
son."

She took the book of the dead back from me.

I felt a cold wind from the window and heard the beach
sand stir as if a great and invisible beast had put a huge paw
down on it.

"I didn't spook Fannie," I said, at last. "I'm not Typhoid
Mary. I don't carry the disease. If it's anywhere tonight, or
here, it's on its own. My stomach's been ruined for days. People are dying or running away, and there's no connection, and
I can't prove anything. I'm around or near when it happens
and I feel guilty I can't see, know, tell, stop it. I have this
god-awful feeling it'll go on more days than I can bear. Everyone I look at, now, I think, I wonder if he or she is next, and
know that if I wait long enough, of course, everyone goes.
They just seem to be going faster this week. That's all I'm
going to say. Now I'll shut up."

She came and kissed the ends of her fingers and put the
fingertips on my mouth. "I won't rile you again. For a custard,
you snap back. What now, another drink? Want to run films?

Midnight dip in my pool? Mercy sex with your film mother?
None of the above?"

I ducked my head so as to avoid her mocking and fiery
gaze.

"Films. I'd like to see Constance Rattigan in *Lace Curtains*.
Last time I saw it, I was five."

"You sure know how to make old folks feel great. *Lace
Curtains*. Stand back while I load the projector. My pa worked
a Kansas City cinema when I was a girl, taught me to run the
machines. Still can. I don't need *anyone* in this house!"

"Yes, you do. Me. To watch the film."

"Damn." She leaped across the pillows and started fiddling
with the projector in the back of the parlor. She yanked a can
of film off a nearby shelf and deftly began to thread it through
the machine. "You're right. I'll watch your face watching me."

While she was busy, humming and adjusting, I turned and
stepped out on the low porch above the sands. My eye traveled
along from the south, roving the shore, past the front of Constance Rattigan's property, and on north until . . .

Down by the tideline, I saw something.

There was a man standing there, motionless, or something
that looked like a man. And how long he had been there, and
whether he had just come in from the surf, I couldn't say. I
couldn't see if he was wet. He looked naked.

I gasped and glanced quickly inside. Constance Rattigan,
whistling between her teeth, was still dickering away at the
projector.

A wave fell like a gunshot. I flicked my gaze back. The man
was still there, hands at his side, head up, legs apart, almost
defiant.

Go away! I wanted to yell. What are you doing here?
We've done nothing.

Are you sure? was my next thought.

No one deserves to be killed.

No?

A final wave came in behind the shape there on the shore. It broke up into a series of cracked mirrors that fell and seemed to envelop the man. He was erased. When the wave pulled back out he was gone, perhaps running away north along the sands.

Back past the lion cage in the canal, past the canary lady's empty windows, back past my apartment with its winding-sheet bed.

"Ready?" Constance Rattigan called from inside.

Not really, I thought.

Inside, Constance said, "Come see the old lady made young."

"You're not old," I said.

"No, by God." She ran around turning off lights and fluffing pillows in the middle of the room. "This health nut's writing a book, out next year. Underwater gymnastics. Sex at low tide. What bicarbs to take after you eat the local football coach. What—my God. You're blushing again. What do you know about girls?"

"Not much."

"How many you had?"

"Not many."

"One," she guessed, and crowed when my head bobbed. "Where is she tonight?"

"Mexico City."

"When's she coming back?"

"Ten days."

"Miss her? Love her?"

"Yes."

"You want to telephone her and stay on the phone all night so her voice protects you from this dragon lady?"

"I'm not afraid of you."

"Like hell you're not. You believe in body warmth?"

"Body?"

"Warmth! Sex without sex. Hugs. You can give this old gila monster canned heat without losing virtue. Just hold and hug, spoon fashion. Keep your eyes on the ceiling. That's where the action is. Films all night until the dawn comes up like Francis X. Bushman's erection. Sorry. Damn. Come on, son. Let's hit the sack!"

She sank into the pillows, pulling me after, at the same time stabbing some buttons on a control console imbedded in the floor. The last lights went out. The sixteen-millimeter projector started humming. The ceiling filled with light and shadow.

"Look. How d'you like that?"

She pointed up with her beautiful nose.

Constance Rattigan, twenty-eight years back in time, on the ceiling, lit a cigarette.

Down beside me, the real lady blew smoke.

"Wasn't I a bitch!" she said.

I woke at dawn not believing where I was. I woke incredibly happy, as if something beautiful had happened in the night. Nothing had, of course, it was just sleeping among so many rich pillows by a woman who smelled like spice cabinets and fine parquetry. She was a lovely chess game carved and set in a store window when you were a kid. She was a freshly built girl's gym, with only the faintest scent of the noon tennis dust that clings to golden thighs.

I turned in the dawn light.

And she was gone.

I heard a wave come along the shore. A cool wind blew in through the open French doors. I sat up. Far out in the dusky waters I saw an arm flash up and down, up and down. Her voice called.

I ran out and dove in and swam halfway to her before I was exhausted. No athlete this. I turned back and sat waiting for her on the shore. She came in at last and stood over me, stark naked this time.

"Christ," she said, "you didn't even take off your underwear. What's happened to modern youth?"

I was staring at her body.

"How you like it? Pretty good for an old empress, huh? Good buzz-um, tight rump, marceled pubic hairs—"

But I had shut my eyes. She giggled. Then she was gone, laughing. She ran up the beach half a mile and came back, having startled only the gulls.

Next thing I knew the smell of coffee blew along the shore, with the scent of fresh toast. When I dragged myself inside she was seated in the kitchen, wearing only the mascara she had painted around her eyes a moment before. Blinking rapidly at me, like some silent screen farm girl, she handed me jam and toast, and draped a napkin daintily over her lap, so as not to offend while I stared and ate. She got strawberry jam on the tip of her left breast. I saw this. She saw me seeing this and said, "Hungry?"

Which made me butter my toast all the faster.

"Good grief, go call Mexico City."

I called.

"Where are you?" demanded Peg's voice, two thousand miles away.

"In a phone booth, in Venice, and it's raining," I said.

"Liar!" said Peg.

And she was right.

And then, quite suddenly, it was over.

It was very late, or very early. I felt drunk on life, just because this woman had taken time to play through the hours, talk through the darkness until the sun, way over in the east, beyond the fogs and mists, threatened to appear.

I looked out at the surf and shore. Not a sign of bodies drowned, and no one on the sand to know or not know. I didn't want to go but I had a full day's work ahead, writing my stories just three steps ahead of death. A day without writing, I often said, and said it so many times my friends sighed and rolled their eyeballs, a day without writing was a little death. I did not intend to pitch me over the graveyard wall. I would fight all the way with my Underwood Standard which shoots more squarely, if you aim it right, than any rifle ever invented.

"I'll drive you home," said Constance Rattigan.

"No, thanks. It's just three hundred yards down the beach. We're neighbors."

"Like hell we are. This place cost two hundred thousand to build in 1920, five million today. What's your rent? Thirty bucks a month?"

I nodded.

"Okay, neighbor. Hit the sand. Come back some midnight?"

"Often," I said.

"Often." She took my two hands in hers, which is to say into the hands of the chauffeur and the maid and the movie queen. She laughed, reading my mind. "You think I'm nuts?"

"I wish the world were like you."

She shifted gears to avoid the compliment.

"And Fannie? Will she live forever?"

My eyes wet, I nodded.

She kissed me on both cheeks and pushed. "Get outa here."

I jumped from her tiled porch into the sand, ran a step, turned, and said, "Good day, princess."

"Shit," she said, pleased.

I ran away.

Nothing much happened that day.

But that night . . .

I woke and glanced at my Mickey Mouse watch, wondering what had pulled me up. I shut my eyes tight and ached my ears, listening.

Rifle fire. Bang, bong and again bang, bong and again bang, down the coast, from the pier.

My God, I thought, the pier's almost empty and the rifle gallery shut, and who could be out there, middle of the night, yanking the trigger and belling the target?

Bang and bang and the sound of the struck gong. Bang and bong. Again and again. Twelve shots at a time and then twelve more and then twelve more, as if someone had lined up three and then six and then nine rifles and jumped from an empty one to a loaded one without a breath and aimed and fired and fired and fired.

Madness.

It had to be. Whoever it was, alone on the pier in the fog, seizing the weapons, firing at Doom.

Annie Oakley, the rifle lady herself? I wondered.

Bang. Take that you son-of-a-bitch. Bang. Take that you bastard runaway lover. Bang. Take that you unholy womanizing—freak. Bang!

Wham and again wham, far off but blowing in the wind.

So many bullets, I thought, to make something impossible die.

It went on for twenty minutes.

When it was over, I could not sleep.

With three dozen wounds in my chest, I groped over to my typewriter and, eyes shut, typed out all the rifle shots in the dark.

"Offisa Pup?"

"How's that again?"

"Offisa Pup, this is Krazy Kat."

"Jesus," said Crumley. "It's you. Offisa Pup, eh?"

"It's better than Elmo Crumley."

"Got me there. And Krazy Kat's right for you, scribe. How goes the Great American Epic?"

"How goes the Conan Doyle sequel?"

"This is embarrassing, but ever since I met you, son, I'm doing four pages a night. It's like a war: should be outa there by Christmas. Krazy Kats, it turns out, are good influences. That's the last compliment you get from the offisa. It's your nickel. Speak."

"I got more possibilities for our list of maybe future victims."

"Jesus in the lilies, Christ on the cross," sighed Crumley.

"Funny how you never notice—"

"It's a laugh riot. Proceed."

"Shrank still leads the parade. Then Annie Oakley, or whatever her real name is, the rifle marksman lady. Someone, last night, was shooting on the pier. It had to be her. Who else? I mean, she wouldn't open up her place, two in the morning, for a stranger, would she?"

Crumley interrupted.

"Get her real name. I can't do anything without her real name."

I felt one of my legs being pulled by him and shut up.

"Cat got your tongue?" said Crumley.

Silence from me.

"You still there?" asked Crumley.

Grim silence.

"Lazarus," said Crumley, "damn it to hell, come outa that Christ-awful tomb!"

I laughed. "Shall I finish the list?"

"Let me grab my beer. Okay. Shoot."

I reeled off six more names, including, though I didn't really believe it, Shapeshade's.

"And maybe," I finished, and hesitated, "Constance Rattigan."

"Rattigan!" yelled Crumley. "What the hell you know about Rattigan? She eats tiger's balls on toast and can whipsaw sharks two falls out of three. She'd walk out of Hiroshima with her earrings and eyelashes intact. Annie Oakley, now, no to her, too. She'd rifle someone's butt off before he—no, only way is some night, on her own, she might toss all her guns off the pier and follow after; *that's* in her face. As for Shapeshade, don't make me laugh. He doesn't even know the real world exists out here with us grotesque normals. They'll bury him in his Wurlitzer come 1999. Got any more bright ideas?"

I swallowed hard and finally decided to at last tell Crumley about the mysterious disappearance of Cal the barber.

"Mysterious, hell," said Crumley. "Where you been? The Mad Butcher skedaddled. Piled his tin lizzie with dregs from his shop just the other day, pulled out of the no-parking zone in front of his place, and headed east. Not west, you notice, toward Land's End, but east. Half the police force saw him make a big U-turn out front the station and didn't arrest him because he yelled, 'Autumn leaves, by God, autumn leaves in the Ozarks!' "

I gave a great trembling sigh of relief, glad for Cal's survival. I said nothing about Scott Joplin's missing head, which was probably what drove Cal off and away forever. But Crumley was still talking. "You finished with your super-brand-new list of possible deads?"

"Well—" lamely.

"Dip in ocean, then dip in typewriter, says Zen master, makes for full page and happy heart. Listen to the detective advising the genius. The beer is on the ice, so that the pee is in the pot, later. Leave your list at home. So long, Krazy Kat."

"Offisa Pup," I said. "Goodbye."

The forty dozen rifle shots from last night drew me. Their echoes would not stop.

And the sound of more of the pier being pounded and compacted and eaten away drew me, as the sounds of war must draw some.

The rifle shots, the pier, I thought, as I dipped in the ocean and then dipped in my typewriter, like the good kat Offisa Pup wished me to be, I wonder how many men, or was it just one, Annie Oakley killed last night.

I wonder, also, I thought, placing six new pages of incredibly brilliant novel in my Talking Box, what new books of drunken doom A. L. Shrank has toadstool-farmed on his catacomb library shelves?

The Hardy Boys Invite Ptomaine?
Nancy Drew and the Weltschmerz Kid?
The Funeral Directors of America Frolic at Atlantic City?
Don't go look, I thought. I must, I thought. But don't laugh

when you see the new titles. Shrank might run out and *charge* you.

Rifle shots, I thought. Dying pier. A. L. Shrank, Sigmund Freud's Munchkin son. And now, there, up ahead of me biking on the pier:

The Beast.

Or, as I sometimes called him, Erwin Rommel of the Afrika Korps. Or, sometimes, simply:

Caligula. The Killer.

His real name was John Wilkes Hopwood.

I remember reading one of those devastating reviews about him in a small local Hollywood theater some years before:

> John Wilkes Hopwood, the matinee assassin, has done it again to another role. Not only has he torn a passion to tatters, he has, madness maddened, stomped on it, ravened it with his teeth, and hurled it across the footlights at unsuspecting club ladies. The damned fools ate it up!

I often saw him riding his bright orange Raleigh eight-speed bike along the ocean walk from Venice to Ocean Park and Santa Monica. He was always dressed in a fine, freshly pressed, brown hound's-tooth English suit with a dark brown Irish cap pulled over his snow-white curls and shading his General Erwin Rommel or, if you prefer, killer hawk's Conrad -Veidt-about-to-smother-Joan-Crawford-or-Greer-Garson face. His cheeks were burned to a wonderful polished nutmeg color, and I often wondered if the color stopped at his neckline, for I had never seen him out on the sand, stripped. Forever, he cycled up and down between the ocean towns, at liberty, waiting to be summoned by the German General Staff or the club ladies over at the Hollywood Assistance League, whichever came first. When there was a cycle of war films, he worked constantly, for it was rumored he had a full closet of

Afrika Korps uniforms and a burial cape for the occasional vampire film.

As far as I could tell, he had only one casual outfit, that suit. And one pair of shoes, fine English oxblood brogues, highly polished. His bicycle clips, brightly clasping his tweed cuffs, looked to be pure silver from some shop in Beverly Hills. His teeth were always so finely polished, they seemed not his own. His breath, as he pedaled past, was Listerine, just in case he had to take a fast call from Hitler on his way to Playa Del Rey.

I saw him most often motionless, astride his bike, Sunday afternoons, when Muscle Beach filled up with rippling deltoids and masculine laughter. Hopwood would stand up on the Santa Monica pier, like a commander in the last days of the retreat from El Alamein, depressed at all that sand, delighted with all that flesh.

He seemed so apart from all of us, gliding by in his Anglo-Byronic-German daydreams . . .

I never thought to see him parking his Raleigh bike outside A. L. Shrank's tarot-card-large-belfry-with-plenty-of-bats-open-at-all-hours shed.

But park he did, and hesitated outside the door.

Don't go in! I thought. No one goes in A. L. Shrank's unless it's for poison Medici rings and tombstone phone numbers.

Erwin Rommel didn't mind.

Neither did the Beast, or Caligula.

Shrank beckoned.

All three obeyed.

By the time I got there, the door was shut. On it, for the first time, though it had probably yellowed there for years, was a list, typed with a faded ribbon, of all the folks who had passed through his portals to be psyched back to health.

H. B. WARNER, WARNER OLAND, WARNER

BAXTER, CONRAD NAGEL, VILMA BANKY, ROD
LA ROCQUE, BESSIE LOVE, JAMES GLEASON . . .

It read like the *Actor's Directory* for 1929.

But Constance Rattigan was there.

I didn't believe that.

And John Wilkes Hopwood.

I knew I *had* to believe that.

For, as I glanced through the dusty window, where a shade
was half-drawn against prying eyes, I saw that someone was
indeed on that couch from which stuffing sprang in mad aban-
don from the burst seams. And the man lying on the couch was
the man in the brown tweed suit, eyes shut, doing lines, no
doubt from a revised and improved last act of *Hamlet*.

Jesus in the lilies, as Crumley had said. Christ fresh to the
cross!

At that moment, intent upon reciting his rosary innards,
Hopwood's eyes flew open with actor's intuition.

His eyes rolled, then his head flicked swiftly to one side.
He stared at the window and saw me.

As did A. L. Shrank, seated nearby, turned away, pad and
pencil in hand.

I stood back, cursed quietly, and walked quickly away.

In total embarrassment, I walked all the way to the end of
the ruined pier, bought six Nestlé's Crunch bars and two Clark
Bars and two Power Houses to devour on the way. Whenever
I am very happy or very sad or very embarrassed, I cram my
mouth with sweets and litter the breezeway with discards.

It was there at the end of the pier in the golden light of late
afternoon that Caligula Rommel caught up with me. The de-
struction workers were gone. The air was silent.

I heard his bicycle hum and glide just behind me. He didn't
speak at first. He just arrived on foot, the bright silver bike clips
around his trim ankles, the Raleigh held in his firm grasp like
an insect woman. He stood at the one place on the pier where

I had seen him, like a statue of Richard Wagner, watching one of his great choruses come in tides along the shore.

There were still half a dozen young men playing volleyball below. The thump of the ball and the rifleshots of their laughs were somehow killing the day. Beyond, two weight-lifting finalists were lifting their own worlds into the sky, in hopes of convincing eight or nine young women nearby that a fate worse than death wasn't so bad after all, and could be had upstairs in the hotdog apartments just across the sand.

John Wilkes Hopwood surveyed the scene and did not look at me. He was making me sweat and wait, daring me to leave. I had, after all, crossed an invisible sill of his life, half an hour ago. Now, I must pay.

"Are you following me?" I said at last, and immediately felt a fool.

Hopwood laughed that famous last-act maniac laugh of his.

"Dear boy, you're much too young. You're the sort I throw back in the sea."

God, I thought, what do I say now?

Hopwood cricked his head stiffly back behind him, pointing his eagle's profile toward the Santa Monica pier a mile north from here, along the coast.

"But, if you should ever decide to follow *me*"—he smiled —"*that* is where I live. Above the carousel, above the horses."

I turned. Far off on that other still vibrant pier was the carousel that had been turning and grinding out its calliope music since I was a kid. Above the big horse race were the Carousel Apartments, a grand eyrie for retired German generals, failed actors, or driven romantics. I had heard that great poets who published small lived there. Novelists of many wits and no reviews lived there. Well-hung artists with unhung paintings lived there. Courtesans of famous film stars who were now prostitutes for spaghetti salesmen lived there. Old English matrons who had once thrived in Brighton and missed the

Rocks lived there with stacks of antimacassars and stuffed Pekingese.

Now it seemed that Bismarck, Thomas Mann, Conrad Veidt, Admiral Doenitz, Erwin Rommel, and Mad Otto of Bavaria lived there.

I looked at that magnificent eagle profile. Hopwood stiffened with pride at my glance. He scowled at the golden sands and said, quietly, "You think I am crazy, allowing myself the tender mercies of one A. L. Shrank?"

"Well—"

"He is a very insightful man, very holistic, very special. And as you know, we actors are the world's most unsettled people. The future is always uncertain, the phone should ring but never does. We have much time on our hands. So it is either numerology or the tarot cards or astrology or the Eastern meditation up under the great tree at Ojai with Krishnamurti, have you *been?* Fine! Or Reverend Violet Greener at her Agabeg Temple on Crenshaw? Norvell the futurist? Aimee Semple McPherson, were you ever saved? I was. She laid on the hands, then I laid her. Holy Rollers? The ecstasy. Or the Hall Johnson Choir down in the First Baptist Church Sunday nights. Dark angels. Such glory. Or it is the all-night bridge or the start-at-noon, play-till-dusk bingo with all the ladies with heliotrope hair. Actors go everywhere. If we knew a good eviscerator we would attend. Caesar's Gut-Readers, Inc. I could make a mint scalpeling doves and fishing out the innards like card-pips where the future lies stinking at noon. I try it all to fill the time. That's what all actors are, time fillers. Ninety percent of our lives, stage-waits. Meanwhile, we lie down with A. L. Shrank to get it up at Muscle Beach."

He had never taken his gaze from the pliant rubber Greek gods who frolicked below, washed by equal parts of salt wind and lust.

"Have you ever wondered," he said at last, a faint line of

sweat on his upper lip, a faint brim of perspiration along the
hairline under his cap, "about vampires who do not appear in
mirrors? Well, now, see those glorious young men down
there? They appear in all mirrors; but no one *else* does. Only
the minted gods show. And when they stare at themselves, do
they *ever* see anyone else, the girls that they ride like seahorses?
I have no such faith. So now"— he went back to his starter
subject—"do you understand why you saw me with the wee
dark mole A. L. Shrank?"

"I wait for phone calls, myself," I said. "Anything's better
than that!"

"You actually understand." He stared at me with eyes that
burned the clothes off my body.

I nodded.

"Come visit me sometime." He nodded at the faraway
Carousel Apartments where the calliope groaned and lamented
over something vaguely resembling "Beautiful Ohio." "I'll tell
you about Iris Tree, Sir Beerbohm Tree's daughter, who used
to live in those apartments, the half-sister of Carol Reed, the
British director. Aldous Huxley sometimes drops up, you
might see him."

He saw my head jerk at that and knew I was on the hook.

"You like to meet Huxley? Well, behave yourself"—he
caressed the words—"and you just might."

I was filled with an inexpressible and insufferable need that
I had to force myself to repress. Huxley was a madness in my
life, a terrible hunger. I longed to be that bright, that witty, that
toweringly supreme. To think, I might meet him.

"Come visit." Hopwood's hand had crept to his coat
pocket. "And I will introduce you to the young man I love best
in all the world."

I forced myself to glance away, as I had often glanced off
from something Crumley or Constance Rattigan said.

"Well, well," murmured John Wilkes Hopwood, his

Germanic mouth curling with delight, "the young man is embarrassed. It's not what you think. Look! No, stare."

He held out a crumpled glossy photograph. I tried to take it but he held it gripped firmly, his thumb placed over the head of the person in the photo.

The rest, sticking out from under the thumb, was the most beautiful body of a young man I had ever seen in my life.

It reminded me of photos I had once seen of the statue of Antinous, the lover of Hadrian, in the lobby of the Vatican Museum. It reminded me of the boy David. It reminded me of a thousand young men's bodies wrestling up and down the beach from my childhood to here, sunburned and mindless, wildly happy without true joy. A thousand summers were compacted down into this one single photograph, as John Wilkes Hopwood held it with his thumb hiding the face to protect it from revelations.

"Isn't it the single most incredible body in the history of the world?" It was a proclamation.

"And it's mine, all mine. Mine to have and hold," he said. "No, no, don't flinch. Here."

He took his thumb off the face of the incredibly lovely young man.

And the face of the old hawk, the ancient German warrior, the African tank general appeared.

"My God," I said. "It's you."

"Me," said John Wilkes Hopwood. And threw his head back with that merciless grin that flashed sabers and promised steel. He laughed silently, in honor of the old days, before films talked.

"It is I, rather," he said.

I took off my glasses, cleaned them, and looked closer.

"No. No fake. No trick photography."

It was like those contest picture puzzles they used to print in newspapers when I was a boy. The faces of presidents, cut in three sections and mixed. Here Lincoln's chin, there Washington's nose, and above, Roosevelt's eyes. Mixed and remixed with thirty other presidents you had to recut and repaste to win a fast ten bucks.

But here a young man's Greek-statue body was fused to the neck, head, and face of a hawk-eagle-vulture ascending into villainy, madness, or both.

Triumph of the Will was in John Wilkes Hopwood's eyes as he stared over my shoulder, as if he had never seen this damned beauty before.

"You think it's a trick, eh?"

"No." But I stole a look at his woolen suit, his fresh clean shirt, his neatly tied old-school tie, his vest, his cufflinks, his bright belt buckle, the silver bike clips around his ankles.

I thought of Cal the barber and Scott Joplin's missing head.

John Wilkes Hopwood stroked his vest and legs with rust-freckled fingers.

"Yes"—he laughed—"it's covered up! So you'll never know unless you come visit, will you? Whether the old half-gone-to-seed Richard   has-been really is the keeper of the Summer Boy flame, eh? How can it be that a miracle of youngness is mated with an old sea-wolf? Why does Apollo lie down with—"

"Caligula?" I blurted, and froze.

But Hopwood didn't mind. He laughed and nodded as he touched my elbow.

"Caligula—yes!—will now speak, while lovely Apollo hides and waits! Will power is the answer. Will power. Health foods, yes, are the center of actors' lives! We must keep our bodies as well as our spirits up! No white bread, no Nestlé's Crunch bars—"

I flinched and felt the last of the bars melting in my pockets.

"No pies, cakes, no hard liquor, not even too much sex. In bed nights by ten. Up early, a run along the beach, two hours in the gym every day, every day of your life, all your friends gym instructors, and two hours of bicycling a day. Every day for thirty years. Thirty years! At the end of which time you stroll by God's guillotine! He chops off your crazed old eagle's head and plants it on a sunburned, forever golden, young man's body! What a price I have paid, but worth it. Beauty is mine. Sublime incest. Narcissus par excellence. I need no one else."

"I believe that," I said.

"Your honesty will be your death."

He put his photo, like a flower, in his pocket.

"You still don't believe."

"Let me see that again."

He handed it to me.

I stared. And as I stared, the surf rolled on the dark shore just last night.

From the surf, a naked man suddenly appeared.

I winced and blinked.

Was this the body, this the man who had come out of the sea to frighten me when Constance Rattigan's back was turned?

I wanted to know. I could only say, "Do you know Constance Rattigan?"

He stiffened. "Why do you ask?"

"I saw her name at Shrank's outside, typed. I thought maybe you were ships that passed in the night."

Or bodies? Him coming out of the surf at three a.m. some night soon, as she plunged in?

His Teutonic mouth shaped itself to merely haughty.

"Our film *Crossed Sabers* was the smash of 1926 across

America. Our affair made headlines that summer. I was the greatest love of her life."

"Were you—" I started to say. Were you the one, I thought, and not the director who drowned himself, who cut her hamstrings with your sword, so she couldn't walk for a year?

But then, last night, I hadn't really had a chance to look for the scars. And the way Constance ran, it was all lies told a hundred years back.

"You should go see A. L. Shrank, a concerned man, pure Zen, all wise," he said, climbing back on his bike. "How so? He told me to give you these."

He took from his other pocket a handful of candy wrappers, twelve of them, neatly paperclipped together, mostly Clark, Crunch, and Power House. Things I had mindlessly strewn in the beach winds and someone had picked up.

"He knows *all* about you," said Mad Otto of Bavaria, and laughed with the soundtrack off.

I took the candy wrappers shamefacedly, and felt the extra ten pounds sag around my middle as I held these flags of defeat.

"Visit me," he said. "Come ride the carousel. Come see if innocent boy David is truly married to old evil Caligula, eh?"

And he biked away, a tweed suit under a tweed hat, smiling and looking only ahead.

I walked back to A. L. Shrank's melancholy museum and squinted through the dusty window.

There was a toppling stack of bright orange, lemon, chocolate-brown candy wrappers filed on a small table near the sunken sofa.

Those can't *all* be mine, I thought.

They are, I thought. I'm plump. But then—he's *nuts*.

I went to find ice cream.

"Crumley?"

"I thought my name was Offisa Pup."

"I think I've got a line on the murderer himself!"

There was a long ocean silence while the policeman put down the phone, tore his hair, and picked the phone up again.

"John Wilkes Hopwood," I said.

"You forget," said the police lieutenant, "there have been no murders yet. Only suspicions and possibilities. There's a thing called a courtroom and another thing called proof. No proof, no case, and they throw you out on your butt so fast you're stopped up for weeks!"

"You ever seen John Wilkes Hopwood with his clothes off?" I asked.

"That did it."

Offisa Pup hung up on me.

It was raining when I came out of the booth.

Almost immediately the telephone rang as if knowing I was there. I snatched at it and for some reason yelled, "Peg!"

But there was only a sound of rain, and soft breathing, miles away.

I won't ever answer this phone again, I thought.

"Son-of-a-bitch," I yelled. "Come get me, you bastard."

I hung up.

My God, I thought, what if he heard and came over to visit?

Idiot, I thought.

And the phone rang for a last time.

I had to answer, maybe to apologize to that breathing far away and tell it to ignore my insolence.

I lifted the receiver.

And heard a sad lady five miles off somewhere in Los Angeles.

Fannie.

And she was crying.

"**F**annie, my God, is that you?"

"Yes, oh, yes, Lord God in heaven," she wheezed, she gasped, she floundered. "Coming upstairs almost killed me. Haven't climbed stairs since 1935. Where have you been? The roof's caved in. Life's over. Everybody's dead. Why didn't you tell me? Oh, God, God, this is terrible. Can you come over? Jimmy. Sam. Pietro." She did the litany and the pressure of my guilt crushed me against the side of the phone booth. "Pietro, Jimmy, Sam. Why did you lie?"

"I didn't lie, I just shut up!" I said.

"And now Henry!" she cried.

"Henry! My God. He isn't—?"

"Fell downstairs."

"Alive? Alive?" I yelled.

"In his room, yes, thank God. Wouldn't go to the hospital. I heard him fall, ran out. That's when I found out what you didn't say. Henry lying there, swearing, naming names. Jimmy. Sam. Pietro. Oh, why did you bring death here?"

"I didn't, Fannie."

"Come prove it. I've got three mayonnaise jars full of quarters. Take a cab, send the driver up, I'll pay him out of the jars! And when you get here, how will I know when you knock at the door it'll be you?"

"How do you know it's me, even now, Fannie, on the phone?"

"I don't know," she wailed. "Isn't that awful? I don't know."

"Los Angeles," I said to the taxi driver, ten minutes later. "Three mayonnaise jars' worth."

"Hello, Constance? I'm in a phone booth across from Fannie's. We've got to get her out of here. Can you come? She's really scared now."

"For good reasons?"

I stared across at the tenement and judged how many thousand shadows were crammed in it, top to bottom.

"This time for sure."

"Get over there. Stand guard. I'll be there in half an hour. I won't come up. You argue her down, damn it, and we'll get her away. Jump."

The way Constance slammed down the phone shot me out of the booth and almost got me run down by a car racing across the street.

The way I knocked on her door, she believed it was me. She threw the door wide and I saw what was almost a crazed elephant, eyes wild, hair in disarray, acting as if a rifle had just shot her through her head.

I launched her back into her chair and threw the icebox wide, trying to decide whether mayonnaise or wine would help. Wine.

"Get that in you," I commanded, and suddenly realized my cab driver was in the door behind me, having followed me upstairs, thinking I was a deadbeat and trying to escape.

I grabbed and handed him one mayonnaise jar full of quarters.

"That enough?" I said.

He did a quick estimate, like someone guessing jelly beans in a vat in a store window, sucked his teeth, and ran off with the coins rattling.

Fannie was busy emptying the wine glass. I refilled it and sat down to wait. At last she said, "Someone's been outside my door every night now for two nights. They come and go, go and come, not like ever before, they stop, they breathe out and in, my God, what are they doing outside an old collapsed ruin of an opera singer fat lady's door at midnight, it can't be rape, can it, they don't rape 380-pound sopranos, do they?"

And here she began to laugh so long and so hard I couldn't tell if it was hysteria or an amazed and self-surprising humor. I had to beat her on the back to stop the laughs and change the color in her face and give her more wine.

"Oh, my, my, my," she gasped. "It's good to laugh. Thank God, you're here. You'll protect me, won't you? I'm sorry I said what I said. You didn't bring that dreadful thing with you and leave it outside my door. It's just the hound of the Baskervilles, hungry, come in on his own to scare Fannie."

"I'm sorry I didn't tell you about Jimmy and Pietro and Sam, Fannie," I said, and gulped my wine. "I just didn't want to read obits to you, all at once. Look here. Constance Rattigan will be downstairs in a few minutes. She wants you to come stay a few days and—"

"More secrets," cried Fannie, eyes wide. "Since when have you known her? And, anyway, it's no use. This is my home. If I left here, I'd waste away, just die. I have my recordings."

"We'll take them with."

"My books."

"I'll carry them down."

"My mayonnaise, she wouldn't have the right brand."

"I'll buy it."

"She wouldn't have room."

"Even for you, Fannie, yes."

"And then what about my new calico cat . . . ?"

And so it went until I heard the limousine shrug in against the curb below.

"So that's it, is it, Fannie?"

"I feel fine, now, now that you're here. Just tell Mrs. Gutierrez to come up and stay a while after you leave," said Fannie cheerily.

"Where does all this false optimism come from, when an hour ago you were doomed?"

"Dear boy, Fannie's fine. That dreadful beast isn't coming back, I just know, and anyway, anyway—"

With a terrible sense of timing, the entire tenement shifted in its sleep.

The door to Fannie's room whispered on its hinges.

As if shot a final time, Fannie sat up and almost gagged on her terror.

I was across the room in an instant and threw the door wide, to stare out into the long valley of the hall, a mile in this direction, a mile in that; endless dark tunnels filled with jet streams of night.

I listened and heard the plaster crack in the ceiling, the doors itch in their frames. Somewhere, a toilet muttered incessantly to itself, an old, cold, white porcelain vault in the night.

There was no one in the hall, of course.

Whoever had been there, if he ever was, had shut a door quickly, or run toward the front or out the back. Where the night came in in an invisible flood, a long winding river of wind, bringing with it memories of things eaten and things discarded, things desired, things no longer wanted.

I wanted to shriek at the empty halls, the things I had wanted to shout along the night shore outside Constance Rattigan's Arabian fort. Go. Let be. We may look as if we deserve to, but we *don't* want to die.

What I shouted to emptiness was, "All right, you kids. Get back in your rooms. Go on, now. Git! That's it. So. There."

I waited for the nonexistent kids to retreat to their nonexistent rooms and turned back in to lean against the door and shut it with a fake smile.

It worked. Or Fannie pretended it did.

"You'd make a good father." She beamed.

"No, I'd be like all fathers, out of mind and out of patience. Those kids should have been doped with beer and slugged into their cots hours ago. Feeling better, Fannie?"

"Better," she sighed, and shut her eyes.

I went and circled her with my arms, like Lindbergh going around the earth and the crowds yelling.

"It will work itself out," she said. "You go now. Everything's all right. Like you said, those kids have gone to bed."

The kids? I almost said, but stopped myself. Oh, yes, the kids.

"So Fannie's safe, and you go home. Poor baby. Tell Constance thanks but no thanks, and she can come visit, yes? Mrs. Gutierrez has promised to come up and stay tonight, on that bed I haven't used in thirty years, can you imagine? I can't sleep on my back, I can't breathe, well, Mrs. Gutierrez is coming up, and you were so kind to come visit, dear child. I see now how kind you are, you only want to save me the sadness of our friends downstairs."

"That's true, Fannie."

"There's nothing unusual about their passing on, is there?"

"No, Fannie," I lied, "only foolishness and failed beauty and sadness."

"God," she said, "you talk like Butterfly's lieutenant."

"That's why the guys at school beat me up."

I went to the door. Fannie took a deep breath and at last said, "If anything does happen to me. Not that it will. But if it does, look in the icebox."

"Look where?"

"Icebox," said Fannie, enigmatically. "Don't."

But I had jerked the icebox open already. I stared in at the light. I saw lots of jams, sauces, jellies, and mayonnaise. I shut the door after a long moment.

"You shouldn't have looked," protested Fannie.

"I don't want to wait, I've got to know."

"Now, I won't tell you," she said, indignantly. "You shouldn't have peeked. I'm just willing to admit maybe it's my fault it came into the house."

"It, Fannie? It, *it!*"

"All the bad things I thought you dragged in on your shoes. But maybe Fannie was responsible. Maybe I'm guilty. Maybe I called that thing off the streets."

"Well, did you, or didn't you?" I yelled, leaning toward her.

"Don't you love me any more?"

"Love you, hell, I'm trying to get you out of here and you won't come. You accuse me of poisoning the toilets, and now tell me to look in iceboxes. Jesus God, Fannie."

"Now the lieutenant is mad with Butterfly." But her eyes were starting to well over.

I couldn't stand any more of that.

I opened the door.

Mrs. Gutierrez had been standing there a long while, I was sure, a plate of hot tacos in her hands, always the diplomat, waiting.

"I'll call you tomorrow, Fannie," I said.

"Of course you will, and Fannie will be alive!"

I wonder, I thought, if I shut my eyes and pretend to be blind . . .

Can I find Henry's room?

⏋ tapped on Henry's door.

"Who that?" Henry said, locked away.

"Who dat say who dat?" I said.

"Who dat say who dat say who dat?" he said, and had to laugh. Then he remembered he was in pain. "It's you."

"Henry, let me in."

"I'm okay, just fell downstairs is all, just almost got destroyed is all, just let me rest here with the door locked, I'll be out tomorrow, you're a good boy to worry."

"What happened, Henry?" I asked the locked door.

Henry came closer. I felt he was leaning against it, like someone talking through a confessional lattice.

"He tripped me."

A rabbit ran around in my chest and turned into a big rat that kept right on running.

"Who, Henry?"

"Him. Son-of-a-bitch tripped me."

"Did he say anything, you sure he was there?"

"How do I know the upstairs hall light is on? Me? I feel. Heat. The hall was terrible warm where he was. And he was breathing, of course. I heard him sucking away at the air and blowing out nice and gentle where he hid. He didn't say nothing as I went by, but I heard his heart, too, wham, wham, or maybe it was mine. I figured to sneak by so he can't see me, blind man figures that if he's in the dark, why not everyone else. And next thing you know—*bam!* I'm at the bottom of the stairs and don't know how I got there. I started yelling for Jimmy and Sam and Pietro, then I said damn fool to myself, they're gone and you, too, if you don't ask for someone else. I started naming names, top speed, doors popped all around the house, and while they was popping, he popped out. Sounded almost barefoot out the door. Smelled his breath."

I swallowed and leaned on the door. "What was it like?"

"Let me think and tell. Henry's going to bed now. I'm sure glad I'm blind. Hate to have seen myself going down stairs like a bag of laundry. Night."

"Goodnight, Henry," I said.

And turned just as the big steamboat of a tenement house rounded a bend of river wind in the dark. I felt I was back at the surf in Mr. Shapeshade's movie house at one in the morning, with the tide glutting and shaking the timbers under the seats, and the big silver-and-black images gliding on the screen. The whole tenement shivered. The cinema was one thing. The trouble with this big old twilight place was the shadows had come off the screen and waited by stairwells and hid in bathrooms and unscrewed lightbulbs some nights so everyone groped, blind as Henry, to find their way out.

I did just that. At the top of the stairs, I froze. I heard breath churning the air ahead of me. But it was only the echo of my own sucks and swallows hitting the wall and bouncing back to feel at my face.

For Christ's sake, I thought, don't trip yourself, going down.

The chauffeur-driven 1928 Duesenberg limousine was waiting for me when I came out of Fannie's. When the door slammed, we were off and halfway to Venice when the chauffeur up front took off his cap and let his hair down and became . . .

Rattigan the Interrogator.

"Well?" she said coldly. "Is she or isn't she upset?"

"She is damn well upset but I didn't upset her."

"No?"

"No, damn it, now just pull up at the next corner and let me the damn hell out!"

"For a bashful boy from northern Illinois, you got some language, Mr. Hemingway."

"Well, hell, Miss Rattigan!"

That did it. I saw her shoulders slump a little. She was losing me, if she wasn't careful, and knew it.

"Constance," she suggested, quieter.

"Constance," I said. "It's not my fault people drown in bathtubs and drink too much or fall downstairs or get taken away by the police. Why didn't you come inside just now? You're Fannie's old, old friend."

"I was afraid that seeing you and me together would over-load and the top of her head fly off and we would never be able to get it back on."

She let the limousine go from a rather hysterical seventy down to a nervous sixty or sixty-two. But she had her claws on the wheel as if it were my shoulders and she was shaking me. I said, "You'd better get her out of there, once and for all. She won't sleep for a week now and that might kill her, just exhaustion. You can't feed a soul on mayonnaise forever."

Constance slowed the limo to fifty-five.

"She give you a rough time?"

"Only called me Death's Friend, like you. I seem to be everyone's goat, handing out bubonic fleas. Whatever is in the tenement is there all right, but I'm not the carrier. On top of which, Fannie has done something stupid."

"What?"

"I don't know, she won't tell me. She's put out with herself. Maybe you can worm it out of her. I got a terrible feeling Fannie brought all this on herself."

"How?"

The limousine slowed to forty. Constance was watching me in the rearview mirror. I licked my lips.

"I can only guess. Something in her icebox, she said. If anything happened to her, she said, look in the icebox. God, how stupid! Maybe you can go back, later tonight on your own and look in the damn icebox and figure out how and why and what it is that Fannie has invited into the tenement that is scaring the hell out of her."

"Jesus at midnight," murmured Constance, shutting her eyes. "Mary at dawn."

"Constance!" I yelled.

For we had just gone through a red light, blind.

Luckily, God was there, and paved the way.

She parked in front of my apartment and she got out while I unlocked the door and she stuck her head in.

"So this is where all the genius happens, huh?"

"A little piece of Mars on earth."

"Is that Cal's piano there? I heard about the music critics who tried to burn it once. Then there were the customers who mobbed the shop one day, yelling and showing their funny hair."

"Cal's all right," I said.

"Have you looked in a mirror lately?"

"He tried."

"Just on one side of you. Remind me, next time you're over, my dad did some barbering, too. Taught me. Why are we standing here in the doorway? Afraid the neighbors will talk if you—hell. There you go again. No matter what I say, it seems to be the truth. You're the genuine article, aren't you? I haven't seen a bashful man since I turned twelve."

She stuck her head further in.

"God, all the junk. Don't you ever pick up? What's this, reading ten books at a time, half of them comics? Is that a Buck Rogers disintegrator there by your typewriter? Did you send away box tops?"

"Yep," I said.

"What a dump," she crowed, and meant it for a compliment.

"All that I have is yours."

"That bed isn't even big enough for club sandwich sex."

"One partner always has to stay on the floor."

"Jesus, what year is that typewriter you're using?"

"1935 Underwood Standard, old but great."

"Just like me, huh, kid? You going to invite the ancient celebrity in and unscrew her earrings?"

"You've got to go back and look in Fannie's icebox, remember? Besides, if you slept over tonight, spoons."

"Plenty of cutlery, but no fork?"

"No fork, Constance."

"The memory of your mended underwear is devastating."

"I'm no boy David."

"Hell, you're not even Ralph. Goodnight, kid. It's me for Fannie's icebox. Thanks!"

She gave me a kiss that burst my eardrums and drove away.

Reeling with it, I somehow made it to bed.

Which I shouldn't have done.

Because then I had the Dream.

Every night the small rainfall came outside my door, stayed a moment, whispered, and went away. I was afraid to go look. Afraid I might find Crumley standing there, drenched, with fiery eyes. Or Shapeshade, flickering and moving in jerks, like an old film, seaweed hung from his eyebrows and nose. . . .

Every night I waited, the rain stopped, I slept.

And then came the Dream.

I was a writer in a small, green town in northern Illinois, and seated in a barber chair like Cal's chair in his empty shop. Then someone rushed in with a telegram that announced I had just made a movie sale for one hundred thousand dollars!

In the chair, yelling with happiness, waving the telegram, I saw the faces of all the men and boys, and the barber, turn to glaciers, turn to permafrost, and when they did pretend at smiles of congratulation their teeth were icicles.

Suddenly I was the outsider. The wind from their mouths blew cold on me. I had changed forever. I could not be forgiven.

The barber finished my haircut much too quickly, as if I were untouchable, and I went home with my telegram gripped in my sweating hands.

Late that night, from the edge of the woods not far from my house, in that small town, I heard a monster crying beyond the forest.

I sat up in bed, with crystals of cold frost skinning my body. The monster roared, coming nearer. I opened my eyes to hear better. I gaped my mouth to relax my ears. The monster shrieked closer, half through the forest now, thrashing and plunging, crushing the wildflowers, frightening rabbits and clouds of birds that rose screaming to the stars.

I could not move or scream myself. I felt the blood drain from my face. I saw the celebratory telegram on the bureau nearby. The monster shouted a terrible cry of death and plunged again, as if chopping trees along the way with its horrible scimitar teeth.

I leaped from bed, seized the telegram, ran to the front

door, threw it wide. The monster was almost out of the forest. It brayed, it shrieked, it knocked the night winds with threats.

I tore the telegram into a dozen pieces and threw them out over the lawn and shouted after them.

"The answer is no! Keep your money! Keep your fame! I'm staying here! I won't go! No," and again, "No!" and a final, despairing, "No!"

The last cry died in the monster dinosaur's throat. There was a dreadful moment of silence.

The moon slid behind a cloud.

I waited, with the sweat freezing over my face.

The monster sucked in a breath, exhaled, then turned and lumbered away, back through the forest, fading, at last gone, into oblivion. The pieces of telegram blew like moth wings on the lawn. I shut and locked the screen and went, mourning with relief, to bed. Just before dawn, I slept.

Now, in bed in Venice, waked from that dream, I went to my front door and looked out at the canals. What could I shout to the dark water, to the fog, to the ocean on the shore? Who would hear, what monster might recognize my *mea culpa* or my great refusal or my protest of innocence or my argument for my goodness and a genius as yet unspent?

Go away! could I cry? I am guilty of nothing. I must not die. And, let the others alone, for God's sake. Could I say or shout that?

I opened my mouth to try. But my mouth was caked with dust that had somehow gathered in the dark.

I could only put one hand out in a gesture, a begging, an empty pantomime. Please, I thought.

"Please," I whispered. Then shut the door.

At which point, the telephone across the street in my special phone booth rang.

I won't answer, I thought. It's him. The Ice Man.

The phone rang.

It's Peg.

The phone rang.

It's him.

"Shut up!" I shrieked.

The phone stopped.

My weight collapsed me into bed.

Crumley stood in his door blinking.

"For God's sake, you know what time it is?"

We stood there watching each other, like boxers who have knocked each other silly and don't know where to lie down.

I couldn't think of what to say so I said, "I am most dreadfully attended."

"That's the password. Shakespeare. Come."

He led me through the house to where coffee, a lot of it in a big pot, was cooking on the stove.

"I been working late on my masterpiece." Crumley nodded toward his bedroom typewriter. A long yellow page, like the tongue of the Muse, was hanging out of it. "I use legal paper, get more on it. I suppose I figure if I come to the end of a regular-sized page I won't go on. Jesus, you look lousy. Bad dreams?"

"The worst." I told him about the barber shop, the hundred-thousand-dollar movie sale, the monster in the night, my shouts, and the great beast moaning away gone and me alive, forever.

"Jesus." Crumley poured two big cups of something so thick it was bubbling lava. "You even *dream* better than I do!"

"What's the dream mean? We can never win, ever? If I stay poor and don't ever publish a book, I lose. But if I sell and publish and have money in the bank, do I lose, too? Do people hate you? Will friends forgive you? You're older, Crumley, tell me. Why does the beast in the dream come to kill me? Why do I have to give back the money? What's it all about?"

"Hell," snorted Crumley. "I'm no psychiatrist."

"Would A. L. Shrank know?"

"With finger-painting and stool-smearing? Naw. You going to write that dream? You always advise others—"

"When I calm down. Walking over here, a few minutes ago, I remembered my doctor once offering to tour me through the autopsy-dissection rooms. Thank God, I said no. Then I really would have been dreadfully attended. I'm over-worked now. How do I clean out the lion cage in my head? How do I smooth the old canary lady's bedsheets? How do I coax Cal the barber back from Joplin? How do I protect Fannie, across town tonight and no weapons?"

"Drink your coffee," advised Crumley.

I grubbed in my pocket and took out the picture of Cal with Scott Joplin except Joplin's head was still missing. I told Crumley where I had found it.

"Someone stole the head off this picture. When Cal saw that, he knew someone was on to him, the jig was up, and got out of town."

"That's not murder," said Crumley.

"Same as," I said.

"Same as pigs flying and turkeys getting carbuncles tap-dancing. Next case, as they say in court."

"Someone gave Sam too much booze and killed him. Someone turned Jimmy over in the bathtub to drown. Someone called the police on Pietro and he was hauled away and that will finish him. Someone stood over the canary lady and very simply scared her to death. Someone shoved that old man into the lion cage."

"Got some further coroner's reports on him," said Crumley. "Blood was full of gin."

"Right. Someone soused him, knocked him on the head, pulled him into the canal, already dead, shoved him behind bars, came out, and walked to his car or his apartment somewhere in Venice, all wet, but who would notice a wet man, no umbrella, in a storm?"

"Shoat. No, let me use a dirtier word, shirt. You couldn't buy a judge doughnuts and java with this garage sale of yours, buster. People die. Accidents happen. Motive, damn it, motive. All you got is that rummy song, last night I saw upon the stair, a little man who wasn't there. He wasn't there again today. My God, I wish he'd go away! Think. If this so-called killer exists, there's only one person we know who's been around it all. You."

"Me? You don't think—"

"No, and calm down. Avert those big pink rabbity eyes. Jesus, let me go find something."

Crumley walked over to a bookshelf on one side of his kitchen (there were books in every room of his house) and grabbed down a thick volume.

He tossed *Shakespeare's Collected Plays* on the kitchen table.

"Meaningless malignity," he said.

"What?"

"Shakespeare's full of it, you're full of it, me, everyone. Meaningless malignity. Don't that have a ring? It means someone running around doing lousy things, a bastard, for no reason. Or none we can figure."

"People don't run around being sons-of-bitches for no reason."

"God." Crumley snorted gently. "You're naive. Half the cases we handle over at the station are guys gunning red lights to kill pedestrians, or beating up their wives, or shooting friends, for reasons they can't recall. The motives are there, sure, but buried so deep it would take nitro to blast them out. And if there is a guy like the one you're trying to find with your beer reason and whiskey logic, there's no way to find him. No motives, no root systems, no clues. He's walking about scot-free and unencumbered unless you can connect the ankle-bone to the legbone to the kneebone to the thighbone."

Crumley, looking happy, sat down, poured more coffee.

"Ever stop to think," he said, "there are no toilets in grave-yards?"

My jaw dropped. "Boy! I never thought of that! No need for restrooms out among the tombstones. Unless! Unless you're writing an Edgar Allan Poe tale and a corpse gets up at midnight and has to go."

"You going to write that? Jesus, here I am, giving away ideas."

"Crumley."

"Here it comes," he sighed, pushing his chair back.

"You believe in hypnotism? Mind regression?"

"You're already regressed—"

"Please." I gathered my spit. "I'm going nuts. Regress me. Shove me back!"

"Holy Moses." Crumley was on his feet, emptying the coffee and grabbing beer out of the icebox. "Outside the nut farm, where do you want to be sent?"

"I've met the murderer, Crumley. Now I want to meet him again. I tried to ignore him because he was drunk. He was behind me on that last big red train to the sea that night I found the old man dead in the lion cage."

"No proof."

"Something he said was proof, but I've forgotten. If you could ticket me back, let me ride that train again in the storm, and listen for his voice, then I'd know who it is and the killings would stop. Don't you want them to?"

"Sure, and after I talk you back with a hypnotic dog act and you bark the results, I go arrest the killer, hmm? Come along now, bad man, my friend the writer heard your voice in a hypnotic seance and that's more than proof. Here are the handcuffs. Snap 'em on!"

"The hell with you." I stood up and jarred my coffee cup down. "I'll hypnotize myself. That's what it's all about, anyway, isn't it? Autosuggestion? It's always me that puts me under?"

"You're not trained, you don't know how. Sit down, for Christ's sake. I'll help you find a good hypnotist. Hey!" Crumley laughed somewhat crazily. "What about A. L. Shrank, hypnotist?"

"God." I shuddered. "Don't even joke. He'd sink me down with Schopenhauer and Nietzsche and Burton's *Anatomy of Melancholy* and I'd never surface again. You got to do it, Elmo."

"I got to get you out and me to bed."

He led me gently to the door.

He insisted on driving me home. On the way, looking straight ahead at the dark future, he said, "Don't worry, kid. Nothing more is going to happen."

Crumley was wrong.

But not immediately, of course.

I awoke at six in the morning because I thought I heard three dozen rifle shots again.

But it was only the annihilators at the pier, the workmen dentists, yanking the big teeth. Why, I thought, do destroyers start so early to destroy. And those rifle shots? Probably just their laughter.

I showered and ran out just in time to meet a fogbank rolling in from Japan.

The old men from the trolley station were on the beach ahead of me. It was the first time I had seen them since the day their friend Mr. Smith who wrote his name on his bedroom wall had vanished.

I watched them watching the pier die, and I could feel the timbers fall inside their bodies. The only motion they made was a kind of chewing of their gums, as if they might spit tobacco. Their hands hung down at their sides, twitching. With the pier gone, I knew, they knew, it was only a matter of time before the asphalt machines droned along and tarred over the railroad tracks and someone nailed shut the ticket office and broomed away the last of the confetti. If I had been them, I would have headed for Arizona or some bright place that afternoon. But I wasn't them. I was just me, half a century younger and with no rust on my knuckles and no bones cracking every time the big pliers out there gave a yank and made an emptiness.

I went and stood between two of the old men, wanting to say something that counted.

But all I did was let out a big sigh.

It was a language they understood.

Hearing it, they waited a long while.

And then, they nodded.

"**W**ell, here's another fine mess you got me in!"

My voice, on its way to Mexico City, was Oliver Hardy's voice.

"Ollie," cried Peg, using Stan Laurel's voice. "Fly down here. Save me from the mummies of Guanajuato!"

Stan and Ollie. Ollie and Stan. From the start we had called ours the Laurel and Hardy Romance, because we had grown up madly in love with the team, and did a fair job of imitating their voices.

"Why don't you do something to *help* me?" I cried, like Mr. Hardy.

And Peg as Laurel spluttered back, "Oh, Ollie, I—I mean —it seems—I—"

And there was silence as we breathed our despair, need, and loving grief back and forth, mile on mile and dollar on Peg's dear dollar.

"You can't afford this, Stan," I sighed, at last. "And it's beginning to hurt where aspirins can't reach. Stan, dear Stanley, so long."

"Oll," she wept. "Dear Ollie—goodbye."

As I said . . .

Crumley was wrong.

At exactly one minute after eleven that night, I heard the funeral car pull up in front of my apartment.

I hadn't been asleep and I knew the sound of Constance Rattigan's limousine by the gentle hiss of its arrival and then the bumbling under its breath, waiting for me to stir.

I got up, asked no questions of God or anyone, and dressed automatically without seeing what I put on. Something had made me reach for my dark pants, a black shirt, and an old blue blazer. Only the Chinese wear white for the dead.

I held on to the front doorknob for a full minute before I had strength enough to pull the door open and go out. I didn't climb in the back seat, I climbed up front where Constance was staring straight ahead at the surf rolling white and cold on the shore.

Tears were rolling down her cheeks. She didn't say anything, but moved the limousine quietly. Soon we were flying steadily down the middle of Venice Boulevard.

I was afraid to ask questions because I feared answers.

About halfway there, Constance said:

"I had this premonition."

That's all she said. I knew she hadn't called anyone. She simply had to go see for herself.

As it turned out, even if she had called someone, it would have been too late.

We rolled up in front of the tenement at eleven-thirty p.m.

We sat there and Constance, still staring ahead, the tears streaking down her cheeks, said:

"God, I feel as though I weigh three-eighty. I can't move."

But we had to, at last.

Inside the tenement, halfway up the steps, Constance suddenly fell to her knees, shut her eyes, crossed herself, and gasped, "Oh, please, God, please, *please* let Fannie be alive."

I helped her the rest of the way up the stairs, drunk on sadness.

At the top of the stairs in the dark there was a vast in-sucked draft that pulled at us as we arrived. A thousand miles off, at the far end of night, someone had opened and shut the door on the north side of the tenement. Going out for air? Going out to escape? A shadow moved in a shadow. The cannon bang of the door reached us an instant later. Constance rocked on her heels. I grabbed her hand and pulled her along.

We moved through weather that got older and colder and darker as we went. I began to run, making strange noises, incantations, with my mouth, to protect Fannie.

It's all right, she'll be there, I thought, making magic prayers, with her phonograph records and Caruso photos and astrology charts and mayonnaise jars and her singing and . . .

She was there all right.

The door hung open on its hinges.

She was there in the middle of the linoleum in the middle of the room, lying on her back.

"Fannie!" we both shouted at once.

Get up! we wanted to say. You can't breathe lying on your back! You haven't been to bed in thirty years. You must always sit up, Fannie, always.

She did not get up. She did not speak. She did not sing. She did not even breathe.

We sank to our knees by her, pleading in whispers, or praying inside. We kneeled there like two worshippers, two penitents, two healers, and put out our hands, as if that would do it. Just by touching we would bring her back to life.

But Fannie lay there staring at the ceiling as if to say: how curious—what is the ceiling doing there? and why don't I speak?

It was very simple and terrible. Fannie had fallen, or been

pushed, and could not get up. She had lain there in the middle of the night until her own weight crushed and smothered her. It would not have taken much to keep her in position so she could not roll over. You didn't have to use your hands on her, around her neck. Nothing had to be forced. You simply stood over her and made sure that she didn't roll to get leverage to gasp herself erect. And you watched her for a minute, two minutes, until at last the sounds stopped and the eyes turned to glass.

Oh Fannie, I groaned, oh Fannie, I mourned, what have you done to yourself?

There was the faintest whisper.

My head jerked. I stared.

Fannie's crank-up phonograph was still turning, slowly, slowly. But it was still running. Which meant that just five minutes ago, she had cranked it up, put on a record, and . . .

Answered the door on darkness.

The phonograph turntable spun. But there was no record under the needle. *Tosca* wasn't there.

I blinked, and then . . .

There was a swift knocking sound.

Constance was on her feet, choking, running. She headed for the door leading out to the balcony overlooking the trash-filled empty lot, with a view of Bunker Hill and the poolhall across the way where laughter came and went all night. Before I could stop her, she was out the screen door and to the balcony rail.

"Constance. No!" I yelled.

But she was out there only to be sick, bending over and leaning down and letting it all come out, as I much wanted to do. I could only stand and watch and look from her to the great mountain where we foothills had stood a moment before.

At last Constance stopped.

I turned, for no reason I could imagine, and went around Fannie and across the room to open a small door. A faint cold light played out over my face.

"Sweet Christ!" cried Constance, in the door behind me. "What're you doing?"

"Fannie told me," I said, my mouth numb. "Anything happened—look in the icebox."

A cold tomb wind blew out around my cheeks.

"So I'm looking."

There was nothing in the icebox, of course.

Or rather there was too much. Jellies, jams, varieties of mayonnaise, salad dressing, pickles, hot peppers, cheesecake, rolls, white bread, butter, cold cuts—an Arctic delicatessen. The panorama of Fannie's flesh was there and how it had been planned and steadily built.

I stared and stared again, trying to see what Fannie wanted me to see. Oh, Christ, I thought, what am I looking for? Is the answer one of these? I almost shoved in to hurl all the jams and jellies to the floor. I had to stop my fist, halfway in.

It's not there, or if it is, I can't see it.

I gave a terrible death groan and slammed the door.

The phonograph, with *Tosca* gone, gave up and quit.

Someone call the police, I thought. Someone?

Constance was out on the balcony again.

Me.

It was all over by three in the morning. The police had come, and everyone had been questioned and names taken and the whole tenement was awake, as if someone had started a fire in the basement, and when I came out the front of the tenement the morgue van was still parked there with the men trying to figure out how to get Fannie out and down the stairs and away. I hoped they wouldn't think of the piano box that Fannie had joked about, in the alley. They never did. But Fannie had to stay in her room until dawn, when they brought a bigger van and a larger carrier.

It was terrible, leaving her up there alone in the night. But the police wouldn't let me stay, and after all, it was a simple case of death from natural causes.

As I went down through the levels of the house, the doors were beginning to close and the lights go out, like those nights at the end of the war when the last conga line, exhausted, drained away into the rooms and down into the streets and there was the lonely walk for me up over Bunker Hill and down to the terminal where I would be taken home in thunders.

I found Constance Rattigan curled up in the back seat of her limousine, lying quietly, staring at nothing. When she heard me open the back door she said, "Get behind the wheel."

I climbed up front behind the steering wheel.

"Take me home," she said quietly.

It took me a full moment of sitting there to say finally, "I can't."

"Why not?"

"I don't know how to drive," I said.

"What?"

"I never learned. There was no reason, anyway." My

tongue moved like lead between my lips. "Since when can writers afford cars?"

"Jesus." Constance managed to prop herself up and get out, like someone with a hangover. She got out and came around walking slowly and blindly and waved. "Get over."

Somehow she started the car. This time we drove at about ten miles an hour, as if there were a fog so you could only see ten feet ahead.

We made it as far as the Ambassador Hotel. She turned in there and drove up just as the last of a Saturday night party came out with balloons and funny hats. The Coconut Grove was putting out its lights above us. I saw some musicians hurrying away with their instruments.

Everyone knew Constance. We signed in and had a bunga-low on the side of the hotel in a few minutes. We had no luggage but no one seemed to mind. The bellboy who took us through the garden to our place kept looking at Constance as if maybe he should carry her. When we were in the room, Constance said, "Would a fifty-dollar tip find the key and unlock the gate to let us in the swimming pool around back?"

"It would go a long way toward finding the key," the bellboy said. "But a swim, this time of night—?"

"It's my hour," said Constance.

Five minutes later the lights came on in the pool and I sat there and watched Constance dive in and swim twenty laps, on occasion swimming underwater from one end to the other without coming up for air.

When she came out, ten minutes later, she was gasping and red-faced and I cloaked her in a big towel and held her.

"When do you start crying?" I said, at last.

"Dummy," she said. "I just did. If you can't do it in the ocean, a pool's fine. If you don't have a pool, hit the shower. You can scream and yell and sob all you want, and it doesn't bother anyone, the world never hears. Ever think of that?"

"I never thought," said I, in awe.

At four o'clock in the morning, Constance found me in our bungalow bathroom, standing and staring at the shower.

"Hit it," she said, gently. "Go on. Give it a try."

I got in and turned the water on, hard.

A t eleven in the morning, we motored through Venice and looked at the canals with a thin layer of green slime on their surface, and passed the half-torn-down pier and looked at some gulls soaring in the fog up there, and no sun yet, and the surf so quiet it was like muffled black drums.

"Screw this," said Constance. "Flip a nickel. Heads we go north to Santa Barbara. Tails, south to Tijuana."

"I don't have a nickel," I said.

"Christ." Constance grubbed in her purse and took out a quarter and tossed it in the air. "Tails!"

We were in Laguna by noon, no thanks to the highway patrol that somehow missed us.

We sat out in the open air on a cliff overlooking the beach at Victor Hugo's and had double margaritas.

"You ever see *Now, Voyager*?"

"Ten times," I said.

"This is where Bette Davis and Paul Henried sat having a love lunch early in the film. This was the location, back in the early Forties. You're sitting in the very chair where Henried put his behind."

We were in San Diego by three and outside the bullring in Tijuana just at the hour of four.

"Think you can stand this?" asked Constance.

"I can only try," I said.

We made it through the third bull and came out into the

late-afternoon light and had two more margaritas and a good
Mexican dinner before we went north and drove out onto the
island and sat in the sunset at the Hotel del Coronado. We
didn't say anything, but just watched the sun go down, lighting the old Victorian towers and fresh-painted white sidings
of the hotel with pink color.

Along the way home we swam in the surf at Del Mar,
wordless and, from time to time, hand in hand.

At midnight we were in front of Crumley's jungle compound.

"Marry me," said Constance.

"Next time I live," I said.

"Yeah. Well, that's not bad. Tomorrow."

When she was gone I walked up the jungle path.

"Where have you been?" said Crumley, in the door.

"Uncle Wiggily says go back three hops," I said.
"The Skeezix and the Pipsisewah say come in," said
Crumley.

The something cold in my hand was a beer.

"Lord," he said, "you look terrible. Come here."

He gave me a hug. I didn't think a man like Crumley ever
hugged anyone, not even a woman.

"Be careful," I said, "I'm made out of glass."

"I heard this morning, friend of mind down in Central. I'm
sorry, kid. I know she was a close friend. You got that list with
you?"

We were out in the jungle with just the crickets sounding
and Segovia, lost inside the house, playing a lament for some
day a long time past when the sun stayed up for forty-eight
hours in Seville.

I found my dumb list crumpled in my pocket and handed it over. "How come you want to see?"

"All of a sudden, I don't know," said Crumley. "You made me curious."

He sat down and began to read:

Old man in lion cage. Killed. Weapon unknown.

Canaries-for-sale lady. Frightened.

Pietro Massinello. In jail.

Jimmy. Drowned in bathtub.

Sam. Dead from alcohol given him by someone.

Fannie.

With an addition made in the last few hours. Smothered.

Other new and possible victims:

Henry, the blind man.

Annie Oakley, the rifle lady.

A. L. Shrank, the fraudulent psychiatrist.

John Wilkes Hopwood.

Constance Rattigan.

Mr. Shapeshade.

With an addition. *No, cross him out.*

Myself.

Crumley turned the list upside down and backward, eyeing it, rereading the names.

"That's quite a menagerie you got there, buster. How come I'm not in your sideshow?"

"There's something broken about all those people. You? You got your own self-starter."

"Just since I met you, kid." Crumley stopped and turned red. "Christ, I'm getting soft. How come you put *yourself* on the list?"

"I'm scared gutless."

"Sure, but you got a self-starter, too, and it works. According to your logic, that should protect you. As for those others? They're so busy running away fast they'll run off cliffs."

Crumley turned the list upside down again, refusing to meet my gaze, and read the names out loud.

I stopped him.

"Well?"

"Well, what?" he said.

"It's time," I said. "Hypnotize me, Crum. Elmo, in the name of the sweet Lord, put me under."

"Jesus," said Crumley.

"You've got to do it, now, tonight. You owe it to me."

"Jesus. Okay, okay. Sit down. Lie down. Do I turn out the lights? God, give me hard liquor!"

I ran to fetch chairs and put them one behind the other.

"This is the big train at night," I said. "I sit here. You sit behind."

I ran to the kitchen and brought Crumley a slug of whiskey. "You got to smell like he smelled."

"For this relief, much thanks." Crumley belted it down and shut his eyes. "This is the dumbest damn thing I have ever done, ever."

"Shut up and drink."

He finished a second one. I sat. Then I remembered and jumped to put on Crumley's African storm record. It began to rain all through the house, all around the big red train. I turned down the lights. "There. Perfect."

"Shut your yap and shut your eyes," said Crumley. "God, I don't know how to do this."

"Sh. Gently," I said.

"Sh, it is. Quiet. Okay, kid. Go to sleep."

I listened closely and carefully.

"Easy does it," drawled Crumley, behind me on the train in the night in the rain. "Serenity. Quiet. Lazy. Easy. Around the curves softly. Through the rain, quietly."

He was getting into the rhythm of it and, I could tell from his voice, beginning to enjoy.

"Easy. Slow. Quiet. Long after midnight. Rain, soft rain," whispered Crumley. "Where are you, kid?"

"Asleep," I said drowsily.

"Asleep and traveling. Traveling and asleep," he murmured. "Are you on the train, kid?"

"Train," I murmured. "Train. Rain. Night."

"That's it. Stay there. Move. On the straightaway through Culver City, past the studios, late, no one on the train but you and—someone."

"Someone," I whispered.

"Someone who's been drinking."

"Drinking," I mourned.

"Swaying, swaying, talking, talking, muttering, whispering. You hear him, son?"

"Hear, talk, murmur, mutter, talk," I said quietly.

And the train moved down the night through dark storm and I was there, a good subject well transported and asleep but hearing, waiting, swaying, eyes shut, head down, hands numb on my knees. . . .

"You hear his voice, son?"

"Hear."

"Smell his breath?"

"Smell."

"Raining harder now."

"Rain."

"Dark?"

"Dark."

"You're underwater on the train, there's so much rain and

someone swaying behind you, behind you, moaning, speaking, whispering."

"Yesssss."

"Can you hear what he says?"

"Almost."

"Deeper, slower, going, moving, swaying. Hear his voice?"

"Yes."

"What's he say?"

"He says—"

"What's he say?"

"He—"

"Deeper, sleeping. Listen."

His breath fanned my neck, warm with alcohol.

"What, what?"

"He says—"

The train screamed around an iron bend in my head. Sparks flew. There was a clap of thunder.

"Gah!" I shrieked. And "Gah!" and a final "*Gah!*"

I writhed in my chair in my panic to escape that maniac breath, the flaming alcohol beast. And something else I had forgotten. But it was back now and it blasted my face, my brow, my nose.

A smell of opened graves, abattoirs, raw meat left too long in the sun.

Eyes slammed tight, I began to retch.

"Kid! Christ, wake up, God, kid, kid!" yelled Crumley, shaking me, slapping my face, massaging my neck, now down on his knees, yanking at my head and cheeks and arms, not knowing where to grab or shake me. "Now, kid, now, for Christ's sake, *now!*"

"Gah!" I shrieked and flailed a final time, and floundered straight up, staring about, falling into the grave with the terrible meat, as the train ran over me and the rain showered into the tomb, with Crumley slapping me and a great gout of sour food jetting from my mouth.

Crumley stood me outside in the garden air, made sure I was breathing right, cleaned me up, then went inside to mop up and came back.

"Jesus," he said, "it worked. We got more than we wanted, yes?"

"Yes," I said, weakly. "I heard his voice. And he said just what I thought he would say. The title I put on your book. But I heard his voice clearly, and I almost know him now. Next time I meet him, wherever it is, I'll know. We're close, Crum, we're close. He won't escape now. But now I'll know him an even better way."

"How?"

"He smells like a corpse. I didn't notice that night, or if I did I was so nervous I forgot. But now it's back. He's dead, or next to dead. Dogs killed in the street smell like him. His shirt, his pants, his coat, are moldy and old. His flesh is worse. So—"

I wandered into the house and found myself at Crumley's desk.

"At last, I have a new title for my own book," I said.

I typed. Crumley watched. The words came out on the paper. We both read them.

"Downwind from Death."

"That's some title," he said.

And went to shut off the sound of the dark rain.

There was a graveside service for Fannie Florianna the next afternoon. Crumley took an hour off and drove me over to the nice old-fashioned graveyard on a hill with a view of the

Santa Monica mountains. I was astonished to see the line of cars outside the place, and more astonished to see the queue of flowers being carried in to be placed by the open grave. There must have been two hundred people there, and a few thousand flowers.

"Criminently," said Crumley. "Look at the mob. See who that is over there. And just beyond. King Vidor?"

"Vidor, sure. And that's Salka Viertel. She wrote films for Garbo a long time back. And that other chap is Mr. Fox, Louis B. Mayer's lawyer. And that one there is Ben Goetz, who headed up MGM's unit in London. And—"

"Why didn't you tell me your friend Fannie knew so many big people?"

"Why didn't Fannie tell *me*?" I said.

Fannie, dear Fan, I thought, how like you, never to tell, never to brag that so many of these came up and down the tenement stairs over the years, for a chat and a remembrance and a song. Lord, Fannie, why didn't you let me in on it, I would have liked to have known. I wouldn't have told anyone.

I looked at all the faces gathered near the flowers. Crumley did likewise.

"Think he's here, kid?" he said, quietly.

"Who?"

"The one you claim did this to Fannie."

"I'll know him when I see him. No, I'll know him when I hear him."

"And then what?" said Crumley. "Have him arrested for being drunk on a train a couple of nights ago?"

I must have shown a terrible frustration in my face.

"Just trying to ruin your day," said Crumley.

"Friends," someone said.

And the crowd grew very quiet.

It was the best kind of graveside service, if there is such a thing. Nobody asked me to speak, why would they do that?

But a dozen others took a minute or three minutes and said things about Chicago in 1920 or Culver City in the mid-Twenties when there were meadows and fields and the false civilization of MGM was a-building and ten or twelve nights a year the big red car pulled up on a siding behind the studio and Louis B. Mayer and Ben Goetz and all the others piled on and played poker training out to San Bernardino where they went to the movie house to see the latest Gilbert or Garbo or Novarro and come home with fistfuls of preview cards: "Lousy!" "Great!" "Terrible!" "Fine!" and sort out the cards along with the kings and queens and jacks and spades to figure out just what in hell kind of hand they had. And pull in behind the studio at midnight, still playing cards, and get off smelling of Prohibition whiskey with happy smiles or grim smiles of determination on their faces, to watch Louis B. toddle to his limousine and go first home.

They were all there and they all spoke with great honesty and clarity. There were no lies. A true grief lay just beneath every word that was said.

In the midst of the hot afternoon, someone touched my elbow. I turned and was surprised.

"Henry! How'd *you* get here?"

"I sure didn't walk."

"How'd you find me in all this mob?" I whispered.

"You're the only Ivory soap, the rest is Chanel and Old Spice. I'm sure glad I'm blind on a day like this. Don't mind listening, but I surely do not want to see this."

The tributes continued. Mr. Fox, Louis B. Mayer's lawyer, was next, a man who knew law but who rarely went to see any of the films they made. Right now, he remembered early days in Chicago when Fannie . . .

A humingbird darted among the bright colors. A dragonfly hummed by soon after.

"Armpits," said Henry, quietly.

Startled, I waited and whispered, "Armpits?"

"On the street outside the tenement," whispered Henry, staring at a sky he could not see, speaking from the corner of his mouth. "Inside, the halls. By my room. By Fannie's room. The smell. Him. The one." A pause. A nod. "Armpits."

My nose twitched. My eyes began to run. I stirred my feet, wanting to get away, go see, find.

"When was this, Henry?" I whispered.

"The other night. Night Fannie went away forever."

"Sh!" said someone nearby.

Henry shut up. When there was a change of speakers I whispered, "Where?"

"Crossing the street early on," said Henry. "That night. Powerful, real powerful smell. Then, later, seemed to me the armpits came into the hall behind me. I mean, it was so strong it cleared my sinuses. Like having a grizzly bear breathe on you. You ever smell that? I froze half-across the street, like I been hit with a baseball bat. Thought, anyone smells like that's got a grudge against God, dogs, mankind, the world. Step on a cat rather than walk around. Bad-ass mean. Armpits, like I said. Armpits. *That* help you any?"

My whole body was frozen. I could only nod. Henry said, "That smell's been around the halls some few nights now, but just got stronger is all, maybe because that dumb son-of-a-bitch was getting closer. I was tripped up by Mr. Smell, I know that now. I got it figured."

"Sh!" said someone.

An actor spoke, and a priest, and a rabbi, and then the Hall Johnson Choir from the First Baptist Church on Central Avenue filed through the tombstones and gathered to sing "Great Day in the Morning," "In the Sweet Bye and Bye," and "Dear God, Joy Me When I'm Gone." And their voices were the voices I had heard in the late Thirties, chanting Ronald Col-

man over the snow peaks and down into Shangri-La, or standing on white clouds in the fields of the Lord in *Green Pastures*.
By the end of their radiant singing, I was overflowed and joyed
and Death had had a new coat of sunlight and time, and the
hummingbird came back for nectar, and the dragonfly sank
down to scan my face and go away.

"That," said Crumley, on the way out of the graveyard,
with Henry walking between us, "is the way I want to be sung
out of the world. God, I'd love to be that whole damn choir.
Who needs money when you can sing like that!"

But I was staring at Henry. He felt my stare.

"Thing is," said Henry, "he keeps coming back. Armpits.
You'd think he'd had enough, sure? But he's hungry-mean,
can't stop. Scaring people is like Cracker Jack to him. Hurt's
his byword. Pain is a living. He figures to get old Henry, like
he got the rest. But I won't fall again."

Crumley was listening with some seriousness.

"If Armpits comes again—"

"I'll call you, *immediamente*. He's fiddling around the
rooms. Caught him fiddling Fannie's locked door. It's padlocked and pasted over by the law, right? He was fiddling it
and I yelled him off. He's a coward for sure. Got no weapons,
just goes around putting his foot out so blind men take a whole
flight of steps in one jump. Armpits! I yelled. Scat!"

"Call us," said Crumley. "Can we give you a lift?"

"Some of the ugly ladies from the tenement brought me,
thanks, and will take me home."

"Henry," I said. I put out my hand. He took it swiftly. It
was almost as if he had seen it coming.

"How do *I* smell, Henry?" I said.

Henry sniffed and laughed. "They don't make heroes like
they used to. But you'll do."

Driving back toward the beach with Crumley, I saw a big

limousine pass us at seventy miles an hour, putting a lot of space between it and the flowered graveyard. I waved and yelled.

Constance Rattigan did not even glance over. She had been at the graveside somewhere, hidden away to one side, and now she was roaring home angry at Fannie for leaving us all and maybe angry with me for somehow bringing Death to present a bill.

Her limousine vanished in a great white-gray cloud of exhaust.

"The harpies and the Furies just screamed by," observed Crumley.

"No," I said, "only a lost lady, running to hide."

J tried calling Constance Rattigan during the next three days, but she wouldn't answer. She was brooding and mad. Somehow, in some dumb way, I was in cahoots with the man who stood in halls and did terrible things to people.

I tried calling Mexico City, but Peg was off lost forever, I was sure.

I prowled around Venice, staring and listening and sniffing, hoping for that dreadful voice, searching for the terrible smell of something dying or long dead.

Even Crumley was gone. I stared, but he was nowhere up ahead, following.

At the end of three days of failed phone calls, unmet killers, furious with fate, and confounded by funerals, I did what I had never done before.

Around ten o'clock at night I strode down the empty pier not knowing where I was going until I got there.

"Hey," someone said.

I yanked a rifle up off the shelf and, without checking to see if it was loaded or if anyone was in the way, I fired it, fired it, fired it, sixteen times!

Wham, wham. And wham wham. And wham wham, and someone was yelling.

I didn't hit any of the targets. I had never handled a rifle in my life. I don't know what I was shooting at, but yes I did.

"Take that, you son-of-a-bitch, take that, you bastard!"

Wham, wham, and wham wham.

The rifle was empty but I kept yanking the trigger. I suddenly knew it was impotent. Someone took the rifle away from me. Annie Oakley, staring at me as if she had never seen me before.

"You know what you're doing?" she asked.

"No, and I don't give a damn!" I glanced around. "How come you're open so late?"

"Nothing else to do. I can't sleep. What's wrong with you, mister?"

"Everybody in the whole damn world is going to be dead by this time next week."

"You don't believe that?"

"No, but it feels like it. Give me another rifle."

"You don't want to shoot any more."

"Yes, I do. And I haven't money to pay, you'll have to trust me!" I cried.

She stared at me for a long time. Then she handed me a rifle. "Sock 'em, cowboy. Kill 'em, Bogie," she said.

I fired sixteen times. This time I hit two targets by mistake, even though I couldn't see them, my glasses were that fogged.

"Had enough?" asked Annie Oakley, quietly, behind me.

"No!" I shouted. Then I said, lower, "Yes. What are you doing outside the gallery on the boardwalk?"

"I was afraid I'd get shot in there. Some maniac just unloaded two rifles without aiming."

We looked at each other and I began to laugh.

She listened and said, "Are you laughing or crying?"

"What's it sound like? I got to do something. Tell me what."

She studied my face for a long time and then she went around shutting off the running ducks and the bobbing clowns and the lights. A door opened in the back of the gallery. She was silhouetted there. She said:

"If you've got to shoot at anything, here's the target." And she was gone.

It was a full half minute before I realized she expected me to follow.

"Do you behave this way often?" asked Annie Oakley.

"Sorry," I said.

I was on one far side of her bed, she on the other, listening to me talk about Mexico City and Peg and Peg and Mexico City so far away it was a dreadful ache.

"The story of my life," said Annie Oakley, "is men in bed with me bored silly or talking about other women, or lighting cigarettes or rushing off in their cars when I go to the bathroom. You know what my real name is? Lucretia Isabel Clarisse Annabelle Maria Monica Brown. My mom gave me all those, so what do I choose? Annie Oakley. Problem is, I'm

dumb. Men can't stand me after the first ten minutes. Dumb.
Read a book, an hour later, it's gone! Nothing sticks. I talk a
lot, don't I?"

"A bit," I said, gently.

"You'd think some guy would like someone as truly dumb
as me, but I wear them out. Three hundred nights a year it's
some damn different male goof lying where you're lying. And
that damn foghorn blowing out in the bay, does it *get* to you?
Some nights, even with a jerk of a cluck in bed with me, when
that foghorn goes off, I feel so alone and there he is, checking
his keys, looking at the door—"

Her telephone rang. She grabbed it, listened, said, "I'll be
damned." She waved it at me. "For you."

"Impossible," I said. "No one knows I'm here."

I took the phone.

"What are you doing at *her* place?" said Constance Rattigan.

"Nothing. How did you find me?"

"Someone called. Just a voice. Told me to check on you
and hung up."

"Oh, my God." I was turning cold.

"Get out of there," said Constance. "I need your help.
Your strange friend has come to visit."

"*My* friend?"

The ocean roared under the Rifle Gallery, shuddering the
room and the bed.

"Down by the shore, two nights in a row. You've got to
come scare him off—oh, God!"

"Constance!"

There was a long silence in which I could hear the surf
outside Constance Rattigan's windows. Then she said, in a
strange numb way, "He's there now."

"Don't let him see you."

"The bastard is down on the shoreline, just where he was

last night. He just stares up at the house, like he's waiting for me. The bastard's naked. What does he think, the old lady is so crazy she'll run out and jump him? Christ."

"Shut the windows, Constance, turn off the lights!"

"No. He's backing off. Maybe my voice carries. Maybe he thinks I'm calling the police."

"*Call* them!"

"Gone." Constance took a deep breath. "Get over here, kid. Fast."

She didn't hang up. She just let the phone drop and walked off. I could hear her sandals slapping the tiled floor making typewriter sounds.

I didn't hang up, either. For some reason I just put the phone down as if it were an umbilical cord between me and Constance Rattigan. As long as I didn't disconnect, she couldn't die. I could still hear the night tide moving on her end of the line.

"Just like all the other men. There you go," said a voice.

I turned.

Annie Oakley sat up in bed, huddled in her sheets like an abandoned manatee.

"Don't hang up that telephone," I said.

Not until I reach the far end, I thought, and save a life.

"Dumb," said Annie Oakley, "that's why you're going. Dumb."

It took a lot of guts to run the night shore toward Constance Rattigan's. I imagined some terrible dead man rushing the other way.

"Jesus!" I gasped. "What happens if I *meet* him?"

"Gah!" I shrieked.

And ran full-tilt into a solid shadow.

"Thank God, it's you!" someone yelled.

"No, Constance," I said. "Thank God, it's *you.*"

"What's so damn funny?"

"This." I slapped the big bright pillows on all sides of me. "This is the second bed I've been in tonight."

"Hilarious," said Constance. "Mind if I bust your nose?"

"Constance. Peg's my girl. I was just lonely. You haven't called in days. Annie asked me for pillow talk, and that's all it was. I can't lie. It shows in my face. Look."

Constance looked and laughed.

"Christ, fresh apple pie. Okay, okay." She sank back. "I scare the hell out of you just now?"

"You should've yelled ahead as you ran."

"I was glad to see you, son. Sorry I haven't phoned. Once I forgot funerals in a few hours. Now, it takes days."

She touched a switch. The lights dimmed and the sixteen-millimeter projector flashed on. Two cowboys knocked each other down on the white wall.

"How can you watch films at a time like this?" I said.

"To rev me up so I can go out and knock Mr. Naked's block off if he shows again tomorrow night."

"Don't even joke about it." I looked out the French windows at the empty shore where only white waves sounded on the edge of night. "Do you think he telephoned you to tell you where I was, with Annie, and then walked up the beach to stand out there?"

"No. His voice wasn't right. It's got to be two different guys. Christ, I can't figure it, but the one guy, the one with no clothes, he's got to be some sort of exhibitionist, a flasher, right?

Or why doesn't he just run up in here and ruin the old lady or kill her or both? It's the other one, the guy on the phone, that gives me the willies."

I know, I thought, I've heard his breathing.

"He sounds like a real monster," said Constance.

Yes, I thought. A long way off I heard the big red trolley shriek around an iron curve in the rain, with the voice behind me, chanting the words of a title for Crumley's book.

"Constance," I said, and stopped. I was going to tell her I had seen the stranger on the shore many nights ago.

"I've got some real estate south of here," said Constance. "I'm going to go check it tomorrow. Call me, late, yes? And meantime, you want to look into something for me?"

"Anything. Well, almost anything."

Constance watched William Farnum knock his brother Dustin down, pick him up, knock him down again.

"I think I know who Mr. Naked on the Shore is."

"Who?"

She searched down along the surf as if his ghost was still there.

"A son-of-a-bitch from my past with a head like a mean German general," she said, "and a body like all the boys of summer who ever lived."

he small motorbike pulled up outside the carousel building with a young man in swimshorts astride, his body bronzed and oiled and beautiful. He was wearing a heavy helmet with a dark visor down over his face to his chin, so I couldn't see his face. But the body was the most amazing I think I have ever seen. It made me think of a day years before when I had seen a beautiful Apollo walking along the shore with a surf of young boys walking after him, drawn for they knew not what reasons, but they walked in beauty with him, loving but not knowing it was love, never daring to name and trying not to think of this moment later in life. There are beauties like that in this world, and all men and all women and all children are pulled in their wake, and it is all pure and wondrous and clean and there is no residue of guilt, because nothing happened. You just saw and followed and when the time on the shore was over, he went away and you went off, smiling the kind of smile that is such a surprise you put your hand up an hour later and find it still attached.

On a whole beach in an entire summer you only see bodies like that, on some young man, or some young woman, once. Twice, if the gods are snoozing and not jealous.

Here was Apollo, astride the motorbike, gazing through his dark, featureless visor at me.

"You come to see the old man?" The laugh behind the glass was rich and throaty. "Good! Come on."

He propped the bike and was in and up the stairs ahead of me. Like a gazelle, he took the steps three at a time and vanished into an upstairs room.

I followed, one step at a time, feeling old.

When I got to his room I heard the shower running. A moment later he came out, stripped and glistening with water, the helmet still over his head. He stood in the bathroom door, looking into me as he might into a mirror, and liking what he saw.

"Well," he said, inside his helmet, "how do you like the most beautiful boy, the young man that I love?"

I blushed furiously.

He laughed and shucked off his helmet.

"My God," I said, "it really *is* you!"

"The old man," said John Wilkes Hopwood. He glanced down at his body and smiled. "Or the young. Which of us do you prefer?"

I swallowed hard. I had to force myself to speak quickly, for I wanted to run back down the stairs before he closed and locked me in the room.

"That all depends," I said, "on which one of you has been standing on the beach, late nights, outside Constance Rattigan's home."

With wondrous timing, the calliope downstairs in the rotunda started up, running the carousel. It sounded like a dragon that had swallowed a corps of bagpipers and was now trying to throw them back up, in no particular order to no particular tune.

Like a cat that wants time to consider its next move, old-young Hopwood turned his tanned backside toward me, a signal that was supposed to fascinate.

I shut my eyes to the golden sight.

That gave Hopwood a moment to decide what he wanted to say.

"What makes you think I would bother with an old horse like Constance Rattigan?" he said, as he reached into the bathroom and dragged out a towel which he now used to swab his shoulders and chest.

"You were the great love of her life, she was yours. That was the summer all America loved the lovers, yes?"

He turned to check on how much irony might show in my face to match my voice.

"Have you come here because she sent you, to warn me off?"

"Perhaps."

"How many pushups can you do, can you do sixty laps of a pool, or bike forty miles in a day without sweating, what weights can you lift, and how many people"—I noticed he did not say women—"can you bed in one afternoon?" he asked.

"No, no, no, no, and maybe two," I said, "to answer all those questions."

"Then," said Helmut the Hun, turning to show me Anti-nous' magnificent facade, something to match the golden hind, "you are in no position to threaten me, *ja?*"

His mouth was a razor slit from which bursts of bright shark teeth hissed and chewed.

"I will come and go on the beach," he said.

With the Gestapo ahead and the summer boys soon after, I thought.

"I admit nothing. Perhaps I was there some nights." He nodded up the coast. "Perhaps not."

You could have cut your wrists with his smile.

He hurled the towel at me. I caught it.

"Get my back for me, will you?"

I hurled the towel away. It fell and hung over his head, masking his face. The Horrible Hun was, for a moment, gone. Only Sun King Apollo, his rump as bright as the apples of the gods, remained.

From under the towel his voice said quietly:

"The interview is over."

"Did it ever really begin?" I said.

I went downstairs as the dragon's sick calliope music was coming up.

There were no words at all on the Venice Cinema marquee. All the letters were gone.

I read the emptiness half a dozen times, feeling something roll over and die in my chest.

I went around trying all the doors, which were locked, and looked into the box office, which was deserted, and glanced at the big poster frames where Barrymore and Chaney and Norma Shearer had smiled just a few nights ago. Now—nothing.

I backed off and read the emptiness a last time to myself, quietly.

"How do you like the double bill?" asked a voice from behind me.

I turned. Mr. Shapeshade was there, beaming. He handed over a big roll of theater posters. I knew what it was. My diplomas from Nosferatu Institute, Graduate School of Quasimodo, Postgraduate in d'Artagnan and Robin Hood.

"Mr. Shapeshade, you can't give these to me."

"You're a romantic sap, aren't you?"

"Sure, but—"

"Take, take. Farewell, goodbye. But another farewell, goodbye, out beyond. Kummen-sei pier oudt!"

He left the diplomas in my hands and trotted off.

I found him at the end of the pier, pointing down and watching my face to see me crumple and seize the pier rail, staring over.

The rifles were down there, silent for the first time in years. They lay on the sea bottom about fifteen feet under, but the water was clear because the sun was coming out.

I counted maybe a dozen long, cold, blue metal weapons down there where the fish swam by.

"Some farewell, huh?" Shapeshade glanced where I was looking. "One by one. One by one. Early this morning. I came running up, yelled, what're you doing!? What does it look like? she said. And one by one, over and down. They're closing your place, they're closing mine this afternoon, so what the hell, she said. And one by one."

"She didn't," I said, and stopped. I searched the waters under the pier and far out. "She didn't?"

"Was she the last one in? No, no. Just stood here a long time, with me, watching the ocean. They won't be here long, she said. Week from now, gone. A bunch of stupid guys will dive and bring them up, yes? What could I say. Yes."

"She leave any word when she went?"

I could not take my eyes off the long rifles that shone in the flowing tide.

"Said she was going somewhere to milk cows. But no bulls, she said, no bulls. Milk cows and churn butter, was the last thing I heard."

"I hope she will," I said.

The rifles suddenly swarmed with fish who seemed to have come to see. But there were no sounds of firing.

"Their silence," said Shapeshade, "is nice, eh?"

I nodded.

"Don't forget these," said Shapeshade.

They had fallen out of my hands. He picked up and handed me my diplomas for all the years of my young life running up and down popcorn aisles in the dark with the Phantom and the Hunchback.

On the way back, I passed a little boy who stood staring down at the remains of the rollercoaster lying like strewn bones on the shore.

"What's that dinosaur doing lying there dead on the beach?" he said.

I had thought of it first. I resented this boy who saw the collapsed rollercoaster as I saw it: a beast dead in the tides.

No! I wanted to yell at him.

But aloud I said, gently, "Oh, Lord, son, I wish I knew."

I turned and staggered away, carrying an armload of invisible rifles down the pier.

I had two dreams that night.

In the first, A. L. Shrank's Sigmund Freud Schopenhauer tarot card shop was knocked to flinders by the great hungry steamshovel, so off in the tide floated the Marquis de

Sade and Thomas De Quincey, and Mark Twain's sick daughters and Sartre on a truly bad day, drowning in the dark waters over the shine of the shooting gallery rifles.

The second dream was a newsreel I had seen of the Russian royal family, lined up by their graves, and shot so that they jerked and jumped like a silent film projection, knocked, blown away, end over end, like popped corks, into the pit. It made you gasp with horrid laughter. Inhuman. Hilarious. Bam!

There went Sam, Jimmy, Pietro, canary lady, Fannie, Cal, old lion-cage man, Constance, Shrank, Crumley, Peg, and *me!*

Bam!

I slammed awake, sweating ice.

The telephone, across the street in the gas station, was ringing.

It stopped.

I held my breath.

It rang again once, and stopped.

I waited.

It rang again, once, and stopped.

Oh, God, I thought—Peg wouldn't do that. Crumley wouldn't do that. Ring once and stop?

The phone rang again, once. Then, silence.

It's him. Mr. Lonely Death. Calling to tell me things I don't want to know.

I sat up, the hairs on my body fuzzed as if Cal had run his Bumblebee Electric barber shears down my neck to strike a nerve.

I dressed and ran out to the shoreline. I took a deep breath, then stared south.

Far away down the coast, all of the windows in Constance Rattigan's Moorish fort were brightly lit.

Constance, I thought. Fannie won't like this.

Fannie?

And then I *really* ran.

I came in from the surf, like Death himself.

Every light in Constance's place was burning, and every door stood wide open, as if she had opened them all to let nature and the world and night and the wind in to clean her place while she was gone.

And she was gone.

I knew without even going in her place, because there was a long line of her footprints coming down to the tideline where I stopped and looked to see where they went in the water, but never came out.

I wasn't surprised. I was surprised that I wasn't surprised. I walked up to her wide-open front door and didn't call, or almost called for her chauffeur and laughed to think I might have been so foolish, and went in without touching anything. The phonograph was playing in the Arabian parlor. Dance music by Ray Noble, from London, in 1934, some Noël Coward tunes. I let the music play. The projector was on, mindlessly whirling its reel, the film done, the white light of the bulb staring at the blank front wall. I didn't think to turn it off. A bottle of Moët et Chandon stood iced and waiting, as if she had gone down to the sea expecting to bring some golden god of the deep back with her.

Cheeses were laid out on a plate on a pillow, along with a shaker of martinis, getting watery. The Duesenberg was in the garage and the footprints still lay in the sand, going only one way. I telephoned Crumley, and congratulated myself on not crying just yet, feeling numb.

"Crumley?" I said into the telephone.

"Crumley. Crum," I said.

"Child of the night," he said. "You bet on another wrong horse again?"

I told him where I was.

"I can't walk very well." I sat down suddenly, clenching the phone. "Come get me."

Crumley met me on the shore.

We stood looking up at that Arabian fort all brightly lit like a festive tent in the middle of a desert of sand. The door opening out on the shore was still wide and the music was playing inside, a stack of records that seemed never to want to stop dropping. It was "Lilac Time," then it was "Diane," then it was "Ain't She Sweet?" followed by "Hear My Song of the Nile" and then "Pagan Love Song." I expected Ramon Novarro to show up at any moment, run in, and come out wild haired and mad of eye, rushing down to the shore.

"But there's just me and Crumley."

"Unh?"

"I didn't know I was thinking out loud," I apologized.

We trudged up the shore.

"You touch anything?"

"Only the phone."

When we reached the door I let him go in and prowl through the house and come out.

"Where's the chauffeur?"

"That's something else I never told you. There never was one."

"What?"

I told him about Constance Rattigan and her role playing.

"She was her own all-star cast, huh? Jesus. Louder and funnier, as they say."

We went back out to stand on the wind-blown porch to look at the footprints that were beginning to blow away.

"Could be suicide," said Crumley.

"Constance wouldn't do that."

"Christ, you're so godawful sure about people. Why don't you grow up? Just because you like someone doesn't mean they can't take the big jump without you."

"There was someone on the shore, waiting for her."

"Proof."

We followed Constance's single line of prints down to the surf.

"He was standing over there." I pointed. "Two nights. I saw him."

"Swell. Ankle deep in water. So no prints for the killer. What else you want to show me, son?"

"Someone called me an hour ago, woke me up, told me to come along the beach. That someone knew her house was empty or soon going to be."

"Phone call, huh? Swell again. Now *you're* ankle deep in water and no prints. That the whole story?"

My cheeks must have reddened. He saw that I had been telling a half-truth. I didn't want to admit I hadn't answered the phone the last time, but ran down the beach on a terrible hunch.

"At least you got integrity, scribe." Crumley looked at the white waves combing in, then at the footprints, then at the house, white, cold, and empty in the middle of the night. "You know what integrity means? Based on the word integers. Numbers. Integrity means to add up. Has nothing to do with virtue. Hitler had integrity. Zero plus zero plus zero makes zero, no score. Phone calls and footprints underwater and blind hunches and dopey faith. These late-night shootings are beginning to tell on me. That about *do* it?"

"No, damn it. I've got a real, live suspect. Constance recognized him. I did, too, went to see him. Find out where he was tonight, you got the killer! You—"

I lost control of my voice. I had to take my glasses off and wipe the tiny wet salt-marks off so I could see.

Crumley patted my cheek and said, "Hey, don't. How do you know this guy, whoever he is, didn't take her in the water and—"

"Drown her!"

"Swim with her, talk nice, and they swam north one hundred yards and walked back to his place. For all you know, she'll be dragging home at dawn with a funny smile on her face."

"No," I said.

"What, am I spoiling the mysterious romance of all this for you?"

"No."

But he could tell I was uncertain.

He touched my elbow. "What else haven't you said?"

"Constance mentioned she had some real estate not far from here, down the coast."

"You sure she didn't just go there tonight? If what you say's true, what if she got spooked, pulled up stakes?"

"Her limousine's still here."

"People walk, you know. *You* do it all the time. Lady could walk a mile south, spooked, in an inch of water, and us no wiser."

I looked south to see if I could see a beautiful lady, escaped along the strand.

"Thing is," said Crumley, "we got nothing to go on. Empty house. Old records playing. No suicide note. No sign of violence. We got to wait for her to come back. And if she doesn't, there's *still* no case, no corpus delicti. I bet you a bucket of beer she'll—"

"Let me take you to the upstairs apartment at the carousel tomorrow. When you see that strange man's face—"

"God. Do you mean who I think you mean?"

I nodded.

"The airy-fairy?" said Crumley. "The fag?"

There was a tremendous flop in the water just then.

We both jumped.

"Jesus, what was that?" cried Crumley, peering out over the midnight waters.

Constance, I thought, coming back.

I stared and at last said, "Seals. They do come and play out there."

There was a series of small flops and splashes which faded as some sea creature departed in darkness.

"Hell," said Crumley.

"The projector's still running there in the parlor," I said. "Phonograph's still playing. Oven's on in the kitchen, something baking. And all the lights in all the rooms."

"Let's shut some off before the damn place burns down."

We followed Constance Rattigan's footprints back up to her fortress of white light.

"Hey," whispered Crumley. He stared at the eastern horizon. "What's that?"

There was a faint band of cold light there.

"Dawn," I said. "I thought it would never come."

Constance Rattigan's footprints blew away off the sand in the dawn wind.

And Mr. Shapeshade came along the shore, looking back over his shoulder, cans of film under his arms. Far off there, at this very moment, his movie house was being trashed by huge steel-toothed monsters that had risen, summoned by real estate speculators, out of the sea.

When Shapeshade saw me and Crumley standing on Con-

stance Rattigan's front porch, he blinked at our faces and then
at the sand and then at the ocean. We didn't have to tell him
anything, our faces were that pale.

"She'll be back," he said again and again, "she'll be back.
Constance wouldn't go away. My God, who would I run films
with, who? She'll be back, sure!" His eyes spilled over.

We left him in charge of the empty fort and drove back
toward my place. On the way, Detective Lieutenant Crumley,
in a burst of invective, using harsh epithets like cow-chappatis,
Bull Durham, bushwah, and watch-out-you'll-step-in-it, refused my offer to go ride on that damn carousel questioning
Field Marshal Erwin Rommel or his pretty pal, dressed up in
rose petals, Nijinsky.

"In one or two days, maybe. If that goony old woman
doesn't swim back from Catalina, sure. *Then* I start asking
questions. But now? I will not shovel horse-flops to find the
horse."

"Are you angry with me?" I asked.

"Angry, angry, why would I be angry? Angry? Christ, you
drive me out of my skull. But angry? Here's a buck, go buy
ten rides on that calliope racetrack."

He dropped me, running, at my door, and roared off.

Inside, I looked at Cal's old piano. The sheet had fallen off
the big white ivory teeth.

"Don't laugh," I said.

◥▛hree things happened that afternoon.
Two were fine. One was terrible.

A letter arrived from Mexico. In it was a photo of Peg. She
had colored her eyes with a blend of brown and green ink, to
help me remember what they looked like.

Then there was a postcard from Cal, postmarked Gila Bend.

"Son," it said, "you keeping my piano tuned? I'm torturing folks part-time in the local beer joint. This town is full of bald men. Me being here, they don't know how lucky they are. Cut the sheriff's hair yesterday. He gave me twenty-four hours to leave town. Will gas up for Sedalia tomorrow. Be happy. Yours, Cal."

I turned the card over. There was a photo of a gila monster with black and white patterns on its back. Cal had drawn a bad portrait of himself seated there as if the creature were a musical instrument and him playing only the dark keys.

I laughed and walked north toward the Santa Monica pier, wondering what I might say to that odd man who lived a double life above the moaning carousel.

"Field Marshal Rommel," I shouted, "how and why did you set out to kill Constance Rattigan?"

But no one was there to hear.

The carousel ran in silence.

The calliope was turned on, but the music was at the end of its roll and the slots flapped around and around.

The carousel owner was not dead in his ticket booth, only dead drunk. He was awake, but seemed not to hear the silence or know that the horses were galloping to the slap of the Swiss cheese roll in the mouth of the big machine.

I surveyed it all with disquiet and was about to trudge upstairs when I noticed a fine-blowing litter on the floor of the circling horse race.

I waited for the carousel to turn twice more, then grabbed a brass pole and hopped on, moving drunkenly among the poles.

Pieces of torn paper blew in the wind made by the horses jumping up and down and the passage of the carousel itself, going nowhere.

I found a thumbtack on the circular floor under the ripped paper. Someone had perhaps tacked the message to the forelock of one of the wooden horses. Someone had found it, read it, torn it, run away.

John Wilkes Hopwood.

I spent a good three minutes picking up the pieces, feeling as hopeless as the carousel's journey, then hopped off and tried piecing it together. It took another fifteen minutes of finding a terrible word here, an awful word there, and a damning word further on, but finally there was a death and a doom. Anyone reading this, anyone, that is, with the wrong old skeleton hung inside his young bright flesh, might wither at these strikes to the groin.

I could not put it all together. There were missing pieces. But the essence was that the reader was an old man, ugly man. Truly ugly. He made love to that body because with that face, who would want him? Nobody for years. It recalled how the studios threw him out in 1929, attacked the fake Kraut voice and broken wrists and strange boyfriends and old sick women. "In bars late at night they say your name and laugh at you when you go away full of cheap gin. And now you have caused death. I saw you on the beach last night when she swam out and did not come back. People will say murder. Goodnight, sweet prince."

That was it. A dreadful weapon, posted and found.

I gathered the pieces and went upstairs, about ninety years older than I had been a few days before.

The door to Hopwood's room whispered open under my hand.

There were clothes all over the place, on the floor and by

several suitcases, as if he had tried to pack, panicked, and gone off traveling light.

I looked out the apartment window. Down on the pier, his bike was still padlocked against a lamppost. But his motorbike was gone. Proving nothing. He might have driven, rather than walked, into the sea.

Christ, I thought, what if he catches up with Annie Oakley, and then the two of them catch up with Cal?

I dumped a small wastebasket out on a flimsy desk by his bed and found some torn bits of fine bright yellow Beverly Hills–type stationery with C.R. for Constance Rattigan along the top. There was typewriting on the paper:

MIDNIGHTS. WAIT. SIX NIGHTS RUNNING ON THE SHORELINE. MAYBE, JUST MAYBE, LIKE OLD TIMES. And the typed initials C.R.

The typeface looked like the machine I had seen open on a desk in her Arabian parlor.

I touched the fragments, thinking, had Constance written Hopwood? No. She would have told me. Someone else must have sent this to Hopwood, a week ago. And he had jogged up the shore like a stallion to wait in the surf for Constance to come laughing down. Had he gotten tired of waiting and dragged her in the water and drowned her? No, no. He must have seen her dive in and never come out. Scared, he ran home, to find what? The last note, the one with the terrible words and awful degradations that shot him below the belt. So he had two reasons to leave town: fright and the insults.

I glanced at the telephone and sighed. No use calling Crumley. No corpus delicti. Just torn paper which I shoved in my jacket pockets. They felt like moth-wings, fragile but poisonous.

Melt all the guns, I thought, break the knives, burn the guillotines—and the malicious will still write letters that kill.

I saw a small bottle of cologne near the phone and took it, remembering blind Henry and his memory and his nose.

Downstairs the carousel still turned in silence, the horses still leaped over invisible barriers toward finish lines that never arrived.

I glanced at the drunken ticketman in his coffin booth, shivered, and, to absolutely no music whatsoever, got the hell out of there.

The miracle came just after lunch.

A special-delivery letter arrived from the *American Mercury* offering to buy a short story if I wouldn't mind their sending a check for three hundred dollars.

"Mind?" I shrieked. "Mind! Good grief, they must be *nuts!*"

I stuck my head out into the empty street and yelled at the houses, the sky, and the shore.

"I just sold to the *American Mercury*! Three hundred bucks! I'm *rich!*"

I lurched over to shove the *Mercury* letter under the bright glass eyes in the small shop window.

"Look!" I cried. "How about that? *See.*

"Rich," I muttered and gasped as I ran to the liquor store to flap the letter in the owner's face. "Look." I waved it around in the Venice train ticket office. "Hey!" I jolted to a halt. For I discovered I had jumped into the bank thinking I had the actual check with me and was about to deposit the damn letter.

"Rich—." I blushed and backed off.

At my apartment, I suddenly remembered the nightmare. That dire beast rising to seize and eat me.

Idiot! Fool! You shouted *good* rice when it should have been *bad.*

That night for the first night in a long while, the small rainstorm did not drench my doormat. There was no visitor, no seaweed on my sidewalk at dawn.

Somehow my truth, my blundering yells, had scared it away.

Curiouser, I thought, and curiouser.

There was no body and so no funeral the next day, just a memorial service for Constance Rattigan that seemed to have been organized by a rat pack of autograph and film-photo fans, so there was a mob of milling extras stomping the sand out front of Constance Rattigan's Arabian fort on the shore.

I stood a long way off from the stampede and watched some aging lifeguards sweat a portable organ across the sands to where someone had forgotten the stool so the lady who played it badly played it standing up, beads of salt on her brow, bobbing her head to conduct the lugubrious choir as the gulls flew down to investigate a scene without food so they flew away, and a fake minister barked and yipped like a poodle and the sandpipers rushed away, frightened, as the sandcrabs dug deeper to hide, and I gritted my teeth halfway between outrage and demon laughter as one by one the various grotesques, come down off the night screen at Mr. Shapeshade's or out from under the midnight piers, staggered down to the surf and hurled withered flower garlands at the tide.

Damn it, Constance, I thought, swim in *now*. Stop this damn freakshow. But my magic thinking failed. The only thing that came in was the wreaths, upchucked by a tide that didn't want them. A few people tried to throw them back again, but the damn things simply returned, and it began to rain. There was a frantic search for newspapers to protect their heads, and the lifeguards grunted the damn organ back across the sand, and I was left alone in the rain with a newspaper draped over my skull and the headlines upside down over my eyes.

FAMED SILENT STAR VANISHES.

I went down to kick the floral wreaths into the surf. This time, they stayed. Stripped down to my swimsuit, I grabbed an armload of flowers and swam out as far as I could before I let go.

Coming back, I almost drowned when my feet caught, tangled in one of the wreaths.

"Crumley," I whispered.

And did not know if his name on my lips was a curse or a prayer.

Crumley opened his door. His face was bright and shining, but not with beer. Something else had happened.

"Hey!" cried the detective. "Where you been? I been calling and calling you. Christ, come see what the old man's got."

He ran ahead to his workroom and pointed dramatically at his desk where a pile of manuscript, half an inch high, lay filled with words.

"Why, you old s.o.b.," I said, and whistled.

"That's me! S. O. B. Crumley. Crumley, S. O. B. Boy howdy."

He ripped a page out of the typewriter.

"Wanta read?"

"I don't have to." I laughed. "It's good, right?"

"Git outa the way." He laughed back. "The dam has broke."

I sat down, snorting with happiness at the sun in his face. "When did all this happen?"

"Two nights ago, midnight, one, two, I dunno. I was just lying here with my teeth in my mouth, staring at the ceiling, not reading a book, not listening to any radio, not drinking beer, and the wind blew outside, and the trees shook, and all of a sudden the damn ideas seethed like maggots on a hotplate. And I just got the hell up and walked over and sat down and next thing I know I'm typing and typing like hell and can't stop, and by dawn there's a big mountain, or molehill, of stuff and I'm laughing and crying all the time. Lookit *that*. And come six in the morning I go to bed and just lie there looking at all this paper and I laugh and laugh and I'm as happy as if I just had a brand-new love affair with the greatest lady in the world."

"You had," I said, softly.

"Funny thing is," said Crumley, "what started it. Maybe the wind outside the house. Somebody leaving seaweed calling cards on the porch? But did the old detective rush out, firing guns, yelling 'Freeze!' Hell, no. No yells, no shots. Just me banging my typewriter, making lots of noise like on New Year's or Halloween. And you know what happened next? Guess?"

My body was cold. A whole population of frosted bumps had come up on my neck.

"The wind went away," I said. "The footsteps outside your house stopped."

"What?" said Crumley, amazed.

"And there's been no seaweed ever again. And he, whoever he was, has not come back since."

"How'd you know that?" gasped Crumley.

"I just did, is all. You did the right thing, without knowing. Just like me. I shouted, and he went away from me, too. Oh, God, God."

I told Crumley about my sale to the *Mercury*, my running around town like a fool, my yelling to the sky, and the rain not raining on my three-o'clock-in-the-morning door any more, maybe forever.

Crumley sat down as if I had handed him an anvil.

"We're getting close, Elmo," I said. "We've scared him off, without meaning to. The further away he gets, the more we know about him. Well, maybe, anyway. At least we know he's put off by loud fools and laughing detectives doing maniac things to typewriters at five in the morning. Keep typing, Crumley. Then you'll be safe."

"Horseradish," said Crumley. But he laughed when he said it.

His smile made me brave. I dug in my pockets and brought out the poison-pen letter that had scared Hopwood, plus the warm love-letter on sun-yellow paper that had lured him down the coast in the first place.

Crumley toyed with the bits and pieces and sank halfway back into his old bathrobe of cynicism.

"Each typed on a different typewriter. Neither signed. Hell, *anyone* could have typed both. And if old Hopwood was the sex freak we took him for, he read that one on yellow paper and really believed Rattigan wrote it, hell, he raced up the shore and waited like a good boy for her to come down and grab his behind. But you know and I know, Rattigan never wrote a note like that in her life. She had an ego like a ten-ton truck. She never begged in the big Hollywood houses, on the streets, or on the shore. So what does that leave us with? She swam at strange hours. I'd run along the beach, my workout, and see that, night after night. Anyone, even me, could have snuck in while she was two hundred yards out in the bay playing with the sharks, anyone could have sat in her parlor, used her typewriter and stationery, and snuck back out, mailed this foreplay sex-note to that Hopwood son-of-a-bitch, and waited for the fireworks."

"And?" I said.

"And," said Crumley, "maybe the whole thing backfired. Rattigan, bugged by the flasher, panicked, swam out to escape him, got caught in a riptide. Then Hopwood, on the shore, watching, waiting, turned chicken when she didn't swim back in, and fled. The next day he gets the second note, the real doomsday attack. He knows someone saw him on the beach, and can finger him as Rattigan's so-called killer. So—"

"He's left town already," I said.

"It figures. Which leaves us still ten miles up from Tampico in Cleopatra's barge with no paddles. What in hell do we have to go on?"

"A guy who makes phone calls and steals Scott Joplin's head off Cal the barber's old photo and scares Cal out of town."

"Check."

"A guy who stands in halls and gets an old man drunk and stuffs him in a lion cage and maybe saves some ticket-punch confetti stolen from the old man's pockets."

"Check."

"A guy who scares the old canary lady to death and steals the newspaper headlines from the bottom of her birdcages. And after Fannie stops breathing, the same guy steals her record of *Tosca* as a keepsake. And then he writes letters to old actor Hopwood and frightens him away forever. Probably stole something from Hopwood's apartment, too, but we'll never know. And, if you checked, probably swiped a bottle of champagne from Constance Rattigan's wine racks just before I got there the other night. The guy can't stop himself. He's a real collector—"

Crumley's telephone rang. He picked it up, listened, handed it to me.

"Armpits," said a mellow voice.

"Henry!" Crumley put his ear to the receiver with me.

"Armpits is back, messing around, hour, two hours ago," said Henry, off in that other country, the tenement far across

Los Angeles in a rapidly dying past. "Someone got to stop him. Who?"

Henry hung up.

"Armpits." I took Hopwood's springtime cologne out of my pocket and placed it on Crumley's desk.

"Nope," said Crumley. "Whoever that bad ass is in the tenement ain't Hopwood. The old actor always smelled like a bed of marigolds and an acre of stardust. You want me to go sniff around your friend Henry's door?"

"No," I said, "by the time you got there, Mr. Armpits'd be back out here, waiting to snuffle around your door or mine."

"Not if we type and shout, shout and type, you forget that? Hey, what was it you shouted?"

I told Crumley more about my *American Mercury* story sale and the billion dollars that came with it.

"Jesus," said Crumley, "I feel like a pa whose boy has just made it through Harvard. Tell me again, kid. How do you do it? What should I do?"

"Throw up in your typewriter every morning."

"Yeah."

"Clean up every noon."

"Yeah!"

The foghorn out in the bay started blowing, saying over and over in a long gray voice, Constance Rattigan would never come back.

Crumley started typing.

And I drank my beer.

That night, at ten minutes after one, someone came and stood outside my door.

Oh, Jesus, I thought, awake. Please. Not again.

There was a fierce bang and a hard bang and then a terrible bang on my door. Someone out there was asking to get in.

God. Coward, I thought. Get it over with. Now, at last . . .

I jumped up to fling the door wide.

"You look great in those lousy torn jockey shorts," said Constance Rattigan.

I grabbed and yelled, "Constance!"

"Who in hell would it be?"

"But—but I went to your funeral."

"So did I. Hell, it's Tom Sawyer time. All those bimbos on the beach and the crappy organ. Shove your ass in your pants. We gotta get out of here. Jump."

Gunning the engine of an old beat-up Ford V-8, Constance made me fast-zip my fly.

Driving south along the sea I kept mourning, "You're alive."

"Hold the funeral and wipe your nose." She laughed at the empty road ahead. "Jesus God, I fooled everyone."

"But why, why?"

"Well, crud, honey, that bastard kept combing the surf line night after night."

"You didn't write, I mean, invite him to—"

"Invite? Jesus, you got no taste."

She braked the car in behind her shut Arabian fort, lit a cigarette, puffed smoke out the window, glared.

"All clear?"

"He's never coming back, Constance."

"Good! He looked better every night. When you're one hundred ten years old it's not the man, it's the pants. Besides, I thought I knew who he was."

"You were right."

"So I decided to fix things for good. I stashed groceries in a bungalow south of here, and parked this Ford there. Then I came back."

She jumped out of the old Ford and led me to the back door of her house.

"I turned on all the lights, music, fixed food that night, opened every door and window, and when he showed up, ran down, yelled, beat you to Catalina! and dove in. He was so stunned he didn't follow, or he might have, part way, and given up. I swam out two hundred yards and lay easy. I saw him on the shore the next half-hour, waiting for me to come in, then he ran like hell. I had really spooked him. I swam south and surfed in by my old el cheapo bungalow near Playa Del Rey. I had a ham sandwich and champagne on the porch, feeling great. Hid there ever since. Sorry to worry you, kid. You okay? Give me a kiss. But no phys. ed."

She kissed me and unlocked the door and we walked through to open the beach-front door and let the wind haunt the curtains and sift sand on the tiles.

"Jesus, who the hell lived here?" she wondered. "I'm my own ghost come home. I don't own this any more. You ever feel, back from vacation, all the furniture, books, radio, seem like neglected cats, resentful. They cut you dead. Feel? It's a morgue."

We walked through the rooms. The furniture, white sheeted in the dust and wind, moved restlessly, perturbed.

Constance leaned out the front door and yelled. "Okay, son-of-a-bitch. Gotcha!"

She turned back. "Find some more champagne. Lock up. Place gives me the creeps. Out."

Only the empty shore and the empty house saw us drive away.

"**H**ow *about* this?" yelled Constance Rattigan against the wind. She had put the top of her Ford down and we drove in a warm-cold flood of night, our hair blowing.

And we pulled up in a great sluice of sand next to a little bungalow by a half-tumbled wharf and Constance was out shucking clothes down to her bra and pants. The embers of a small fire burned in the front-yard sands. She stoked it with kindling and paper and, when it flared, shoved some forked hotdogs into it and sat knocking my knees like a teenage ape, drinking the champagne, and tousling my hair.

"See that hunk of driftwood there? All that's left of the Diamond Dance Pier, 1918. Charlie Chaplin sat at a table there. D. W. Griffith beyond. Me and Desmond Taylor at the far end. Wally Beery? Well, why go on. Burn your mouth. Eat."

She stopped suddenly and looked north along the sands.

"They won't follow, will they? He or they or them or whatever. They didn't see us, did they? We're safe forever?"

"Forever," I said.

The salt wind stirred the fire. Sparks flew up to shine in Constance Rattigan's green eyes.

I looked away.

"There's just one last thing I have to do."

"What?"

"Tomorrow, around five, go in and clean out Fannie's icebox."

Constance stopped drinking and frowned.

"Why would you want to do that?"

I had to think of something so as not to spoil the champagne night.

"Friend of mine, Streeter Blair, the artist, used to win blue ribbons at the county fair every autumn with his baked bread. After he died they found six loaves of his bread in his home freezer. His wife gave me one. I had it around for a week and ate a slice with real butter once in the morning, once at night. God, it was swell. What a great way to say goodbye to a wonderful man. When I buttered the last slice, he was gone for good. Maybe that's why I want Fannie's jellies and jams. Okay?"

Constance was disquieted.

"Yes," she said at last.

I popped another cork.

"What do we drink to?"

"My nose," I said. "At last, my damn head cold is over. Six boxes of Kleenex later. To my nose."

"Your lovely big nose," she said, and drank.

We slept out on the sand that night, feeling safe two miles south of those funeral flowers touching the shore by the late Constance Rattigan's former Arabian lean-to, and three miles south of an apartment where Cal's piano smile and my battered Underwood waited for me to come save earth from Martians on one page and Mars from earthmen on the next.

In the middle of the night I awoke. The place next to me on the sand was empty, but still warm from where Constance had lain cuddling the poor writer. I got up to hear her thrashing and chortling with seal-bark commotions out in the waves. When she ran in, we finished the champagne and slept until almost noon.

That day was one of those no-excuses-needed-for-living-weather days when you just lie and let the juices flow and drip. But finally I had to say, "I didn't want to ruin last night. God, it was good to find you alive. But the truth is, it's one down, one to go. Mr. Devil-in-the-Flesh on the beach ran away because he thought he had caused you to drown. He never intended anything but skin diving, anyway, and midnight frolics like 1928. What he got was you drowned, it seemed.

"So, he's gone, but there's still the one who sent him."

"Jesus," whispered Constance. Her eyelids flinched like two spiders over her shut eyes. At last she sighed, exhausted, "So it's not over after all?"

I clenched her sand-gritty hand in mine.

After a long silent time of thinking she said, her eyes still shut, "About Fannie's icebox? I never made it back that night five centuries ago, to look in. You looked, saw nothing."

"That's why I've got to go look again. Trouble is, the law has padlocked her apartment."

"You want me to go jimmy the lock?"

"Constance."

"I'll go in, clear the halls, chase out the spooks, you hit 'em with a club, then we both crack the padlock, spoon Fannie's mayonnaise, and at the bottom of the third jar, we find the answer, the solution, if it's still there, if it hasn't spoiled or been taken away—"

A fly buzzed, touched my brow. An old notion stirred.

"Reminds me, that story, years ago in some magazine. Girl fell and froze in a glacier. Two hundred years later, the ice melts and there she is, beautiful, young as the day she was frozen."

"That's no beautiful girl in Fannie's fridge."

"No, it's something terrible."

"And when and if you find and take whatever it is out— do you kill it?"

"Nine times, I guess. Yeah. Nine should do it."

"How," said Constance, her face pale under her tan, "does that damn first aria from *Tosca* go?"

I got out of her car in front of the tenement just at dusk. The night looked even darker just inside the waiting hall. I stared at it for a long moment. My hands trembled on the door of Constance Rattigan's roadster.

"Want old Ma to come in with you?" she said.

"Good grief, Constance."

"Sorry, kid." She patted my cheek, gave me a kiss that made my eyelids fly up like windowshades, handed me a piece of paper, and shoved. "That's my bungalow phone, listed under the name Trixie Friganza, the I-Don't-Care Girl, remember her? No? Nuts. If someone kicks your bung downstairs, yell. If you find the bastard, form a conga line and throw him off the second-floor porch. You want me to wait here?"

"Constance," I moaned.

Down the hill, she found a red light and went through it.

I came up the stairs to a hall that was dark forever. The lightbulbs had been stolen years ago. I heard someone run. It was a very light tread, like a child's. I froze, listening.

The footsteps diminished and ran down the steps at the rear of the tenement.

The wind blew down the hall and brought the smell with it. It was the scent that Henry had told me about, of clothes that had hung in an attic for a hundred years, and shirts that had been worn for a hundred days. It was like standing in a midnight alley where a pack of hounds had gone to lift their legs with mindless panting smiles.

The smell pulled me into a jumping run. I made it to

Fannie's door and braked myself, heart pounding. I gagged because the smell was so strong. He had been here only a few moments ago. I should have run after, but the door itself stopped me. I put out my hand.

The door scraped softly inward on unoiled hinges.

Someone had broken the lock on Fannie's door.

Someone had wanted something.

Someone had gone in to search.

Now, it was my turn.

I stepped forward into a dark remembrance of food.

The air was pure delicatessen, a warm nest where a great, kind, strange elephant had browsed and sung and eaten for twenty years.

How long, I wondered, before the scent of dill and cold cuts and mayonnaise would blow away lost down the tenement stairwells. But now . . .

The room was a ramshackle mess.

He had come in and tumbled the shelves and closets and bureaus. Everything was flung to the linoleum floor. All of Fannie's opera scores were strewn among the broken phonograph records that had been kicked against the wall or toppled in his search.

"Jesus, Fannie," I whispered. "I'm glad you can't see this."

Everything that could have been searched and wrecked was wrecked. Even the great throne chair where Fannie had queened it for half a generation or more was tossed down on its back, as she had been tossed down to stay.

But the one place he had not looked, the last place, I looked now. Stumbling on the shambles, I grabbed the icebox door and pulled.

The cool air sighed out around my face. I stared as I had stared many nights ago, aching to see what was right there before me. What was the thing the stander in the hall, the stranger on the night train, had come to find but left behind for me?

Everything was just as it had always been. Jams, jellies, salad dressings, wilted lettuce, a rich cold shrine of colors and scents where Fannie had worshipped.

But suddenly, I sucked my breath.

I reached out and shoved the jars and bottles and cheese boxes way to the back. They had been placed all this while on a thin folded paper of some size which, until now, I had simply taken as a sheet to catch drippings.

I pulled it out and read by the icebox light, *Janus, the Green Envy Weekly.*

I left the box door wide and staggered over to put Fannie's old chair upright and collapse in it, to wait for my heart to slow.

I turned the green-tinted newspaper pages. On the back were obits and personals. I ran my eye down, found nothing, ran it down again, and saw—

A small box, circled faintly with red ink.

And this was what *he* had searched for, to take away forever.

How could I know? Here were the words:

WHERE HAVE YOU BEEN ALL THESE YEARS? MY HEART CRIES OUT, DOES YOURS? WHY DON'T YOU WRITE OR CALL? I CAN BE HAPPY IF ONLY YOU'D REMEMBER ME AS I RE-MEMBER YOU. WE HAD SO MUCH AND LOST IT ALL. NOW, BEFORE IT'S TOO LATE TO REMEM-BER, FIND YOUR WAY BACK.
CALL!

And it was signed:

SOMEONE WHO LOVED YOU, LONG AGO.

And in the margin were these words, scrawled by some-one:

SOMEONE WHO LOVED YOU, WITH A FULL
HEART, LONG AGO.

Jesus at midnight, Mary in the morn.
I read it six times in disbelief.
I let the paper fall, walked on it, stood in the icebox draft
to cool off. Then I went back to read the damn message for a
seventh time.

What a piece of work it was, what a beaut, what a come-on,
what a baited trap. What a Rorschach test, what a piece of
palmistry, what a numbers game that anyone could sum and
win with. Men, women, old, young, dark, light, tall, thin.
Listen, look! This means YOU.

It applied to anyone who had ever loved and lost, meaning every single soul in the whole damned city, state, and universe.

Who, reading it, would not be tempted to lift a phone, dial,
wait, and whisper at last, late at night:
Here I am. Please—come find me.

I stood in the middle of the linoleum floor of Fannie's
apartment and tried to imagine her here, the ship's deck creaking underfoot as her weight shifted this way and that, as *Tosca*
lamented from the phonograph, and the icebox door stood
wide with its enshrined condiments, her eyes moving, her
heart beating like a hummingbird trapped in a vast aviary.

Christ. The Fifth Horseman of the Apocalypse *had* to be
the editor of a paper like this.

I checked all the other advertisements. The telephone
number was the same in each. You had to call one number to
get referrals to all the ads. And that phone number belonged

to the publishers of, damn them to hell forever, *Janus, the Green Envy Weekly*.

Fannie had never in her life bought a paper like this. Someone had given it to her or . . . I stopped and glanced at the door.

No!

Someone had left it for her to find with the red ink circling this one ad, so she would be sure to see.

SOMEONE WHO LOVED YOU, WITH A FULL HEART, LONG AGO.

"Fannie!" I cried in dismay. "Oh, you damn, damn fool."

I waded through broken shards of *La Bohème* and *Butterfly*, then remembered and stumbled back to slam the icebox door.

hings were no better on the third floor.

Henry's door was wide open. I had never seen it open before. Henry believed in shut doors. He didn't want anyone having a sighted advantage on him. But now . . .

"Henry?"

I stepped through, and the small apartment was neat, incredibly neat and clean and filed, everything in place, everything fresh—but empty.

"Henry?"

His cane lay in the middle of the floor, and by it a dark string, a black twine with knots in it.

It all looked scattered and impromptu, as if Henry had lost these in a fight, or left behind when he ran . . .

Where?

"Henry?"

I handled the twine, and looked at the knots. In a line, two knots, a space, three knots, a long space, then a series of three, six, four, and nine knots.

"Henry!" Louder.

I ran to knock on Mrs. Gutierrez's door.

When she opened it and saw me, she welled over. Tears dropped from her eyes as she saw my face. She put her tortilla-scented hand out to touch my cheeks. "Aw, poor, poor. Come in, oh, poor, sit down. Sit. You wanta eat? I bring something. Sit, no, no, sit. Coffee, yes?" She brought me coffee and wiped her eyes. "Poor Fannie. Poor *man*. What?"

I unfolded the newspaper and held it out for her to see.

"No read *inglese*," she said, backing off.

"Don't have to read," I said. "Did Fannie ever come up to phone and bring this paper with her?"

"*No, no!*" Her face changed color with memory. "*Estupido! Sí.* She came. But I don't know who she call."

"Did she talk a long while, a long time?"

"Long time?" She had to translate my words for a few seconds, then she nodded vigorously. "*Sí.* Long. Long she laugh. Oh, how she laugh and talk, talk and laugh."

While she was inviting Mr. Night and Time and Eternity to come over, I thought.

"And she had this paper with her?"

Mrs. Gutierrez turned the paper over like it was a Chinese puzzle. "Maybe *sí*, maybe *no*. This one, some other. I dunno. Fannie is with God."

I turned, weighing 380 pounds, and leaned toward the door, the folded newspaper in my hands.

"I wish I were," I said. "Please, may I use your phone?"

On a hunch I did not dial the *Green Envy* number. Instead, counting the knots, I dialed the numbers of blind Henry's twine.

"Janus Publications," said a nasal voice. "*Green Envy*. Hold."

The phone was dropped to the floor. I heard heavy feet shuffling through wintry mounds of crumpled paper.

"It fits!" I yelled, and scared Mrs. Gutierrez, who jumped back. "The number fits." I yelled at the *Green Envy* paper in my hand. For some reason Henry had knotted the Janus publication's number onto his remembrance twine.

"Hello, hello!" I shouted.

Far off in the *Green Envy* office I could hear some maniac shrieking because he was trapped and electrocuted by a bin of wildly berserk guitars. A rhinoceros and two hippos were dancing a fandango in the latrine to rebut the music. Someone typed during the cataclysm. Someone else was playing a harmonica to a different drummer.

I waited four minutes, then jammed the phone down and stormed out of Mrs. Gutierrez's, raving.

"Mister," said Mrs. Gutierrez, "why you so upset?"

"Upset, upset, who's upset!" I cried. "Christ, people don't come back to phones, I got no money to get out to that damn place, wherever it is in Hollywood, and there's no use calling back, the damn phone's off the hook, and time's running out, and where the hell is Henry. He's dead, damn it!"

Not dead, Mrs. Gutierrez should have said, merely sleeping.

But she didn't say and I thanked her for her silence and stormed down the hallway, not knowing what to do. I didn't even have money for the stupid red trolley car to Hollywood. I . . .

"Henry!" I shouted down the stairwell.

"Yes?" said a voice behind me.

I whirled around. I yelled. There was nothing but darkness there.

"Henry. Is that—?"

"Me," said Henry, and stepped out into what little light there was. "When Henry decides to hide, he truly hides. Holy

Moses Armpits was here. I think he knows that we know what he knows about this mess. I just skedaddled out my apartment door when I heard him prowl the porch outside my view window, I just dropped and jumped. Left stuff, I don't care, on the floor. You find it?"

"Yes. Your cane. And the string with knots for numbers."

"You want to know about them knots, that number?"

"Yes."

"I heard crying in the hall, day before Fannie's gone forever. There she is, at my door. I open it to let all that sadness in. Not often I see her upstairs, it kills her to climb. I shouldn't've done it, no, shouldn't have done it, she says, all my fault she says, over and over. Watch this junk, Henry, take this junk, here, what a fool I am she says, and she gave me some old phonograph records and some newspapers, special, she said, and I thanked her and thought what the hell and she went down the hall crying for herself being a fool and I just put the old newspapers by and the records and didn't think a long while till after Fannie was tributed and sung after and gone, and then this morning I ran my hand over those fool papers and thought, what is this? And I called Mrs. Gutierrez and said, "What?" and in Mexican and English she looked over the paper and saw the words, you see 'em, circled in ink, the same words in five different issues of the paper and the same number, and I got to thinking, why was Fannie crying so hard, and what's this number, so I knotted the knots and called. You call?"

"Yes, Henry," I said. "I found the same paper in Fannie's place now. Why didn't you tell me you had them?"

"What for? Sounded foolish. Woman stuff. I mean, did you read it? Mrs. Gutierrez read it, bad, but read it out loud. I laughed. God, I thought, that's trash, real trash. Only now, I think different. Who would read and believe junk like that?"

"Fannie," I said, at last.

"Tell me this, now. When you called that number, some dumb son-of-a-bitch come on, talk, and not come back again ever?"

"Some son-of-a-bitch."

Henry started steering me back toward the open door of his apartment. As if I were the blind one, I let him.

"How they *run* a business like that?" he wondered.

We were at his door. I said, "I guess when you don't give a damn, people throw money at you."

"Yeah, that was always my trouble. I cared too much. So nobody ever threw nothing. Hell, I got plenty cash anyway—uh."

He stopped, for he had heard me suck my breath.

"That," he said, with a quiet nod and smile, "is the sound of someone wants to borrow my life's savings."

"Only if you come with, Henry. To help me find the guy who hurt Fannie."

"Armpits?"

"Armpits."

"This nose is yours. Lead on."

"We need money for a taxicab to save time, Henry."

"I never been in a taxi in my life, why would I take one now?"

"We got to get out to that newspaper before it closes. The sooner we find out what we need to know, the safer it'll be. I don't want to spend one more night worrying about you here in this tenement, or me at the beach."

"Armpits has teeth, huh?"

"You'd better believe it."

"Come on." He circled his room, smiling. "Let's find where a blind man hides his money. All over the place. You want eighty bucks?"

"Hell, no."

"Sixty, forty?"

"Twenty, thirty will do."

"Well, hell then." Henry snorted, stopped, laughed, and yanked a great wad of bills out of his hip pocket. He began to peel the lettuce. "Here's forty."

"It'll take awhile to pay it back."

"If we get whoever pushed Fannie over, you don't owe nothing. Grab the money. Find my cane. Shut the door. C'mon! Let's go find that dumb bunny who answers phones and goes off on vacation."

In the taxicab, Henry beamed around at sources of scent and odor he could not see.

"This is dandy. I never smelled a cab before. This one's new and going fast."

I couldn't resist. "Henry, how'd you save up so much?"

"I don't see 'em, touch 'em, even smell 'em, but I play the horses. Got friends at the track. They listen, and lay on the lettuce. I bet more and lose less than most sighted fools. It mounts up. When it gets too big, I trot along to one of those ugly ladies, so they tell me, in the bungalows out front near the tenement. They say ugly but I don't mind. Blind is blind, and —Well, now. Where *are* we?"

"Here," I said.

We had pulled into an alley behind a building in a run-down block in Hollywood south of the boulevard. Henry snuffed a deep breath. "It ain't Armpits. But it's his first cousin. Watch out."

"I'll be right back."

I got out. Henry stayed in the back seat, his cane in his lap, eyes restfully shut.

"I'll just listen to the meter," he said, "and make sure it don't run fast."

The dusk was long since gone and it was full night as I picked my way along the alley, looking up at a half-lit neon sign on the backstairs of a building, with the great god Janus painted facing two ways above it. Half of one face had flaked off in the rains. The rest would be soon gone.

Even the gods, I thought, are having a bad year.

I dodged upstairs among various young men and women with old faces, hunched like beaten dogs, smoking, begging their pardon, excusing myself, but nobody seemed to mind. I stepped in at the top.

The offices looked as if they hadn't been cleaned since the Civil War. There was paper balled, wadded, tossed over every inch, foot, and yard of the floor. There were hundreds of old newspapers, crumpled and yellowing, in the windows, on the desktops. Three wastebaskets stood empty. Whoever had thrown the paper wads had missed ten thousand times. I waded in through a tide that reached my ankles. I walked on dried cigars, cigarette stubs, and, by the crackling sound of their small thoraxes, cockroaches. I found the abandoned phone under a snow-piled desk, picked it up, listened.

I thought I could hear the traffic going by under Mrs. Gutierrez's window. Crazy. She must have hung up, long ago.

"Thanks for waiting," I said.

"Hey, man, what gives?" said someone.

I hung up and turned.

A tall, skinny man, with a clear drop of water on the end of his thin nose, came wading through the paper tide. He sized me up with nicotine-stained eyes.

"I called about half an hour ago." I nodded at the phone. "I just hung up on me."

He gazed at the phone, scratched his head, and finally got it. He managed a feeble smile and said, "Shee-it."

"Those are my very thoughts."

I had a feeling he was proud of never coming back to the phone; it was better to make up your own news.

"Hey, man," he said, getting another idea to replace the first. He was the sort of thinker who has to move out the furniture before he can bring in the cows. "You, you wouldn't happen to be the fuzz."

"No, just the Goofer Feathers."

"Unh?"

"Remember the Two Black Crows?"

"Huh?"

"Nineteen twenty-six. Two white men in blackface talked about Goofer Feathers. The fuzz. From peaches. Forget it. Did you write this?" I held out the *Janus, Green Envy* page with the terribly sad advertisement at the bottom.

He blinked at it. "Hell, no. It's legit. It was sent in."

"You ever stop to think what you're doing with an ad like that?"

"Hey, man, like we don't read, we just print 'em. It's a free country, right? Lemme see that!" He grabbed the ad and peered at it, moving his lips. "Oh, sure. That one. Funny, huh?"

"You realize someone just might look up that geek and believe in him?"

"Them's the breaks. Hey, look, why don't you fall downstairs outa my life?" He thrust the paper back at me.

"I don't leave without the home phone number of this weirdo."

He blinked at me, stunned, then laughed. "That's Q.T. information, like no one knows. You want to write him, sure. We pass mail on. Or he comes, picks it up."

"This is an emergency. Someone's dead. Someone——." I ran out of gas and looked around at the ocean of paper on the floor and, without thinking about it, took out a box of small stick matches.

"Looks like a fire hazard here," I said.

"What fire hazard?"

He glanced around at the year's growth of paper wadding, empty beer cans, dropped paper cups, and old hamburger wrappings. A look of immense pride overcame him. His eyes almost danced when he saw the five-or-six-quart wax milk cartons busy manufacturing penicillin on the window sills, next to some tossed men's jockey shorts that gave the place its real touch of class.

I struck a match to get his attention.

"Hey," he said.

I blew out the first match, to show what a good sport I was, and when he made no further offer of help, lit a second.

"What if I dropped this on the floor?"

He gave the floor a second look around. The paper junk seethed and lapped at his ankles. If I had dropped the match the flames would have reached him in about five seconds.

"You ain't going to drop that," he said.

"No?" I blew it out and lit a third.

"You got the goddamnedest sense of humor, don't you?"

I dropped the match.

He yelled and jumped.

I stepped on the flame before it could spread.

He took a deep breath and let it blast.

"Now you get the hell outa here! You—"

"Wait." I lit a final match and crouched, guarding the flame, close down to a half-ton of wadded rewrites, old calling cards, torn envelopes.

I touched the flame here and there and the paper started burning.

"What in hell you want?"

"Just a phone number. That's all. I still won't have an address, so I can't get at the guy, trace him. But I do, damn it to hell, want that phone, or the whole place burns."

I realized my own voice had gone up about ten decibels, to maniac. Fannie was fighting in my blood. A lot of other dead people were screaming in my breath, wanting out.

"Give it here!" I shouted.

The flames were spreading.

"Shit, man, stomp out the fire, you'll get the goddamn dumb number. Shit, hold on, jump!"

I jumped on the fire, dancing around. Smoke rose and the fire was out by the time Mr. Janus, the editor who faced two ways at once, found the number on his Rolodex.

"Here, goddamn it, here's the crapping number. Vermont four-five-five-five. Got that? Four-five-five-five!"

I struck a final final match until he shoved the Rolodex card under my nose.

"Someone who loved you," it read, and the telephone.

"Okay!" shrieked the editor.

I blew out the match. My shoulders sank with sudden relief.

Fannie, I thought, we'll get him now.

I must have said it out loud, for the editor, his face purple, sprayed me with his saliva. "*What* you going to get?"

"Myself killed," I said, going downstairs.

"I hope so!" I heard him yell.

I opened the door of the taxicab.

"Meter's ticking like crazy," said Henry, in the back seat. "Thank God I'm rich."

"Be right with you."

I beckoned the taxi driver to follow me out to a corner where there was an outdoor phone booth.

I hesitated for a long while, afraid to call the number, afraid someone might really answer.

What, I wondered, do you say to a murderer during suppertime?

dialed the number.

Someone who loved you, long ago.

Who would answer a dumb ad like that?

All of us, on the right night. The voice from the past, making you remember a familiar touch, a warm breath in the ear, a seizure of passion like a strike of lightning. Which of us is not vulnerable, I thought, when it comes to that three-in-the-morning voice. Or when you wake after midnight to find someone crying, and it's you, and tears on the chin and you didn't even know that during the night you had had a bad dream.

Someone who loved you . . .

Where is she now? Where is he? Still alive somewhere? It can't be. Too much time is gone. The one who loves me can't still be in the world somewhere. And yet? Why not, as I was doing, call?

I called three times and went back to sit with Henry in the back seat of the taxi, listening to the meter tick. "Don't worry," he said. "That meter don't bother me. There's plenty of horses waiting and lots of lettuce up ahead. Go dial the number again, child."

The child went to dial.

This time, a long way off in another country, it seemed, a self-appointed funeral director picked up the phone.

"Yes?" said a voice.

At last I gasped, "Who's this?"

"For that matter, who's *this?*" said the guarded voice.

"What took you so long to get to the phone?" I could hear cars going by on the other end.

It was a phone booth in an alley somewhere in the city. Christ, I thought, he does as I do. He's using the nearest pay booth for his office.

"Well, if you're not going to say anything—" said the voice on the other end.

"Wait," I said. I almost know your voice, I thought. Let me hear more. "I saw your ad in *Janus.* Can you help me?"

The voice on the other end relaxed, pleased by my panic. "I can help anyone, anywhere, anytime," he said, easily. "You one of the Lonelies?"

"What?" I cried.

"You one of the—"

Lonelies he had said. And that did it.

I was back at Crumley's, back in time, back on the big train in the cold rain rounding a curve. The voice on the phone was that voice in the night storm half a lifetime ago, saying its say about death and lonely, lonely and death. First the memory of a voice, then the session with Crumley knocking my head, and now this real sound on the phone. There was only one missing piece. I still couldn't put a name on the voice. Close, familiar, I almost had it, but. . . .

"Speak up," I practically shouted.

There was an interval of suspicion on the other end. In that moment I heard the most beautiful sounds of half a lifetime.

The wind blowing at the far end of the line. But more than that: surf rolling in, louder and louder, closer and closer, until I almost felt it roll under my feet.

"Oh, Jesus, I know where you *are!*" I cried.

"No way," said the phone voice, and broke the connection.

But not soon enough. I stared wildly at the empty phone in my hand and squeezed it in my fist.

"Henry!" I yelled.

Henry leaned out of the taxicab, staring at nothing.

I fell getting in the cab.

"You still with me?"

"If I ain't," said Henry, "where am I? Speak to the driver."

I spoke. We went.

The taxicab rolled to a stop with its windows down. Henry leaned forward, his face like the prow of a dark ship. He sniffed.

"Ain't been here since childhood. That smell's the ocean. That other smell, rotten? The pier. This where you live, scribe?"

"The Great American Novelist? Sure."

"I hope your novels smell better than this."

"If I live, maybe. Can we keep the cab waiting, Henry?"

Henry licked his thumb, peeled off three twenty-dollar bills, held them over the front seat of the cab.

"That keep you from being nervous, son?"

"That"—he cab driver took the money—"will buy you midnight."

"It'll all be over by then," said Henry. "Child, you know what you're doing?"

Before I could answer, a wave came in under the pier.

"Sounds like the New York subway," said Henry. "Don't let it run over you."

We left the cab waiting at the foot of the Venice pier. I tried to steer Henry along in the night.

"Don't need no steering," said Henry. "Just warn me on

wires, ropes, or loose bricks is all. But I got a nervous elbow, don't like touching."

I let him walk proudly on.

"Wait here," I said. "Step back about three feet. There, you can't be seen. When I come back I'll just say one word, 'Henry,' and then you tell me what you smell, okay? And then just turn and go to the cab."

"I can still hear the motor running, sure."

"Tell the taxi to take you to the Venice Police Station. Ask for Elmo Crumley. If he's not there, have them call his home. He's to come here with you, fast as possible, once we get the whole thing rolling. That is, *if* it rolls. Maybe we won't use your nose tonight, after all."

"I hope I do. I brought my cane to hit that guy. You let me hit him, once?"

I hesitated. "Once," I said. "You okay, Henry?"

"Br'er Fox, he lie low."

Feeling like Br'er Rabbit, I walked away.

I t was the elephants' graveyard, the pier at night, all dark bones and a lid of fog over it and the sea rushing in to bury, reveal, and bury again.

I picked my way along past the shops and shoebox apartments and shut poker parlors, noting, on my way, various phones here or there, standing in their unlit caskets, waiting to be taken away tomorrow or next week.

I walked out along the plankings, over the sighs and rustles and stirs of moist and dry wood. The whole structure creaked and heaved like a sinking ship, as I passed red warning flags and signs which read DANGER, as I stepped over strung chains and found myself as far as I could go, at the edge of the pier, looking back at all the nailed-shut doors and rolled-down-and-pinned canvas fronts.

I slid into the last phone booth, rummaged my pockets, cursing until I found the nickels Henry had given me. I dropped one in the phone slot and dialed the number given me by the *Janus* editor.

"Four—five—five—five," I whispered, and waited.

At this moment, the frayed strap on my Mickey Mouse wristwatch broke. The watch fell to the booth floor. Cursing, I picked it up, and shoved it on the shelf under the phone. Then, listened. Far off, I could hear the phone ringing at the other end.

I let my receiver drop and hang. I stepped out of the booth and stood listening, eyes shut. At first there was only one great roll of surf traveling under my feet, shaking the timbers. It passed. At last, straining, I could hear.

Far down at the halfway point on the pier, a phone rang.

Coincidence? I thought. Phones ring everywhere all the time. But this phone, a hundred yards away, now—had I dialed its number?

Half in, half out of the booth, I grabbed the receiver and planted it back on its hook.

Far off in the windy darkness, that other phone stopped ringing.

Which still proved nothing.

I dropped my nickel back in and redialed.

A deep breath and . . .

That telephone in its glass coffin, half a light-year away, started ringing again.

It made me jump and hurt in my chest. I felt my eyes widen and my breath suck in cold.

I let the phone ring. I stood out of my booth, waiting for someone off there in the night to run from the alleys or out of the damp canvas or from behind the old Knock the

Milk Bottles game. Someone, like me, would have to answer.
Someone who, like myself, jumped up at two in the morning to run in the rain and talk to the sunlight in Mexico City
where life still walked and lived and seemed never to die.
Someone. . . .

The whole pier stayed dark. No shack windows lit. No
canvasses whispered. The phone rang. The surf wandered
under the boards, looking for someone, anyone, to answer.
The phone rang. It rang. I wanted to run answer the damn
thing myself, just to shut it up.

Jesus, I thought. Get your nickel back. Get . . .

Then it happened.

A crack of light appeared swiftly and went out. Something
stirred down there, across from that telephone. The phone
rang. The phone rang. And someone stood in the shadows
listening to it, tentatively. I saw a whiteness turn and knew that
whoever it was was looking along the pier, fearful, careful,
searching.

I froze.

The phone rang. At last the shadow moved, the face turned
back, listening. The phone rang. The shadow suddenly ran.

I leaped back into my booth and grabbed the receiver just
in time.

Click.

On the far end, I heard breathing. Then, at last, a man's
voice said,

"Yes?"

Oh, my God! I thought. It's the same. The voice I heard
an hour ago, in Hollywood.

Someone who loved you, long ago.

I must have said it aloud.

There was a long pause, a wait, an in-sucked gasp from the
far end of the line.

"Yes?"

It shot me through the ear, then the heart.

I know that voice now, I thought.

"Oh, Christ," I said hoarsely, "it's you!"

That must have shot him through the head. I heard him seize in a great storm of breath and blast it out.

"Damn you," he cried. "Damn you to hell."

He didn't hang up. He just let the red-hot telephone drop, bang, dance on its hangman's noose. I heard his footsteps rush away.

By the time I got out of the booth, the pier was empty in all directions. Where the brief light had been was dark. Only bits of old newspaper blew along the plankings as I forced myself to walk, not run, the hundred long yards to that other phone. I found it dangling and tapping the cold glass of the booth.

I picked it up and listened.

I could hear my ten-dollar Mickey Mouse watch ticking at the other end, back in that other phone booth, a hundred miles away.

If I was lucky and alive, I'd go save the Mouse.

I hung up this telephone and turned, staring at all the little buildings, shacks, shop fronts, shut-down games, wondering if I would do something crazy now.

I did.

I walked about seventy feet to a small shop front and stood in front of it, listening. Someone was in there, moving around, perhaps shoving himself into street clothes in the dark. I heard rustles and someone whispering angrily to himself, someone talking under his breath, telling him where to find socks, where shoes, and where, where the damn tie? Or maybe it was just the tide under the pier, making up lies no one could ever check.

The muttering stopped. He must have felt me outside the door. I heard footsteps move. I fell backward, clumsily, realizing my hands were empty. I hadn't even thought to bring Henry's cane as weapon.

The door opened with savage swiftness.

I stared.

Crazily, I saw two things at once.

Beyond, on a small table in half-light, a stack of yellow and brown and red Clark Bar and Nestlé's Crunch and Power House wrappers.

And then . . .

The small shadow, the little man himself, staring out at me with stunned eyes, as if wakened from a forty-year sleep.

A. L. Shrank, in person.

Tarot card reader, phrenologist, dime-store psychiatrist, day- and nighttime psychologist, astrologer, Zen/Freudian/Jungian numerologist, and full Life Failure stood there, buttoning his shirt with mindless fingers, trying to see me with eyes that were either fixed by some drug or shocked numb by my inept bravado.

"Damn you to hell," he said, quietly, again.

And then added, with some quick sort of impromptu quiver of a smile,

"Come in."

"No," I whispered. Then I said it louder. "No. You come out."

The wind was blowing the wrong way, or perhaps the right way, this time.

My God, I thought, cringing back, then holding my ground. All those other days, how did the wind blow? How could I not have noticed? Because, I thought, oh damn simple fact: I had had a head cold for a solid ten days. No nose at all. No nose.

Oh, Henry, I thought, you and your always lifted, always curious beak, connected to all that bright awareness within. Oh, smart Henry crossing an unseen street at nine of an evening, and sniffing the unwashed shirt and the unlaundered underclothes as Death marched by the other way.

I looked at Shrank and felt my nostrils wince. Sweat, the first smell of defeat. Urine, the next smell of hatred. Then, what mixtures? Onion sandwiches, unbrushed teeth, the scent of self-destruction. It came like a storm cloud, full flood, from the man. I might have been standing on an empty shore with a ninety-foot tidal wave poised to crush me, for the sick fear I suddenly knew. My mouth baked dry even as sweat broke on my body.

"Come in," said A. L. Shrank again, uncertainly.

There was a moment when I thought he might suck backward like a crayfish. But then he saw my glance at the phone booth directly across from his shop, and my second glance down the pier to the phone at the far end where my Mickey Mouse watch ticked, and he *knew*. Before he could speak again, I called into the shadows.

"Henry?"

Dark stirred in dark. I felt Henry's shoes scrape as his voice called back, warm and easy, "Yes?"

Shrank's eyes jerked from me to where Henry's voice stirred the shadows.

At last I was able to say:

"Armpits?"

Henry took a deep breath and let it out.

"Armpits," he said.

I nodded. "You know what to do."

"I hear the meter running," said Henry.

From the corners of my eyes, I saw him walking away, then stop and throw his hand up.

Shrank flinched. So did I. Henry's cane sailed through the air to land with a sharp clatter on the planks.

"You might need that," said Henry.

Shrank and I stood staring at the weapon on the pier.

The sound of the taxi driving off jerked me forward. I grabbed the cane and held it to my chest, as if it might really work against knives or guns.

Shrank looked at the vanishing lights of the taxi, far off.

"What in hell was that all about?" he said.

Behind him, Schopenhauer and Nietzsche and Spengler and Kafka all leaned on their mad elbows, sank in their dusts, and whispered, yes, what was *that* all about?

"Wait'll I get my shoes." He vanished.

"Don't get anything else," I cried.

That made him laugh a choking laugh.

"What would I get?" he called, unseen, rummaging around. In the door he showed me a shoe in each hand. "No guns. No knives." He shoved them on, but didn't lace them.

I couldn't believe what happened next. The clouds, over Venice, decided to pull back, revealing a full moon.

Both of us looked up at it, trying to decide if it was bad or good, and for which of us?

Shrank's gaze wandered to the shoreline and along the pier.

"He wept like anything to see such quantities of sand," he said. Then hearing himself he snorted softly. "Come oysters, said the carpenter, and took them close in hand. A pleasant walk, a pleasant talk, along the golden strand."

He began to walk. I stayed. "Aren't you going to lock your door?"

Shrank gave the merest nodding glance over his shoulder

at the books clustered like vultures with their black feathers and dusty golden stares, waiting on shelves for the touch that gave life. In invisible choirs, they sang forth wild tunes I should have heard long days ago. My eye ran and reran the stacks.

My God, why hadn't I truly seen?

That dreadful escarpment inhabited by dooms, that lineup of failures, that literary Apocalypse of wars, squalors, diseases, pestilences, depressions, that downfall of nightmares, that pit of deliriums and mazes from which mad mice and insane rats never found light or made exit. That police lineup of degenerates and epileptics dancing the rims of shelved library cliffs with teams replacing teams of nausea and revulsion waiting in the higher darkness.

Single authors, single books—fine. A Poe here or a Sade there is a spice. But this was no library, it was an abattoir, a dungeon, a tower where ten dozen men in iron masks were penned, silently raving, forever.

Why hadn't I seriously seen and known?

Because Rumpelstiltskin was in charge.

Staring at Shrank even now I thought, at any moment he'll grab his foot and rip himself straight up in half and fall in two pieces!

He was hilarious.

Which made him all the more terrible.

"Those books," said Shrank at last, breaking the spell, not looking at them, staring up at the moon, "they don't care for me. Why should I care for them?"

"But—"

"Besides," said Shrank, "would anyone really want to steal *Decline of the West*?"

"I thought you loved your collection!"

"Loved?" He blinked once. "My God, don't you see? I hate everything. Name it, there's nothing in the world I like."

He strode off in the direction Henry had taken with his taxicab.

"Now," he said, "coming or not?"

"Coming," I said.

▐ s that a weapon?"

We walked slowly, feeling each other out. I was amazed to find Henry's cane in my hands.

"No, an antenna, I think," I said.

"Of a very large insect?"

"A very blind one."

"Can he find his way without it, and where's he going this time of night?"

"Running errands. Back immediately," I lied.

Shrank was a lie detector. He almost writhed with delight at my voice. He quickened his pace, then stopped to examine me.

"I take it he steers by his nose. I heard what you asked and what he answered back."

"Armpits?" I said.

Shrank shriveled inside his old clothes. His eyes darted first to his left, then to his right underarm and down along a vast history of stains and time's discolorings.

"Armpits," I said again.

It was a bullet in the heart.

Shrank staggered, then firmed himself.

"Why and where are we walking?" he gasped. I could sense the rabbit palpitation under his greasy tie.

"I thought you were leading the way. I only know one thing." I moved, this time half a step ahead of him. "Blind

Henry was searching for some unwashed shirts, dirty underclothes, bad breath. He found and named them for me."

I did not repeat the dread epithet. But Shrank, with each
word, was diminished.

"Why would a blind man want me?" said Shrank at last.

I didn't want to give it all away at once. I had to test and
try. "Because of *Janus, the Green Envy Weekly,*" I said. "I've
seen copies in your place, through your window."

That was pure lie, but it struck midriff.

"Yes, yes," said Shrank. "But a blind man, and you—?"

"Because." I took a deep breath and let it out. "You're Mr.
Fixit."

Shrank shut his eyes, spun his thoughts, chose a reaction.
Laughed.

"Fixit? Fixit! Ridiculous! Why would you think?"

"Because." I walked on, making him dog-trot to follow. I
talked to the mist which gathered ahead. "Henry smelled
someone crossing the street, many nights ago. The same smell
was in his tenement hall, and here now tonight. And the smell
is you."

The rabbit palpitation shook the little man again, but he
knew he was still clear. Nothing was proven!

"Why," he gasped, "would I prowl some downtown lousy
tenement I wouldn't dream to live in, why?"

"Because," I said, "you were looking for Lonelies. And
damn fool stupid dumb me, blinder than Henry, helped you
find them. Fannie was right. Constance was right! I was the
death goat after all. Christ, I was Typhoid Mary. I carried the
disease, you, everywhere. Or at least you followed. To find
Lonelies." A drumbeat of breath. "Lonelies."

Almost as I said it, both Shrank and I were seized with
what were almost paroxysms. I had spoken a truth that was like
a furnace lid thrown back so the heat scorched out to sear my
face, my tongue, my heart, my soul. And Shrank? I was de-

scribing his unguessed life, his need; all yet to be revealed and admitted, but I knew I had at last yanked the asbestos up and the fire was in the open.

"What was that word?" asked Shrank, some ten yards off and motionless as a statue.

"Lonelies. You said the word. You described them last month. Lonelies."

And it was true. A funeral march of souls went by in a breath, on soundless feet, in drifts of fog. Fannie and Sam and Jimmy and Cal and all the rest. I had never put a proper label on them. I had never seen the carry-over that tied them all and made them one.

"You're raving," said Shrank. "Guessing. Making up. Lying. None of this has to do with me."

But he was looking down at the way his coat was run up on his skinny wrists and the weathermarks of late-night sweats down his coat. His suit seemed to be diminishing even as I watched. He writhed in his own pale skin, underneath.

I decided to attack.

"Christ, you're rotting even as you stand there. You're an affront. You hate everything, all, anything in the world. You told me that just now. So you attack it with your dirt, your breath. Your underwear is your true flag, so you run it up a pole to ruin the wind. A. L. Shrank. Proprietor of the Apocalypse!"

He was smiling, he was overjoyed. I had complimented him with insults. I was paying attention. His ego roused. Without knowing it, I had made and baited a trap.

What now? I thought. What, what, for God's sake do I say now, now? How draw him out? How finish him?

But he was walking ahead again now, all inflated with insults, all magnificent with the medals of ruin and despair I had pinned to his greasy tie.

We walked. We walked. We walked.

My God, I thought, how long do we walk, how long do we talk, how long does this go on?

This is a movie, I thought, one of those unbelievable scenes that continue and continue when people explain and others talk back and people say again,

It can't be.

It is.

He's not sure what I know and I'm not sure that I know, either, and both of us wonder if the other is armed.

"And both of us are cowards," said Shrank.

"And both are afraid to test the other."

The Carpenter went on. The Oyster followed.

We walked.

And it was not a scene from a good or bad film where people talked too much; it was a scene growing late at night and the moon vanishing to reappear as the fog thickened and I was having a dialogue with Hamlet's father's idiot psychiatrist's friend's ghost.

Shrank, I thought. What a name. Shrink from this, shrink from that, you wind up shrunk! How had it started? Out of college, on top of the world, hang a shingle; then the great earthquake of some year, did he recall? the year his legs and mind broke and there was the long slide without a toboggan, just on his skinny backside, and no women between him and the downfall pit to ease the concussion, lubricate the nightmare, stop his crying at midnight and hatred at dawn? And one morning, he got out of bed and found himself, where?

Venice, California, and the last gondola long since departed and the lights going out and the canals filling with oil and old circus wagons with only the tide roaring behind the bars. . . .

"I have a little list," I said.

"What?" said Shrank.

"*The Mikado,*" I told him. "One song explains you. Your object all sublime, you will achieve in time. To make the punishment fit the crime. The Lonelies. All of them. You put them on your list, in the words of the song, they never will be missed. Their crime was giving up or never having tried. It was mediocrity or failure or lostness. And their punishment, my God, was you."

He was puffed now, with a peacock stride.

"Well?" he said, walking ahead. "Well?"

I loaded my tongue and took aim and fired a round.

"I imagine," I said, "that somewhere nearby is the decapitated head of Scott Joplin."

He could not help the impulse that moved his right hand to his greasy coat pocket. He pretended to pat it in place, found himself staring with pleasure at that hand, glanced away, and went on walking.

One shot, one hit. I glowed. Detective Lieutenant Crumley, I thought, wish you were here.

I fired a second round.

"Canaries for sale," I said in a tiny voice like the faded lead-pencil lettering on the cardboard in the old lady's window. "Hirohito ascends throne. Addis Ababa. Mussolini."

His left hand twitched with secret pride toward his left coat pocket.

Christ! I thought. He's carrying her old bottom-of-the-birdcage headlines with him!

Bull's-eye!

He strode. I followed.

Target three. Aim three. Fire three.

"Lion cage. Old man. Ticket office."

His chin dropped toward his breast pocket.

There, by God, would be found punchout ticket confetti from a train never taken!

Shrank plowed on through the mist, absolutely oblivious of the fact that I was butterfly-netting his crimes. He was a happy child in the fields of the Antichrist. His tiny shoes flinted on the planks. He beamed.

What next? My mind swarmed. Ah, yes.

I saw Jimmy in the tenement hall with his new choppers, all grin. Jimmy in the bathtub, turned over and six fathoms deep.

"False teeth," I said. "Uppers. Lowers."

Thank God, Shrank did not pat his pockets again. I might have shouted a terrible laugh of dread to think he carried a dead grin about. His glance over his shoulder told me it was back (in a glass of water?) in his hut.

Target five, aim, fire!

"Dancing Chihuahuas, preening parakeets!"

Shrank's shoes did a dog-dance on the pier. His eyes jumped to his left shoulder. There were bird-claw marks and droppings there! One of Pietro Massinello's birds was back there in the hut.

Target six.

"Moroccan fort by an Arabian sea."

Shrank's little lizard tongue made a tiny whiplash along his thirsty lips.

One bottle of Rattigan's champagne, shelved behind us, leaning on De Quincey in his dope, Hardy in his gloom.

A wind rose.

I shuddered, for suddenly I sensed that ten dozen candy wrappers, all mine, were blowing along after Shrank and me, ghost rodent hungers from other days, rustling along the night pier.

And at last I had to say and could not say but finally made myself say the terrible final sad words that broke my tongue even as something burst in my chest.

"Midnight tenement. Full icebox. *Tosca.*"

Like a black discus hurled across the town, the first side of *Tosca* struck, rolled, and slid under A. L. Shrank's midnight door.

The list had been long. I was poised on the near rim of hysteria, panic, terror, delight at my own perception, my own revulsion, my own sadness. I might dance, strike, or shriek at any moment.

But Shrank spoke first, eyes dreaming, the whispered arias of Puccini turning and turning in his head.

"The fat woman's at peace now. She needed peace. I gave it to her."

I hardly remember what happened next.

Somebody yelled. Me. Someone else yelled. Him.

My arm thrust up, Henry's cane in it.

Murder, I thought. Kill.

Shrank fell back only in time as the cane chopped down. Instead of him, it struck the pier and was shocked from my grip. It fell, rattled, and was kicked by Shrank so it sailed over the edge of the pier and down into the sand.

Now I could only lunge at the little man with empty fists and lurch to a halt as he stepped aside because a final thing had broken in me.

I gagged, I wept. Days ago, the crying in the shower was only a start. Now the full flood came. My bones began to crumble. I stood weeping and Shrank, astounded, almost reached out to touch me and murmur, there, there.

"It's all right," he said at last. "She's at peace. You should thank me for that."

The moon went behind a great bank of fog and gave me time to recover. I was all slow motion now. My tongue dragged and I could hardly see.

"What you mean is," I said, at last, underwater, "they're all gone and I should thank you for all of them. Yes?"

It must have been a terrible relief for him, having waited all these months or years to tell someone, no matter who, no matter where, no matter how. The moon came out again. His lips trembled with the renewed light and the need for release.

"Yes. I helped them all."

"My God," I gasped. "Helped? Helped?"

I had to sit down. He helped me to do that and stood over me, astonished at my weakness, in charge of me and the night's future, the man who could bless people with murder, keep them from suffering, put off their loneliness, sleep them from their private dooms, save them from life. Benefit them with sunsets.

"But you helped, too," he said, reasonably. "You're a writer. Curious. All I had to do was follow, collecting your candy wrappers as you went. Do you know how easy it is to follow people? They never look back. Never. You never did. Oh dear, you never knew. You were my good dog of death, for more times than you guess. Over a year. You showed me the people you were collecting for your books. All the gravel on the path, chaff in the wind, empty shells on the shore, dice with no spots, cards with no pips. No past, no present. So I gave them no future."

I looked up at him. My strength was coming back. The sadness was just about over for now. My anger built a slow pressure.

"You admit it all, do you?"

"Why not? It's all sour breath on the wind. If when we finish here and I actually walk you to the police station, which I will, you have no proof of what I've said. It's all lost hot air."

"Not quite," I said. "You couldn't resist taking one thing from each victim. Your godawful place is full of phonograph records, champagne, and old newspapers."

"Son-of-a-bitch!" said Shrank, and stopped. He barked a laugh and then made a grin. "Pretty smart. Got it out of me, eh?"

He rocked on his heels, thinking about it.

"Now," he said, "I'll just have to kill *you*."

I jumped up. I was a foot taller and not brave, but he jumped back.

"No," I said. "You can't do that."

"Why not!"

"Because," I said, "you can't lay hands on me. You didn't lay hands on them. It was all hands off. I see it now. Your logic was to get people to do things to themselves, or destroy them indirectly. Right?"

"Right!" His pride was involved again. He forgot me standing there and looked off at his bright and glorious past.

"Train ticket office old man. All you did was get him drunk? Knock his head on the edge of the canal, maybe, then jump in and make sure he got in the lion cage."

"Right!"

"Canaries-for-sale old lady. All you did was stand over her bed and make faces?"

"Right!"

"Sam. Gave him enough hard liquor to put him in the hospital."

"Right!"

"Jimmy. Made sure he had three times too much booze.

You didn't even have to turn him over in the bathtub. Rolled over himself, gone."

"Right!"

"Pietro Massinello. You wrote the city government to come get him and his ten dozen dogs, cats, and birds. If he isn't dead now, soon will be?"

"Right!"

"Cal the barber, of course."

"I stole Scott Joplin's head," said Shrank.

"So Cal, scared, left town. John Wilkes Hopwood. Him and his immense ego. Wrote him using Constance Rattigan's stationery, got him to come naked on the beach every night. Scaring Constance out to drown herself?"

"Indeed!"

"Then got rid of Hopwood by letting him know you had seen him on the beach the night Constance vanished. You added a really terrible dirty letter, calling him everything vile."

"Everything he was."

"And Fannie Florianna. Left your ad by her door. And when she called and you made an appointment, all you did was come over, burst in, same as with the old canary lady, frighten Fannie so she ran backward, yes, fell and couldn't get up, and all you had to do was stand over her to make sure she didn't, yes?"

He knew better than to say yes to this, to say anything, for I was furious now, still shaky but getting strength from my own madness.

"You made only one mistake all along the way over the weeks. Sending the papers to Fannie, leaving them, marked. When you remembered this and went back and broke in, you couldn't find them. The one place you didn't think to look was the icebox. Your newspaper notice put under the jars to catch drips. I found it there. That's why I'm here. And not about to be the next on your list. Or do you have other plans?"

"Yes."

"No, and do you know why not? For two reasons. One, I'm not a Lonely. I'm not a failure. I'm not lost. I'm going to make it. I'm going to be happy. I'm going to marry and have a good wife and children. I'm going to write damned fine books and be loved. That doesn't fit your pattern. You can't kill me, you damn stupid jerk, because I'm okay. You see? I'm going to live forever. Secondly, you can't lay a finger on me. No one else has been touched by you. If you touch me, it spoils your record. You got all your other deaths by fear or intimidation. But now if you try to prevent my going to the police, you'll have to commit *real* murder, you sick bastard.

I plowed off with him running after in utter confusion, almost tugging at my elbows for attention. "Right, right. I almost killed you a year ago. But then you made those sales to magazines and then you met that woman and I decided to just follow you and collect people, yes, that was it. And it really began that night on the Venice train, in the storm, and me drunk. You were so close to me that night on the train, I could have reached out and touched. And the rain came down and if you had just turned, but you didn't, you would have seen me and known me, but you didn't and—"

We were off the pier and in the dark street by the canal now and moving swiftly over the bridge. The boulevard was empty. I saw no cars, no lights. I rushed.

In the middle of the bridge over the canal, by the lion cages, Shrank stopped and caught hold of the railing.

"Why don't you understand me, help me!" he wailed. "I wanted to kill you, I *did*! But it would have been like killing Hope, and there has to be some of that in the world, doesn't there, even for people like me?"

I stared at him. "Not after tonight."

"Why?" he gasped, "why?" looking at the cold oily water.

"Because you're utterly and completely insane," I said.

"I'll kill you now."

"No," I said, with immense sadness. "There's only one person left to kill. One last Lonely. The empty one. You."

"Me?" shrieked the little man.

"You."

"Me?" he screamed. "Damn, damn, damn you!"

He spun. He grabbed the rails. He leaped.

His body went down in darkness.

He sank in waters as oiled and scummy as his coat, as terrible and dark as his soul, to be covered and lost.

"Shrank!" I yelled.

He did not rise.

Come back, I wanted to yell.

But then, suddenly, I was afraid he would.

"Shrank," I whispered. "Shrank." I bent over the bridge rail, staring at the green scum and the gaseous tide. "I know you're there."

It just couldn't be over. It was too simple. He was somewhere out of the light, brooding like a dark toad, under the bridge, maybe, eyes up, waiting, face green, sucking air, very quietly. I listened. Not a drip. Not a ripple. Not a sigh.

"Shrank," I whispered.

Shrank, echoed the timbers under the bridge.

Off along the shore, the great oil beasts lifted their heads up at my summons, sank them down again, in time to a long sighing roll of water on the coast.

Don't wait, I thought I heard Shrank murmuring. It's nice down here. Quiet at last. I think I'll stay.

Liar, I thought. You'll come up when I least expect it.

The bridge creaked. I whirled.

Nothing. Nothing but fog sifting across the empty boulevard.

Run, I thought. Run telephone. Call Crumley. Why isn't he here? Run. But no. If I did, Shrank might go free.

Far away, two miles off, the big red trolley bucketed along, whistling, wailing, sounding like the terrible beast in my dream, come to take my time, my life, my future away, heading for a tar pit at the end of the line.

I found a small pebble and dropped it in.

Shrank.

It hit and sank. Silence.

He's escaped me. I wanted to pay him back for Fannie.

Then, Peg, I thought. Call her.

But no, she would have to wait, too.

My heart pounded so loudly that I feared the waters would stir below and the dead rise. I feared that my very breathing would knock down the oil derricks. I held onto my heart and breath and made them slow, eyes shut.

Shrank, I thought, come out. Fannie's here, waiting. The canary lady's here, waiting. The old man from the ticket office is beside me. Pietro's here and wants his pets. Come out. I'm here, along with the rest, waiting.

Shrank!

This time he must have heard.

He came to get me.

He shot out of the black water like a cannonball off a springboard.

Christ, I thought, *fool!* Why did you call to him?

He was ten feet tall, a dragon yeasted up from a dwarf. Grendel, who was once a jockey.

He snatched up like a Fury, talons out. He hit me like a balloon full of scalding water, with thrash and yell and shriek. He had long since forgotten his good intentions, his plans, his myth, his murderous integrity.

"Shrank!" I yelled.

There was something slow-motion and terrible about it, as if, frame by frame, I might stop him along the way and examine his astonishing arc and growth, and how his eyes blazed and his mouth ached with hate and hands gripped with rage as he seized my coat, my shirt, my neck in iron grapples. His mouth was blooded with my name as he heaved back. The tar waters waited. Christ, not there, I thought. The lion cages waited with doors flung wide.

"No!"

The slow motion stopped. The swift fall followed.

Fused by his rage, we fell down, sucking air in flight.

We struck like two concrete statues and sank, loving each other with a mindless frenzy of passion, climbing each other to keep each other down, making ladders to air and light.

On the way down I thought I heard him whining, wailing, "Get in there, get in there, get in," like a boy at some rude game without rules, and I was playing wrong. "Get in!"

But now, under, we went from sight. We whirled around like two crocodiles at each other's necks. From up top we must have seemed like a moil and welter of piranhas self-feasting, or a great propeller off center and amok in rainbow oils and tars.

And at center of the drowning there was a small pinpoint flash of hope which burst but to fire again behind my eyes.

This is his first real murder, I must have thought, or was there time? But I am flesh and will not behave. I fear dark more than he fears life. He must know that. I must win!

Not proven.

We rolled and struck something that knocked most of the air from my lungs. The lion cage. He was shoving and kicking me through the open door. I thrashed. We whirled and in the surge and white water I suddenly thought:

God. I'm inside. The cage. The whole thing ends as it began! Crumley comes to find—me! beckoning behind the bars at dawn. Christ. My lungs ballooned with fire. I tried to whirl and knock free. I wanted to shout him off with my last breath. I wanted to . . .

It was over.

Shrank relaxed his grip.

What? I thought. What? What!

He almost let go.

I seized him to push but it was like grabbing a dummy that had suddenly lost its ability to gesticulate. It was like handling a corpse that had leaped out of the grave and now wanted back.

He's quit, I thought. He knows he must be the last one. He knows he can't kill me, it doesn't fit.

He had indeed made up his mind and as I held him I could see his face, the merest pale ghost, and the shrug that said I was to at last go free and move up toward night and air and life. In the dark water, I saw his eyes accept his own dread as he opened his mouth, flexed his nostrils, and let out a terrible gaseous illumination. Whereupon he took a deep breath of black water and sank away, a lost man seeking his final loss.

He was a cold marionette I left behind in the cage as blindly I thrashed for the door, pushed out, and pushed up, wildly praying to live forever, to seek the fog, to find Peg, wherever she was in all the dread damned world.

I broke up and out into a mist that had begun to rain. As my head burst out, I gave a great cry of relief and sorrow. All the souls of all the people lost and not wanting to be lost in the last month wailed out of me. I gagged, threw up, almost sank again, but made it to the bank and dragged myself out to sit and wait on the rim of the canal.

omewhere in the world I heard a car pull up, a door slam, running feet. Out of the rain, one long arm reached and a big hand clutched to shake my shoulder. Crumley's face, like a frog's under glass, came to view in a movie closeup. He looked like a father in shock, bending to his drowned son.

"You okay, you all right, you okay?"

I nodded, gasping.

Henry came up behind, sniffing the rain, alert for dread smells and finding none.

"He okay?" said Henry.

"Alive," I said, and truly meant it. "Oh, God, alive."

"Where's Armpits? I got to give him one for Fannie."

"I already did, Henry," I said.

I nodded down at the lion cage, where a new ghost drifted like pale gelatin behind the bars.

"Crumley," I said, "he's got a whole shack full of stuff, evidence."

"I'll check it."

"Where the hell have you guys been?" I wondered.

"Damn-fool taxi driver's blinder than me." Henry felt his way to the canal rim and sat down on one side of me. Crumley sat on the other, all of us letting our feet dangle over almost into the dark water. "Couldn't even find the police station. Where's he at? I'll give him a hit, too."

I snorted a laugh. Water flew out of my nostrils.

Crumley leaned close to look me over.

"You hurt?"

Nowhere anyone could ever see, I thought. Ten years from now, some night, it'll all surface. I hope Peg won't mind a few screams just to get a little mothering.

In a moment, I thought, got to go phone. Peg, I'll say.

Marry me. Come tonight, come home. We'll starve together but by God we'll live. Marry me at last, Peg, and protect me from the Lonelies. Peg.

And she would answer yes and come home.

"Not hurt," I answered Crumley.

"Good," said Crumley, " 'cause who in hell would read my novel, if not you?"

I barked with laughter.

"Sorry." Crumley ducked his head with embarrassment at his own honesty.

"Hell." I grabbed his hand and put it on the back of my neck, showing him where to massage. "I love you, Crum. I love you, Henry."

"Damn," said Crumley, gently.

"Bless you, boy," said the blind man.

Another car arrived. The rain was stopping.

Henry took a deep sniff. "I know that limo smell."

"Jesus God," said Constance Rattigan, leaning out. "What a sight. World's champion Martian. World's Greatest Blind Man. And Sherlock Holmes's Bastard Son."

We all responded one way or another to this, too tired to keep it up.

Constance got out and stood behind me, looking down.

"Is it all over? Is that him?"

We all nodded, like an audience at a midnight theater, not able to take our eyes away from the canal waters, and the lion cage and the ghost behind the bars that rose and fell and beckoned.

"God, you're drenched; you'll catch your death. Let's get the kid stripped and warm. All right if I take him to my place?"

Crumley nodded.

I put my hand on his shoulder and held tight.

"Champagne now, beer later?" I said.

"See you," said Crumley, "at my jungle compound."

"Henry," said Constance, "come along?"

"Couldn't keep me away," said Henry.

And more cars arrived and police were getting ready to dive in to get whatever that was out of the cage and Crumley was walking over toward Shrank's hut, and I stood there trembling as Constance and Henry peeled off my wet jacket and helped me into the limousine and we drove along the middle of the night coast among the big, sighing derricks, leaving behind a strange, small apartment where I worked and leaving behind the dark, small lean-to where Spengler and Genghis Khan and Hitler and Nietzsche and a few dozen old candy wrappers waited and leaving behind the shut trolley station where tomorrow some lost old men would sit again waiting for the last trains of the century.

Along the way, I thought I saw myself passing on a bike, twelve years old, delivering papers in the dark morn. Further on, my older self, nineteen, wandered home, bumping into poles, lipstick on his cheek, drunk with love.

Just before we turned in at Constance's Arabian fort, another limousine came roaring the other way, along the shore highway. It passed like thunder. Is that me too, I wondered, some year soon? And Peg, in an evening gown, with me, coming back from a dance? But the other limousine vanished. The future would have to wait.

As we pulled in to Constance's sandlot backyard, I knew a simple present and the best kind of alive happiness.

With the limo parked and Constance and me waiting for him to move, with a grandiose wave Henry raised his arm.

"One side or a leg off."

We stood aside.

"Let the blind man show you the way."

He did.

We gladly followed.

A NOTE ABOUT THE AUTHOR

RAY BRADBURY has published some 500 short stories, novels, plays, and poems since his first story appeared in *Weird Tales* when he was twenty years old. Mr. Bradbury was Idea Consultant for the United States Pavilion at the 1964 World's Fair, has helped design a ride for Disney World, and is doing consultant work on city engineering and rapid transit. When one of the Apollo astronaut teams landed on the moon, they named Dandelion Crater there to honor Mr. Bradbury's novel *Dandelion Wine*.

Death Is a Lonely Business is Mr. Bradbury's first novel since the publication of *Something Wicked This Way Comes*. *A Graveyard for Lunatics* is his most recent novel.